Fly Me to Paris

Helga Jensen is an award-winning British/Danish best selling author and journalist. Her debut novel was a winning entry in the 2017 Montegrappa First Fiction competition at Dubai's Emirates Literary Festival. Her debut was also a contender for the coveted 2021 Joan Hessayon Award for new writers. Helga holds a BA Hons in English Literature and Creative Writing, along with a Creative Writing MA from Bath Spa University. She is currently working on a PhD.

T0022812

Also by Helga Jensen

Twice in a Lifetime
A Scandinavian Summer

HELGA JENSEN
Fly Me *to* Paris

San Diego, California

CANELO US

Canelo US
An imprint of Printers Row Publishing Group
9717 Pacific Heights Blvd, San Diego, CA 92121
www.canelobooksus.com

Printers Row Publishing Group is a division of Readerlink Distribution
Services, LLC. Canelo US is a registered trademark of Readerlink
Distribution Services, LLC.

This edition originally published in the United Kingdom in 2023 by
Canelo.

Published in partnership with Canelo.

Correspondence regarding the content of this book should be sent to Canelo
US, Editorial Department, at the above address. Author inquiries should be
sent to Canelo, Unit 9, 5th Floor, Cargo Works, 1–2 Hatfields, London SE1
9PG, United Kingdom, www.canelo.co.

Publisher: Peter Norton • Associate Publisher: Ana Parker
Art Director: Charles McStravick
Senior Developmental Editor: April Graham
Editor: Traci Douglas
Production Team: Beno Chan, Julie Greene

Library of Congress Control Number: 2023948263

ISBN: 978-1-6672-0747-6

Printed in India

28 27 26 25 24   1 2 3 4 5

To the woman who once carried a BOAC bag around London so that people would assume she was a glamourous air hostess of the '60s.

This is dedicated to my late mother, Jan, who always encouraged me to see the world.

Everyone has a soulmate.
You just have to find them.

Chapter 1

The customers who come into Little Darlings aren't always as the name would imply. Perhaps I should have expected the patrons to be a teeny bit demanding when I took the job at an exclusive children's designer wear boutique in Cardiff. But the tantrums I have to witness are worse than anything I have seen on *Real Housewives*, even the episodes when the ladies have imbibed too much Sauvignon!

Of course, it isn't only the children who are demanding; the mums can be worse. This morning, we had a bit of a scene in the shop because we didn't have a matching handbag for a girl's red velvet dress. There were tears, and the stamping of feet, as though the whole cast of *Riverdance* were tapping along beside me, and that was just from mum.

The poor beauty salon that rents out the basement below us has to listen to so many feet stomp around all day. I do feel sorry for them. It can't be very pampering for the clients when they're getting their lashes extended by three feet and trying to listen to relaxing whale music.

Whilst I am busy in the fitting room trying to put ten little dresses on hangers after they were thrown on the floor, the bell on the door rings as it flies open.

I watch the mother and her mini-me daughter as they enter the shop. I love seeing mums out shopping with their daughters. How I wish I had a lovely little girl I could dress up and spoil. Sadly, it is too late for children now. With all those weird twinges I am getting in my ovaries I am sure my eggs are failing by the day. What a waste. Sometimes I feel I should have at least donated my eggs. That is, if they ever worked, but I guess now I will never find out.

You could say the decision not to try for a baby is the only niggle in my relationship with my lovely boyfriend, Geraint. Apart from that we are the perfect match. It isn't always easy when only one of you wants a family with children, dogs and a hamster. Sadly, Geraint seems to be allergic to anything furry or, for that matter, that makes a noise. But, as he always tries to convince me, 'Why do we need anyone else in our lives, when we have each other?'

I smile and look back at the mum and her lovely daughter. That is one of the things I like about working here: that at least I get to spend time with children and I don't even have to spend long with the naughty ones!

I much prefer it here to my last job, doing administration for a plumber. It was so stressful telling people on the phone that their estimate for a new boiler would be £3,500, plus labour.

The stories that people told you as to why they couldn't afford their boiler repairs were heartbreaking. If I were rich, I would have paid for their boilers myself. In fact, at one point, I went through a phase of buying lottery tickets so that I could donate new boilers to the elderly. Then, one day, a lady called Jane rang. She needed a boiler for her shop and told me about her new venture. That is how we met. We got on well from the beginning, and I never had to charge the elderly for a basic essential need again. I still wish I could hand out free boilers though. It is so different here at Little Darlings, where people are excited to spend money.

Immediately, I can tell this mum and her daughter are on a mission to spend. They have that look of determination we see here so often. I leave them to pull out a few items and watch them discreetly in case they need some help. I always try to be as helpful as I can for Jane's sake. Her parents left her some money and she invested it all in Little Darlings, which, since the days of that boiler installation, has so far been a great success.

Little Darlings is now featured in all the fancy magazines and anyone who is anyone shops here, although some customers can be more demanding than others. In fact, I have a foreboding sense that I will be required to put my diplomatic skills to good use at any moment.

I smile at the mum in front of me and offer the little girl a marshmallow from the glass jar by the till.

'Ta,' she says. At least she said thank you. It's surprising how many youngsters don't nowadays.

'Do you have this in age nine?' asks the wealthy-looking mum. She holds a red tartan dress up with one arm; a designer bag hangs from her other muscular arm.

'Let me check what we have in the stock room,' I say.

The mini-me daughter looks at me and smiles. What a sweetie. I rummage through the designer childrenswear searching for the right age, but I only have bad news to deliver.

'I'm so sorry, no, we don't have any left. I think that particular dress was hand-made by artisan tailors in Peru, or was it Nepal? I can never remember. But, yes, I'm afraid that means we can't order any more in. Would you like something like this?' I ask, searching through the racks for a similar designer dress, with a slightly smaller check, that

I know we have in stock. Jane always trained me to offer an alternative when something isn't available, although I would anyway. Such an angelic smile on this little girl; I am very keen to find her something she will like.

'This looks lovely on,' I say with a smile. The little girl gives me a look that scarily reminds me of Veruca Salt in *Charlie and the Chocolate Factory*. Her angelic smile has suddenly disappeared.

'Is that a joke? Mummy and I chose that dress. We don't want any old dress off the rack for my birthday. It's artisan or nothing.'

I know I should hide my expression, but my face must give away my shock at her outburst. I stumble over my words for a moment and don't know what to say. I didn't even know about artisan tailors when I was her age.

'Oh, I am so sorry. Umm,' I stutter.

'Tabby was only telling you what she was looking for. What's that big face for? What's your name?' demands the mum.

'Umm, Penny,' I manage.

'Well, Penny, I came to this shop because it has an excellent reputation, but I think you need to improve your customer service skills. I shall be leaving a review on the shop's Facebook page.'

'Come on, Tabby. Let's go,' says the mum.

Young Tabby gives me evil stares, then glares with equal hatred at the beautiful antique wooden rocking horse we have beside the shop window. Jane has owned it since childhood. She was a little hesitant to put it in the shop at first, but all the children love it, even the stroppy ones. It usually calms them down on the way out if they don't get what they want. But it doesn't seem to have

4

that effect on little Tabby. In fact, it seems to incense her further.

'Urgh, stop staring at me, rocking horse,' says Tabby. Then, I look on in complete shock as she grabs his beautiful leather reins and tries to snap them.

'Umm, sorry, that's quite precious. Can you be careful please?' I say.

Tabby doesn't listen and instead kicks the beautiful rocking horse on the leg, leaving a big black mark and flaking off some of his cream paint.

'Oh my goodness!' I say. Tabby and her mother don't care. They leave the shop like a pair of posh thugs.

'Poor Smokey,' I say, stroking his mane as if it will make everything better.

I love Smokey as if he were one of the dogs at the shelter I help out at. Helping at the shelter is one of the highlights of my existence in this world. I suppose I have always liked to help people and animals. Perhaps it is having sick parents that made me want to save the world and everyone in it. If I could cure cancer with my bare hands, I would. But, for now, it is Smokey who is in need of help.

I worry about the chipped paint. Jane is going to be in bits if she finds out that a little devil has ruined a leg on her childhood rocking horse. What a mean little girl. I scold myself for not calling them back. I'm fifty years old and didn't have the courage to summon a little nine-year-old back. What on earth? I shouldn't have allowed the pair to leave. I should have got Tabby's mum to pay for the damage. How could her mum not tell her off? She clearly saw what she did.

This will surely have to go to a specialist repair shop. For a moment I wonder if that repair shop on the telly could fix it; any excuse to meet the lovely presenter, Jay Blades. I will have to think of something.

I take a photo of the damage and send it to Geraint. He knows the answer to everything. He will know what to do.

> How can I fix it?

He doesn't answer. I don't know why he can't answer my calls when his phone is never far away, but I get on with the rest of the day.

Despite a dramatic morning, the afternoon gets slightly better. I sell three party dresses and two of our bestselling skirts. I mentally add up all the commissions in my head. Hopefully, it will be enough for a bit of petrol to get to work next month and to cover the electricity to put a light on. Jane pays a fair wage, but I don't always get enough hours. If it wasn't for the commission then I probably wouldn't be able to work here.

Sometimes I think I may have to look for a new job, despite me loving it here so much. But then I also remember I have never been very good at interviews. I made a right fool of myself at the last one I went to. It was for a checkout assistant at the local supermarket. Unfortunately, I didn't do very well when one of their questions was, 'What would you do if a pigeon flew into the store?' I mean, what sort of question is that? I said I would probably scream and run away. Well, I believe it always pays to be truthful, but that obviously wasn't the answer they wanted. I still wonder what the right answer would have been, to be honest.

I am about to lock up the shop when Geraint finally messages me back. I am so relieved. I know I shouldn't depend on him as much as I do, but I can't help it. He's all I have.

> Hiya, babe, oh, don't know. Think Farrow and Ball have a shade of cream like that. Works well on wood too. Have a look. Fancy dinner tonight? My treat?

Geraint really does know about everything. I don't know how he does it. He's an electrician, but should be some kind of interior designer; he has such an eye for detail. Perhaps it is having to get all those wires together correctly. I am the luckiest woman alive, even though we are still 'only' dating after ten years together. Of course, I try to be a strong independent woman, so would never be needy and try to push him to name the date. Everything is perfect just the way it is, although he does go away on charity cycling trips with his best friend quite a bit. That can be a bit annoying when I have nobody to go out and do things with. As I don't have many friends, I rely on Geraint for everything. But the fact is that when I was in secondary school, Yvonne, my best friend, ditched me overnight and I never really got over it. It was almost like a death. We went everywhere together, whether it was shopping in Boots for cheap make-up to experiment with, C&A for bras, or school roller discos; we were inseparable. We had even planned to go backpacking around Australia when we finished school. It was our dream. We would get a job picking grapes that would culminate in a bottle of Australian Chardonnay. It sounded fun, especially when the only wine I had ever come across was Blue Nun and Concorde.

But then one day, our friendship ended via a letter posted in my letterbox. Mum woke me up before school and told me that the writing on the envelope looked like it was something from Yvonne.

'Why would Yvonne be sending you a letter?' she asked.

I couldn't answer. It was very unexpected.

Reading the letter, it was as though my heart had been torn in two. It was devastating. She accused me of flirting with Craig, the hottest boy in our class. My hands began to shake as I started reading the letter. I remember it as though it were yesterday.

What sort of friend are you? You know how much I fancy Craig. I want nothing more to do with you.

I didn't even like Craig. That was the odd thing. I never went for the cool boys in school. I much preferred the quieter unassuming boy who read books, let alone fall out with a friend over a boy. I wasn't that type of person. My friendship with Yvonne meant everything.

I tried to speak to her at school but she wanted nothing more to do with me. Mum said that perhaps she had used Craig as an excuse. That perhaps we had grown apart, which sometimes happens. Maybe there was something going on in her life that I didn't know about. Mum promised me it wasn't me; it was Yvonne.

I spent the last few terms at school alone as I didn't want to ever have a close friendship like that again to then lose it. When a friendship ends nobody thinks it hurts; people have sympathy for you when you lose a partner, but not so much when it is a friendship. Yvonne was the sister I never had and it was horrendous to lose her friendship overnight like that. The only person who cared for my loss was Mum and then a year later she died suddenly. It was a shock, but everyone who knew her said that it was losing my dad two years earlier that exacerbated the cancer. She never got over him. So, that was the moment that I found myself truly alone in the world. Everyone I had ever been close to had left me. That was when I chose to never let anyone get near me again. That is, until I met Geraint a very long time later. He came to do some wiring at my flat as the landlord had called him out when my lights kept flickering.

I didn't mind the lights flickering. I thought it was Mum and Dad making contact with me. I used to talk to the small living room chandelier as if they were there in the room with me. I am glad nobody saw me!

'Mum, Dad, is that you?' I would ask, as the lights flickered on and off. I was sure they were trying to make contact with me. There was no way they'd have deserted me, even in death. However, there never was any response, but I assumed it was because ghosts couldn't talk; they could only make electrical disturbances, for some reason.

Then, one evening, the landlord came around to collect his rent and noticed the lights.

'Does that happen a lot?' he asked.

'Yes, but it's okay,' I said.

'No, it could mean an electrical fault. I'll get someone over,' he said.

I pleaded with him not to bother. I didn't want it fixed. If it was Mum and Dad then that would mean they would be gone forever. But he was quite insistent and so, one morning, whilst I was sitting in my Mickey Mouse nightshirt, having just dribbled the milk from my cornflakes down the front of me, there was a knock on the door.

9

'Hiya, I'm here to fix your lights?' this man with dazzling white teeth and dark hair said.

I welcomed him in and ran to the bedroom to brush my hair and put on a bit of mascara. My fair eyelashes never had been a good look in the morning. I put a dressing gown over my thin nightshirt and went back in to offer him a coffee.

Over his coffee, we got along well. He was so easy to talk to. I don't know if I had been starved of companionship for too long, or if Geraint genuinely was incredibly charming, but we swapped phone numbers in case I needed an electrician. Perhaps he also realised I needed more than just someone to fix my wiring in my life.

After we met, the lights stopped flickering and I always wondered if it was down to a loose connection, or if my parents left me alone as they knew there was now someone in my life to keep an eye on me.

Chapter 2

Getting ready for my date night with Geraint, I consider what to wear and throw some bits out of the wardrobe. I want to look my best tonight when he picks me up. I fling the first dress I take out onto the exercise bike in the corner of the room. I only bought the bike to try and keep up with Geraint's cardio anyhow, but it is much more useful as extra clothing storage space. Everyone should have one.

Finally, I choose a long flowing white cotton skirt and a Bardot top, lace-up some cerise espadrilles around my ankles and my look is complete. Geraint, being the fashion-loving person he is, will no doubt approve. Not that this is why I am dressing up, of course. I always like to make an effort, but especially tonight.

We are going to our favourite tapas bar in Cardiff and it is full of glamorous people, so I don't want to look out of place. It is always packed; sometimes you even get minor celebrities in there. I am sure I saw someone off *Songs of Praise* once. It wasn't Aled Jones or anything, rather someone from a local choir, but still. They are still celebs who have been on TV!

By the time we arrive at Signor Tapas the place is a hive of activity. Geraint is looking quite hot in his white shirt and tight jeans. He has such a great body for a fifty-one-year-old. I suppose between his cycling and his work, it all helps. Unlike me and my stomach, which seems to have herniated since my last birthday. My waistband feels tighter every morning, although ordering all my favourite tapas doesn't help.

'I'll have the prawn ceviche, croquetas de jamon, and chorizo al vino,' I say to Miguel, our favourite waiter there.

'Is that it?' asks Geraint.

He knows me too well.

'Okay then, I'll have the tuna empanada as well. Thank you.'

Miguel takes the order and dashes off.

'Cheers,' I say with a smile, clinking my glass of cider against Geraint's bottle of lager.

'Cheers,' says Geraint. I look up at his chestnut eyes. Oh, he is a handsome man! I swear all the women stop and stare when we walk into places. Sometimes, even the guys do too. If I didn't know better, I would think that even lovely Miguel has a soft spot for him.

'Anyway, I thought we would have a bit of a chat, Penny.'

'Oh, about what, lovely?' I say.

'Our future. We've been together such a long time now.' Geraint takes a sip from his bottle and swallows.

'I think it's only fair we have this chat. It's long overdue,' he says, smiling. I notice that his smile doesn't quite reach his eyes. Does he look nervous or am I imagining things? He really needn't be nervous with me. We know each other inside out.

'Go on,' I say, smiling.

'Well, I'm sure you want some sort of commitment from me. It's only natural, so I've been thinking that we should…' Geraint takes a sip of his beer again. This time, some dribbles down the bottle, splashing his lovely white shirt. That isn't going to look good in the photos I have a suspicion I am going to post all over Instagram to my two followers when he asks me to marry him. I wonder if he has a ring somewhere.

'Oh, I thought you'd never ask,' I say, grinning. I don't think I have ever felt happier in my life.

'Sorry, did you want me to call Miguel over for you to get another drink? I didn't realise you were empty. You need a drink for what I'm about to say,' says Geraint. He calls Miguel over and I wonder if it is too soon to order some champagne, presuming Geraint is still paying for tonight.

'Ooh, Miguel, what shall I order for a special occasion? What do you suggest?'

'Brandy? I think you need something strong,' says Miguel seriously.

'Give me some kind of cocktail with brandy in it then, please.'

The champagne can wait. I can already feel it's going to be a long night. Who cares if I'm hungover tomorrow? It's my day off.

'So, what were you saying, my gorgeous Geraint?' I smile.

'Oh, is that the woman who's on that cake programme on TV? Look,' says Geraint.

'You're right. It's her. She does lush cakes, it has to be said. Maybe she could do one for our...' I stop myself from saying wedding. We haven't even had our engagement yet. Perhaps we can try her out for our engagement cake first. He is bound to want a party with all his family and friends. No doubt Geraint will want his cycling friends Nathan and Alex there. It would be great to finally meet

Alex, whom Geraint doesn't stop talking about. That's the problem when I have no interest in cycling, apart from my unused exercise bike. These cyclists seem to have their own little clique that I don't fit into.

'Here you go,' says Miguel, interrupting my imaginary engagement party plans.

'Thank you, Miguel. You're fabulous,' I say.

'Drink up then and I'll tell you what I want to say,' says Geraint.

I remove my cocktail umbrella and the pink plastic flamingo that is dangling from my drink, placing them beside my handbag. I have a habit of collecting mementoes to remind me of important events. There are drawers full of tacky plastic things at home.

'So, as I was saying… We've been together a long time and it's time I told you. We have had so many wonderful adventures together and now I have got to tell you something really important.'

I grin from ear to ear. I hope everyone is listening and will clap when I say yes!

'Oh my gosh,' I squeal.

Geraint looks at me seriously.

'You don't seem to be getting what I'm saying. Why are you smiling?'

'Umm, aren't you about to propose?'

'Well, yes, I am. But not to you,' says Geraint.

'What? To who?' I ask.

It feels as though I have had the biggest punch in the stomach. I am aware that my mouth is hanging wide open, like some kind of baby bird waiting to be fed. Only I am waiting to be fed the next shocking words to come out of Geraint's mouth. My head feels like it is spinning and I can't stop the room from whirring about. I have to hold on to the table to steady myself.

After a few moments of silence, my shock turns into curiosity. Who is he about to propose to if it isn't me?

I grab my drink and take a sip to ease my dry mouth. I almost want to throw it over him. It might be wise not to waste it at this point, though.

'Is it that horrible woman in the builder's yard you go to? You're always talking about her.'

I have seen the way she drives that bobcat around the yard while she flicks her long auburn ponytail. It's her. I know it. Why didn't I realise before?

'No, it's not her. It's Alex. It was always Alex.'

'Your cycling buddy, Alex? One of the lads you go off on weekends cycling with?'

I feel like I am about to fall on the floor. How could I not know he was gay? How could I not know he was cheating?

'Didn't you realise that Alex is a woman? Alexandra, innit. I'm sorry. I know you don't have anyone in your life apart from me, and so I couldn't bring myself to tell you before. But Alex said it would be kinder in the long run, especially now we have decided to make it official. To be honest, Nathan doesn't really come on the trips any more. Well, not since Alex and I…'

'I thought those rides were for charity. I thought you were incredibly kind and what happened to "Why do we need anyone else in our lives when we have each other?"'

My voice is getting screechy now. Someone turns from the table next to me and stares.

I start to cry as the words sink in. He was doing these charity cycles so that he could be with Alex! I always thought it was because he was so kind that he wanted to spend his time helping charities, but now I wonder if it was all a ruse to be with her. How long has he been lying to me? For all I know, he never even went cycling; perhaps he just went to stay weekends with Alex. I feel so stupid. How could I not guess something was going on? How could he be so good at hiding his feelings in front of me? What if it was I who was his charity case? Poor old orphaned Penny. I shudder at the thought.

'Look, I'm sorry. I really am. I thought it was about time I was honest. It's for your own good in the long run. Alex knows I'm telling you tonight.'

Geraint looks at his phone and picks it up.

'Aww, that's Alex messaging, she's checking I'm okay,' he says.

I look at him, my eyes wide with fury. What about me? Am I okay? No, I am bloody not.

'Look, again, sorry. Are you okay? Your face has gone red like when you get really angry.'

'Why would you stay with me for ten years, Geraint? I was thirty-nine when we met. I could have met someone else. Even tried for children with someone. You always said you never wanted any and I accepted that. You've messed my life up. Why tell me now?'

Geraint doesn't look at me whilst I am talking. He looks down and fiddles with my plastic flamingo. I feel like grabbing it off him and telling him that is *my* flamingo. Not his. How dare he. But fighting over a plastic flamingo cocktail stirrer right now is the last thing I need. It's not the flamingo that is the problem. The flamingo is simply an innocent bystander.

Finally, Geraint lifts up his head and looks at me, then quickly looks away again.

'Alex is pregnant. I'm sorry.'

I feel dizzy. My head starts to spin again and my heart races so much that it makes me feel sick.

'Look, it was an accident. I didn't want kids, but now Alex is pregnant I'm coming around to it a bit more.'

The whole room is spinning. It is as if I have been caught up in a tornado. I am struggling to breathe.

'Have you got a tight chest? You're doing that thing, trying to gasp for breath, like when you have a fever?' says Geraint.

'Why do you think I have a tight chest, Geraint?' I gasp. 'I can't believe you are saying this. How could you do this to me?'

'Well, it's better I'm honest with you,' says Geraint.

'I don't know if I want to hear any of it, to be *honest*,' I say.

I can't get my head around all these confessions in one night. It's all too much.

'We always got on well, didn't we? I tried my best for you. I do love you, Penny. I know the sex is great between us, but I thought maybe you realised that things weren't quite right with our relationship.'

'"The sex was great between us but things weren't quite right." Did you really just say that out loud? I haven't come to terms with the fact you've got someone pregnant yet. I'd just shut up if I were you,' I shout.

The woman at the table next to me gasps and gives Geraint a filthy look. At least I have an ally.

I see Miguel coming towards us and then turning as he hears me. I ignore the looks I am getting from others who can't quite make out what is happening. How are you supposed to remain quiet when the person you love, the person who is your whole world, is telling you that it has all been such a joke to him? He is in love with a woman who wears skintight cycling shorts and got her pregnant, goddammit.

'Is this why you never moved in with me when my rent went up and I hinted I may have to move?'

'Yeah, well, I did say at the time I needed my own space and I was a confirmed bachelor. I thought you'd get the hint.'

'Yes, but I thought you were just one of those guys who needed his own space. Not that you wanted to be with someone else. You just felt sorry for me, didn't you? Maybe you never loved me,' I say.

'I did love you. I do. We were happy, Pen. We really had some fab times, didn't we?' Geraint leans toward me to touch my hand.

'Get off me,' I say.

'Look, I was attracted to you when we first met. I promise. You're lovely and funny and nice. You have fabulous calves,' says Geraint.

'I have fabulous calves!'

'Yeah, you do. And if you ever fancy cycling with us, you'd be good at it. I hope we can stay friends. It's not like I'm leaving you because you're a bad person. We just don't have as much in common as Alex and I do. You have a lovely kind heart and I am sure another guy would be very happy with you,' says Geraint.

At this point, I want to slap him in the face. Would that be acceptable in a full restaurant when people have camera phones everywhere? I decide probably not, despite the extreme circumstances, and so I refrain from violence and finally feel that it is appropriate to splash my drink over him. But even that misses and makes me wonder if I am good at anything at all.

'Umm, excuse me. Sorry, but I have prawn ceviche here for the madam,' says Miguel, standing back.

Tears fill my eyes now until I can hardly see the prawns.

'I don't want them,' I say.

'Oh, come on, you need to eat,' says Geraint.

Not surprisingly, I have lost my normally voracious appetite.

'I'm going to the toilet,' I say.

I wish to sob in peace and don't want these trendy types and the cake lady seeing me in this state.

Miguel brushes past me on the way to the toilet.

'He told you then?' he says.

'Miguel, you knew?'

'Hell, yeah, Alex is one of our regulars. I'm surprised you haven't bumped into her and her...'

'What, bump? Why wouldn't you tell me?' I start to cry. 'How could everyone be a part of such a big lie?'

'It's not my place, is it? I'm here to dish out food, not bad news. Anyway, sorry, this is getting cold,' says Miguel, looking at the tray full of tapas in his hand.

I manage to get to the toilet in one piece, avoiding making eye contact with a happy crowd of girls on a hen night who rush out of the toilet. I suddenly feel sorry for myself as I realise how I've never had a hen night, nor a baby shower, or anything remotely like that and now I never will. I should never have let my guard down; everyone always disappoints me.

I close the cubicle door and sob quietly. Then loud sobs, and by this stage, I don't care who hears. Two women chat and compliment each other on their outfits. They seem merry and like new best friends. But then my sobs drown them out and I don't hear the rest of their amicable conversation.

This was supposed to be one of the best nights of my life, but instead, it has quickly become the worst.

Chapter 3

I wake up in a daze. Am I at Geraint's? When I see the pale blue pillowcase beside me that doesn't have his head imprinted on it, everything floods back. The break-up, the shock that Alex is a woman and the baby. The baby that I always wanted but doesn't belong to me. My stomach rumbles loudly, which also reminds me that I didn't eat last night. I wasted all the tapas. My stomach is angry, but the rest of me feels even worse. How could I have had no idea? As I shuffle my way to the bathroom, I regret drinking that brandy cocktail on an empty stomach; it's not helping my mood, or the pain in my head. I look in the mirror and notice how puffy my eyes are. I must have cried myself to sleep. I was in such a state that I don't remember much about getting home, except that Miguel eventually felt sorry for me and offered to drive me back when he finished his shift. A memory of him leaning over to undo my seatbelt flashes before me. Did I try to kiss him? Oh my, I did. Why would I do that? I thought he was being kind and at that moment I was overcome with gratitude, even though Miguel has been with Tony for years. Do I have a thing subconsciously for men who aren't interested in me? I hang my head in shame as I think of Miguel. How could I possibly do such a thing?

My phone rings and I throw it across the room. If that is Geraint saying sorry then he can shove it. The damage he has done is irreparable. I am hurt, shocked. Broken, even.

Sometimes, in the early days of our relationship, I used to have flashbacks to the terrific sex we had just had. It would make me blush when I was in the supermarket, or wherever it came back to me at an inappropriate time.

Now, all I can see are flashbacks to last night. A baby. His face as he told me that Alex thought I should know about them. The cheek; she doesn't even know me. The anger makes me want to explode. I am angry at him, at her, and I am angry at myself. Did I choose to ignore the red flags? Were they waving at me in the face the whole time? Did I kid myself that he was just a cheeky chappy who was a commitmentphobe? I question everything during our whole relationship. What was I thinking? If someone doesn't commit after ten years, I guess that is the biggest red flag of all. But he always had an excuse and I thought I was empowered enough not to need a man to commit. We were happy the way things were. We never argued, we had fun; what more could we ask for?

Commitment? Babies? my head reminds me.

It makes me think that I was just some fun for him until the right person came along. The right person, who is she-who-shall-not-be-named, wears cycling shorts and has the cardiovascular capacity to ride a bike from Cardiff to North Wales.

I make some coffee before checking my phone, secretly disappointed that it was not him. I so wanted him to call so that I could ignore him. Damn.

Instead, there is a voicemail from Jane.

'Hey, I'm so sorry, I know it's your day off but I don't suppose you could come in this afternoon? The dentist just got a cancellation and I've been on that waiting list forever. Can you let me know ASAP?'

The last thing I want to do is to face the world today, but I know how important it is to Jane so I don't have much choice. Dentist appointments are like gold dust.

One steaming hot shower, two Anadin and a Twix later, I am in the shop with puffy eyes and a wedding party looking for two little bridesmaids' dresses.

'We want it to be special, don't we, 'Chelle,' says a bride to her sister.

'Oh, it must be. We want Nana to be proud,' says 'Chelle.

'Yeah, we brought the wedding forward as she doesn't have long left,' the bride whispers to me.

'Oh, I'm so sorry,' I say. There I am devastated that my boyfriend has dumped me for his cycling buddy and Nana's on her last legs, bless her. It's a reminder that I mustn't feel sorry for myself forever. We only get one life and I have already wasted the first half.

Whilst I am here heartbroken, I bet Geraint hasn't given me a moment's thought since last night. He will be happily planning his vows and a christening by now.

I try to avoid thinking of christenings and look towards a dark-haired woman in a pretty pink summer dress who walks in and joins the bride and her sister.

'Sorry I'm late, lovelies, flight got delayed out of LA, phew. Anyway, here now.' She smiles.

'Oh wow, have you just come back from LA?' I ask.

I could do with a holiday. I would never be able to stretch to a trip to LA, though. Maybe Paris; I have always dreamed of going there. I even had it in mind as a honeymoon destination for a moment last night.

Last night. Another flashback comes to me. I can't cry in front of this gorgeous woman with her perfect dress and perfect make-up.

I must not cry in front of customers, I chant to myself. *I must not cry. I must not cry.* I gulp back the tears that are desperate to escape.

'Just twenty-four hours. Didn't have time to get down Venice Beach this trip, just did a bit of shopping instead,' she replies.

'Oh, you go frequently?' I ask. I try to be polite but I can hear a wobble in my voice. Any second, I'm going to cry. I have no control over it.

I force myself to focus on this woman and her travels. I think how she must be rich to fly off to LA often. Perhaps she is a movie star that I don't recognise. I am not always up on the latest movies.

'Not that much. San Fran usually, always getting JFK and Newark flights,' she says.

'Wow, you go to the US quite a bit then,' I say.

I realise that I need to check on the two little girls and their mums to make sure they have all they need. I can hear them talking behind the fitting room curtain, but if I go near them and they mention Nana again I am going to be inconsolable on the floor.

So, I distract myself by listening to the stories that this woman starts telling me.

'Yeah, but it's Tokyo next. Few days off first, though,' she says.

'Oh,' I say, trying to remain focused.

'Glad of the break, to be honest. I don't know if I'm coming or going. I was in India on a different time zone the week before. Thank god for the melatonin I pick up in the States.'

'Melatonin?'

'Yeah, I swear by it. That and lots of water.'

'Oh right. Well, you have beautiful skin,' I say.

Why would I say to a stranger that she has beautiful skin?

'Aw, thank you. It's all the products I pick up in duty-free,' she says, laughing.

What on earth can she be doing to have such a life? It sounds like a dream, although I wouldn't want to do the melatonin bit; I'd be far too scared of side effects. Would it be rude to ask her why she travels like this? I am supposed to be the professional one here. But I find my mouth opening before I can stop it.

'How come you travel so much?' I ask. 'That was so cheeky. Sorry, I really shouldn't have asked but my boyfriend just ditched me for his cycling buddy. My life is so miserable and…'

Then I can't control myself. It's too late. I knew I couldn't keep a brave face much longer. I shouldn't have said all that. How on earth could I blurt out something like this to a complete stranger? I haven't even told Jane what happened yet. First, I tell a customer that she has beautiful skin and then I tell her about my personal life. I am officially emotionally unstable.

'Sorry. I'm not usually like this. I can't believe I just said that,' I say.

I wipe my eyes with the sleeve of my pullover.

'Sorry, again,' I snivel.

The seasoned traveller puts her arm around me comfortingly.

'Men, hey. You know, sometimes it's for the best. I wouldn't have lived the life I have if I hadn't been dumped by my miserable fiancé. It was a very long time ago now.'

I wipe my tears and look up at her. I must look in such a state with my mascara running everywhere.

A head pops around the curtain of the fitting room and looks at me. I really must go and help them; this is not a good look for Jane's cherished business. But I have to find out about this woman's fiancé. In the midst of heartbreak, there is nothing like comparing notes with someone else who loved a ratbag. Somehow, I feel a connection with this stranger. I can't explain it, but perhaps it is easier to confide in someone who doesn't know me and, more importantly, doesn't know Geraint.

'How do you mean?' I ask.

'Well, we had the venue set, family were flying over from Italy for the wedding. Then he told me he couldn't go through with it. Said he was too young. I thank every god there is for that decision now. One day, I was flicking through *Cosmopolitan* and a beautiful young lady was smiling out from the page in a uniform. There was a heading on top that said "See the world and get paid for it", and it had a photo of a plane. It got my attention right away.'

'That certainly doesn't sound like a normal job advert,' I say.

I think back to the old Job Centres and their adverts. I was always hanging around job centres looking for something that would excite me. I never really found anything though, apart from a hostess job on the buses, way back. The buses went to London and you would have to serve hot chocolate and coffees to the passengers on the National Express. But then they stopped that due to cost cutting, I presume, so I never got a chance to apply. It was the nearest I got to an adventure and travelling out of here.

'I don't really think of it as a job. More a lifestyle. I mean, you get paid to travel the world, get allowances to spend. I love my lifestyle more than anything,' she says.

'Well, that sounds too good to be true to me,' I say.

I am beginning to wonder if she is some kind of fantasist. Nobody would pay you to travel the world like that. Have I missed a documentary on Netflix about this woman? Is she like that Tinder scammer in reverse?

The woman smiles. 'Don't get me wrong, it can be hard work. You're on your feet for hours on end...'

'I do that here,' I interrupt.

'You have to jump down slides and know the safety procedures, it's not always easy...' she says.

'Okay, what is it you do? Jump down slides, you say?'

'I'm cabin crew, flying long haul,' she says.

My heart sinks. For a moment I thought this might be something I would be able to do, although just the travel bit and not jumping down slides. I'm not that adventurous. But it is far too late to become cabin crew at this stage in my life.

'Wow, sounds awesome for you,' I say sadly.

'It is, wouldn't change it for the world. Joined when I was twenty-four, still at the same airline.'

'Great,' I say miserably.

'Take my advice, it's time for a new start by the looks of you. Don't hang around here,' she says.

'Well, my boss is really lovely. I'm not sure I'd leave her in the lurch. It's just I don't get enough hours sometimes, but...'

'Do you have a passport?' she asks.

'Well, yes, I think it's in a drawer somewhere,' I say.

'Great, there's nothing stopping you then. Travel the world.'

'Ha, I don't have that kind of money,' I say. I don't know what sort of salary she thinks I am on.

'You don't need much money. Get a flight to Thailand, get a job in a bar. But whatever you do, you look like you need to take some time out to me,' she says.

'I've just turned fifty. I don't think a trendy bar in Phuket is exactly going to take me on,' I say.

'Now, come on. Don't be like that. Ageism isn't everywhere. It used to be that you'd have to hang your cabin shoes up at thirty. That would be discrimination and highly illegal nowadays. Well, in the UK, anyhow. My airline has no upper age limit. Why don't you apply? I'm a purser now, I could even end up on one of your flights.' She smiles.

'You're so incredibly kind, aren't you?' I say.

'I'm cabin crew, I'm used to sorting out everyone's problems,' she says, laughing. 'Anyway, look at me, giving you career advice when we don't even know each other's names yet! I'm Carys. Pleased to meet you.' Carys holds out her hand and we share a handshake.

'But listen, if you really do like the idea of it and feel in need of a change, there are plenty of airlines recruiting right now. I'm sure you could get a Cardiff or Bristol base. Take a look when you get home perhaps; see what's out there. If you need any tips or advice, give me a shout. Look me up on Facebook. Carys Edwards.'

What a wonderful person Carys is. There should be more Caryses in the world.

Standing in the shop, I think about what would have happened if I had been more adventurous, like Carys. I imagine myself rollerblading down Venice Beach with the stars, visiting the most eminent landmarks around the world like the Leaning Tower of Pisa, or the Eiffel Tower.

It sounds like the most exciting job in the world. Though knowing my luck, I'd be flat on my face in Venice Beach and come back on a stretcher.

'Have you two finished chatting now? We'll take these,' says 'Chelle. She throws down two pale gold bridesmaids' dresses and some girls' white tights on the counter at the till.

'So sorry, Carys is just so interesting,' I say, looking at her.

I forget for a moment that I probably still have mascara down my face from my earlier tears.

'Yeah, she's led an interesting life, all right. Lucky thing she is, and she's a fab friend too. She even takes me on trips for free sometimes, don't you, Carys? That will stop now I'm getting married though, I'm trying for a boy next,' says 'Chelle looking at her two girls.

'How wonderful.' I smile.

As I ring up the purchases, I feel a little brighter. I picture myself in a uniform, travelling the world. Ha, that would show Geraint not to feel sorry for me.

–

When I get home, I don't bother with dinner. I still can't face eating anything much, except the odd chocolate bar. The only thing I manage is a chocolate Freddo. I bite his head off and apologise to him immediately.

Then I open a bottle of wine that Jane gave me ages ago when I hit a sales target, before scrolling through social media. I must be in a bad state of mind that I want a glass of wine on a hangover day. Usually, I wouldn't drink for at least a week or two.

The first thing I do is find Geraint and block him. If he thinks we can still be Facebook friends he is very wrong. I notice he has already changed his profile picture to him at a cycling event. Luckily it isn't with she-who-shall-not-be-named, or I would be tempted to report his account as spam.

Then I search for Carys to send her a friend request. Carys has a photo of her in her uniform, standing in front of a Boeing 747. Even I recognise the plane with its upstairs windows. It looks so cool. I can't wait to see what other pictures she has on her Facebook page. I am going to be stalking her all night once she accepts my friend request.

Scrolling through my remaining thirty-two acquaintances, all I notice are people living their best lives. I can't even find anyone drunk-ranting about their ex or annoying husband, like my Facebook friend Cheryl, who is always moaning about her husband after two wines. I go on her page to see if I have missed anything, but no, all she has posted about is that they've gone to see a concert and are having a date night. Even they are getting on well tonight.

There's not one 'are you okay, hun' comment at all. What's going on tonight? I consider posting about my break-up with Geraint as I could certainly do with some support, but I decide not to bother. I am sure people will figure it out soon enough.

I carry on scrolling and see that John and Steff, who were both in school with me, are celebrating their twenty-fifth wedding anniversary at some romantic restaurant. They're posting pictures of themselves under some cute fairy lights in the restaurant's garden. Too sickly, yuck. I want to know where all the people are who don't have the energy to get the clothes out of the laundry basket. The people who are about to collapse into bed and realise their sheets are still in the washing machine. Where are they? Where are the ones who have been dumped for their pregnant lover as they reach their fifties? Or am I the only one?

Stop wallowing in self-pity, I remind myself. Carys turned heartache into a positive and I must do the same. I might not need anyone in my life, but perhaps I do need a new career. A voice in my head reminds me that she was a lot younger than me when she got her heart broken. What if I have left it too late to do anything? It's been almost twenty-four hours since Geraint broke up with me. I need to be kind to myself for a while and then consider my future. I must not do anything impulsive. I look at the lights in my living room. Please, Mum and Dad, give me a sign. But there is nothing. Damned electricians.

Out of boredom, I search on the internet for cabin crew jobs, merely out of curiosity more than anything. What are the requirements? I left school at sixteen. I don't have a degree or anything. None of my friends got degrees in those days. I do sometimes regret that now, but it was different back then where I am from.

I come across a job advert for Carys' airline and read through it. I am surprised to see that being degree educated is not one of the requirements at all. I just about have the minimum number of GCSEs that they stipulate.

I read on and notice that you must be over five foot two; okay, I can just about scrape that. Weight in proportion to height; yikes. I make a mental note to stop eating chocolate Freddos from tomorrow morning. Must be able to swim unaided fifty metres. I am not that good a swimmer. I had a horrendous swimming lesson once in school and it put me off swimming for life after they took us down the deep end. I shudder as I think about it.

Then I notice it says that customer service experience is desirable. If I can deal with all the tears and tantrums in Little Darlings then I am pretty sure I have the customer service experience they require. Seeing this stipulation makes me think that I might be able to apply for the job after all. Perhaps I should be a little more open-minded.

The advert says to send your CV if you're interested in working a job where no two days are the same, to work with a multicultural team where you see the world. After another glass of wine, I am sold. I haven't updated my CV in a long while, but fortunately I manage to find it on the computer. After a bit of a drunken tweak, I find myself sending it off before I bottle out.

As I send it off, I see that Carys has accepted my friend request. I think about telling her what I have just done, but it's too early. Plus, she might think I am one of those weird people who copy everything someone else does. I don't want to freak her out when she has only just met me. I have already said far too much. Though I do spend the rest of the night secretly stalking her Facebook photos, even if that is a bit weird. Is there anywhere this woman hasn't been? One minute she is in Bahrain at a Gold Souk, then Bangkok standing outside a temple and then standing in front of a big white Merlion in Singapore. She even has a Singapore Sling at Raffles hotel in another picture. I don't know anyone who is not a billionaire who lives like this. Not that I know any billionaires. The latest photos she has posted are of her in a fun-sounding place called Bongo Bazar in Dhaka. A status above it says she is snapping up designer clothes for next to nothing. I feel a pang of jealousy.

As I continue scrolling through, I almost accidentally click 'Like' on a photo of Carys sitting in front of the Taj

Mahal from five years ago. Fortunately, I manage to move my finger in time. What a life to lead; no wonder she is glad she was ditched. I would swap a guy for her lifestyle any day.

Thinking of guys, I check my phone and notice there is still nothing from Geraint. What did I expect? I know he isn't going to change his mind, but I thought at least he would check up on me. Especially when he notices that I have blocked him on all my social media accounts. I haven't blocked his phone number so that I can see if he tries to contact me. Having met Carys and looking at her photos, I begin to wonder if meeting her was a sign from the universe, telling me that I need to go in a different direction, just as Geraint did. What if Geraint and I had drifted on for another ten years? I would have been sixty, sat on the sofa watching *Escape to the Country* and having my weekly Friday night takeaway, drinking too much cider or wine when he was away on his cycling trips. I thought it was just what happened when you were in a relationship for a long time. You had your own space.

But, looking at Carys' photos makes me realise that there is so much more out there. I am annoyed with myself that I lived but I didn't live properly. I simply existed and went along with what turned up in front of me. I chased nothing. Just accepted my fate.

Carys has taught me that you don't need to live a life sitting on the sofa watching other people reach their dreams on social media, or the telly. There is a big wide world just waiting to be discovered and everyone has the potential to reach their dreams; you just have to do something about it.

Chapter 4

I don't usually have to do favours for Jane, but a dress is urgently needed for a photo shoot at a castle in a nearby town. One of the local Welsh magazines needs it and Jane was thrilled to be included in the fashion feature. So, she sent me off on a mission.

At first, I am happy to get out of the shop for a bit and have a change of scenery. However, as I get lost on the windy roads in my beloved yellow Seventies Beetle, Dolly, I start to feel a bit panicky. I knew I shouldn't have trusted my dodgy satnav. I pull over to let a herd of cows pass the narrow one-track lane and squirm in my seat as a cow with the biggest eyelashes I've ever seen stares at me through the windscreen. Twenty-year-old girls would pay good money for lashes like those.

I avert my eyes so that I don't look as though I am a threat to the confused cow. They don't show this bit on *Escape to the Country*, do they? Where on earth am I? As if I am not in enough of a flap, I see that Jane is calling me. Since I am stuck on the road, I accept the call.

'Penny, where on earth are you?'

'I'm sorry, I'm so lost I think I am going to burst into tears in a minute,' I say.

'Right, calm down, lovely. What can you see?' Jane asks. I look at the cows going past the car. This could be any back road.

'A cow. He's black and white and giving me evil stares,' I manage to say.

'Okay, that's not really helping. Take some deep breaths and send me your location from your phone. I'll help you get back on the right road.'

Jane is always so understanding. She was amazing when I told her about Geraint when I walked in this morning. In fact, I think that's why she wanted me to deliver the dress instead of her. She normally keeps these important jobs for herself so she can do a bit of networking with the stylists. She went ballistic when I told her what Geraint had done.

'That sneaky little narcissist, well I won't be using him for the electrics ever again, I can promise you.'

The thought that he has lost a good customer in the form of Jane cheered me up slightly; after all, it would be rather awkward if Geraint turned up to fix a plug point. I mean, I might be tempted to boot him up the bottom when he was crouched down, so it is for everyone's safety really.

The last cow eventually passes as I am fantasising about booting Geraint up the bum. I breathe a sigh of relief; it was getting a bit claustrophobic being surrounded for a moment. How on earth could I be cabin crew dealing with emergencies and travelling the world when I can't even get to a castle in the next town and feel threatened by a herd of cows? Imagine if I came face to face with a hijacker! I'd never stay calm in a crisis which is one of the airline requirements and I would imagine quite essential in any unnerving moment.

Jane sends through the directions and, according to her, all I need to do is stay straight. I drive in the direction she suggests and am relieved when ten minutes later I see the main road with a sign for the castle. Hooray! I am finally on the right track, which is more than can be said for my life.

The castle comes into full view in front of me. It is absolutely stunning with a drawbridge, turrets and peacocks wandering about. Then I notice a sign at the side of the moat advertising their exquisite weddings. That's not what I need to see today, and why are weddings bothering me so much? It wasn't as if Geraint and I had ever planned on marrying, but since that night I realise that secretly I wanted to be Mrs Lloyd-Jones. The Mrs Lloyd-Jones with the children and hamster – and now that title will fall to someone else. I wonder if they'll get a hamster together next.

Grabbing the carefully wrapped dress from the car, I head inside the castle to find the stylist, trying to avoid the peacocks as I rush in.

'Oh, finally. We've been waiting,' says a distinguished woman in a long black dress with lots of beads and a grey ponytail. I notice her Doc Martins suit her perfectly. Why is everyone so fabulous nowadays? She must be in her mid-sixties and I am pretty sure I have never looked as good. I imagine she would model some of the time too. I explain about the cows and the cheap satnav I had installed in Dolly. None of this makes her accept my tardy timekeeping so I make my way back to the exit.

I head through the reception area first with its beautiful floral displays and red seating area. You could just imagine a king and queen in this castle with the vibrant red velvet throne-like chairs. I notice some leaflets in the reception area about their weddings; there are even business cards for a harpist! How sickening. I would have loved a harpist at my wedding. I'd have requested those beautiful

Welsh hymns, 'Calon Lan' and 'Myfanwy'. The thought of Geraint comes over me, like a massive wave crashing me to the ground. How could he do this to me? If only he'd admitted the truth sooner, my life could have been different. I could have travelled, had babies with someone who wanted them, or had some pets with someone I love at the very least.

I begin to cry as I reach outside and almost bump into the peacock. The peacock looks at me and I put my head down. *Not today, Mr Peacock.* Or is it Mrs Peacock? I can never remember which are the ones with the plume of feathers. I assume it's a male as he seems to be posing about a bit, just the way Geraint and the other guys used to at the gym.

For some reason, animals don't seem to like me this morning and the peacock starts displaying his feathers and getting quite high-pitched. For a second it looks like he is going to chase me, so I run towards the safety of Dolly. But, as I hear more peacocks chipping in and look back to see a crowd of them gathered, I fall on a stone. As I bang down on my cheek, I feel the pain of it cutting open. I imagine the peacocks swarming all around me. What if they're like vultures? I hurry back up but notice that the peacocks aren't interested in me after all. It must be a male thing.

From the safety of Dolly, I wipe the blood on my face with a tissue. Oh, what a morning it has been. I start my way back to the shop where I am needed for the rest of the day but get side-tracked by a garden centre on the corner of the road selling lovely hanging baskets. The sight of the pretty flowers starts to cheer me up. It is the first time in my life I find myself interested in hanging baskets and am slightly concerned as I take two colourful baskets filled to the brim with petunias and begonias to the till. It's finally happened. I have turned into a middle-aged woman. I console myself with the fact that at least I didn't plant them myself; it could have been worse.

To make myself feel a little less middle-aged, I blast out some Def Leppard and sing in the car all the way back to the shop, despite not really being in the mood to sing. I might be miserable but at least I'm still a rock chick at heart, even if my cheek is feeling rather sore as I screech out the words about pouring sugar all over myself. You see, that's not stereotypical middle-aged behaviour. I am a mere youngster.

'My goodness, what happened to you?' says Jane, looking at my blood-stained face when I arrive back.

'I thought a peacock wanted to chase me, don't ask,' I say.

'Oh dear, you do look like you've been through it. What a day you've had. Looks nasty. Are you sure you don't need stitches?'

'No, it's okay. It looks a lot worse than it is. I have got a bit of a headache though,' I say.

'Poor thing, why don't you have an early finish? You've done so much for me today. It was never in your job description to go around castles running from peacocks to be fair,' says Jane.

She really is wonderful.

'Thank you. I might just do that. Think I could do with a lie down.'

'You so deserve an early finish. I still feel terrible about calling you in yesterday when you'd been through so much the night before. I'd have told the dentist to forget that cancellation had I known. I do wish you'd have told me, you'd always come first,' says Jane.

'No, it's fine. Honestly. It was probably for the best. No point moping about at home alone, is there,' I say. Then it hits me yet again. Alone at home, as always.

'Oh, lovely girl. I wish I could do something for you. It's unfair how he treated you. He always was a bit slimy I suppose. You often find those charming guys are love rats. Charm the pants off anyone,' says Jane.

'Why didn't you say something before?' I ask.

'Well, it's only in hindsight, isn't it? When you put all the pieces together you think about it. You don't realise at the time. You just think they are genuinely charming. Don't you worry. Once a cheat, always a cheat. That Alex woman doesn't know what she's let herself in for. It's not a loss at all for you. It's a gift. They both did you a favour.'

'Yeah, I'm really not seeing that right now.'

'You will. I tell you what. How about a boozy lunch Friday afternoon so we can have a good chat? We'll close the shop for a few hours. We'll call it staff training.'

Jane flicks her short brown bob about as she waits for me to accept the invitation.

'You can't do that,' I say.

'I bloody well can. It's my business. Is it a yes? I'll get Chris to pick us up and he can drop you home. No expense spared, you even have your own driver, so no excuses. And, wait for it, I'll pay you for a full day.'

'Oh, Jane, are you sure? I feel terrible that you'd close the shop to take me out. I don't want you to lose any sales. It does sound lovely though,' I say.

'It will indeed be lovely. I'll tell Chris tonight that he's on taxi duty.'

Jane and Chris have been married for thirty years. He is such a dependable bloke. Why couldn't Geraint be like him? Jane has no idea how lucky she is to have picked a good one.

On the way home I forget about my decision to keep my calories controlled and treat myself to an Indian takeaway. At least I have added new foods to my diet this week.

I notice the big bruise on my cheek in Dolly's mirror as I get out of the car. The mark on my face reminds me of the one I had when Kezza, the school bully at the comprehensive, smacked me in the face with her satchel.

Unlike that day though, it is nobody's fault but mine today. I shouldn't have been scared of the peacock when he was causing me no harm. I really don't seem to understand the male species at all, whether human or the peacock variety. From now on I am staying well clear of all of them.

As I am munching on my onion bhaji I get a notification that an email has arrived on my phone.

I click on it and am surprised when I see the heading.

RE: Cabin crew application.

That was quick. Oh well, it was only for a bit of fun. I completely understand their decision to not take this any further. Gingerly, I open the email.

Dear Penny,
Many thanks for your application as cabin crew. We are pleased to invite you for an interview at nine a.m. on 18 June at our head office...

I drop the phone down in shock. I got selected for an interview! Oh, I never thought that would happen.

Perhaps I didn't put my date of birth down and they don't realise my age. Surely they are not going to take on a fifty-year-old with no flying experience?

Then it dawns on me that the interview is only a week away. How can I go to an interview with a big bruise on my face? Besides, I have the best boss in the world closing her business for the afternoon, especially for me. I am not the same person I was when I hastily sent off the application.

I immediately want to reach out to Carys to tell her what's happened, but still feel a little embarrassed that I want to live a life like she does. Even though she was helpful and probably wouldn't mind, I decide not to say anything. I am not going to go anyway and will stay in the shop for the rest of my life. I can't do it to Jane.

I forget about the interview when I see that a call is coming through. It's Geraint. Finally, he is calling to check on me. He took his time. I don't want to answer but find myself accepting the call. I am desperate to know what he has to say and, if I am honest with myself, to hear his voice. Will he sound apologetic? Or be cocky and confident? Despite so many warnings, I need to know for sure what sort of person he is after Jane's remarks earlier. Did I not ever notice that he was a snarky snake narcissist?

'All right babe,' he says chirpily as I answer.

'No, not really,' I say.

'Aww, not coming down with something are you?'

'No, I'm not,' I say incredulously. Does he still not realise how upset I am about everything?

'What is it, Geraint?' I ask.

'Was wondering if I could come round and collect my Duran Duran LP. I think I left it there and we're having an Eighties party next week so I need it.'

I roll my eyes. I feel as though I could snap his LP if I knew where it was.

'I don't know. I haven't seen it anywhere,' I manage to say.

'You can come if you want,' says Geraint.

'You what?'

'You can come to the party if you like. You can bring the album with you at the same time.'

'I don't think so, Geraint. I'll have a look for it and if I find it I'll send it to you. In the post, all right?'

'What's wrong with you?' says Geraint.

'What do you think is wrong with me?' I say.

'Don't be like that now, Pen. We had a good time together, didn't we? I want us to stay friends. I know I did the wrong thing but I don't see why we can't stay on good terms.'

'How can I stay friends with someone who cheated on me and hurt me so badly and strung me along for all these years?'

'Well, that's what I mean. We've been together ages. Everyone knows us as Ger and Pen. It's like Morecambe and Wise, or Ant and Dec. It was us two. We can't throw away all that just because I met someone I'm more compatible with. Oh, and have you blocked me on Facebook?'

'Oh my god. Can you not see what you've done to me?'

'Well, yeah. I'm sorry. I didn't mean to hurt you. But I don't want us to fall out and never speak again just because it was time for us to be with other people.'

'*You* to be with other people. Not me,' I say firmly.

'Yeah, well, like I said. Soz, innit. Shit happens.'

'Soz! Soz! Shit happens? I have spent ten years with a two-timing snake who says "soz, shit happens". My god, I've wasted my life. I'm going now, Geraint. I don't want to speak to you ever again. And, yes, I have blocked you and I should have blocked your number on here too. Goodbye, Geraint. I wish you the best with that woman. You two suit each other.'

'Oh, thanks babe. I think we do too. Ta-ra then,' says Geraint.

I put the phone down, not bothering to say my farewell. Then I block his number. I need to move on quickly from him. I can't waste my life for a second longer. He is not worth a moment of my time. Now I must consider my next move as though I am playing a game of chess. But I don't want a king; I want to be the powerful queen and make sure that my next move is the winning one.

Chapter 5

At lunch with Jane, she tells me what a valuable employee I am. In fact, the more wine she has, the more fabulous she tells me I am. It is wonderful to be so appreciated. My boyfriend may not have held me in high regard, but at least Jane does.

'Let's get another bottle,' says Jane, as we empty the first one.

'Are you sure?' I ask. I feel terrible knowing that Jane is being so extravagant. She ordered lobster for us and everything. I can't possibly take any more from her.

'Expenses, lovely,' she says.

'Yes, but it all comes out of your bottom line,' I remind her.

'Think of it as a staff party, but it's just us. Cheers,' she says.

'Cheers,' I say, drinking the last drop of wine in my glass. I feel tipsy already.

As much as Jane is practically the only friend I have, I am always a little guarded in front of her since she is my boss too. I would hate to overstep any boundaries.

But, as the wine flows, so does Jane's tongue.

'You know, some days I think of flogging it all,' she says.

'Flogging what?'

'The business,' she says.

I look at her in alarm. Is this just drunk talk or is she serious?

Despite all the wine, she seems to detect the look on my face. I really must get better at hiding my expressions.

'Oh, it's a silly thought. No, I don't mean it. I've built the business up from scratch to what it is today. Why would I want to give all that up? Except to live on a Caribbean island.'

I can't tell if she is joking about the Caribbean island or not, but it terrifies me. I need the stability of Jane and my job right now.

'It's just, you know when you get bored and start looking online at stuff. Well, there was this stunning place in the Cayman Islands. Is that the Caribbean or Pacific? I was never very good at geography. Anyway, it looked lush. Swimming pool, palm trees, three bedrooms. The boys could visit with their families. The grandkids would love the pool. Hmm, yeah.'

Jane looks wistful as she says this. Oh my god, she is actually serious. Her dream is to run off to the Cayman Islands, leaving me behind. Backpacking with Yvonne was my dream when I was younger, but now what aspirations do I have? Nothing.

The lunch goes a little flat after Jane's revelation. I should be incredibly happy that Jane is in the position to think about selling up one day and moving away. But all I can think about is being left yet again.

After Chris has dropped me off at home, I plonk myself down on the sofa and scroll through social media and quietly observe everyone's perfect lives. One of which is Carys'. In a new photo she is standing in front of some baby elephants with a group of women of all different ages. A comment above it reads, *What a fab crew on this five-day stay in Columbo.* She gets paid to have five days in Sri Lanka with elephants. Quite unbelievable.

As I am looking through her fabulous life, I see a message come through from her on Facebook. I hope she doesn't have some device that tells her I was looking through her pics.

> Hello, lovely, How's things?

I can see she is online so I answer right away.

> Great, just had a lovely lobster lunch with my boss.

> Ah, that's great. Glad you're feeling better than when we met.

> Yeah, I'm okay. How's things with you?

> Just landed in Dominican, now sat on the beach. Bit jet-lagged but still, sunbathe first, sleep later! That's my motto.

> Sounds like a great motto.

I put the kettle on and wonder how much longer I can continue plodding on with no aspirations in life. It is time I had a great motto too.

By the time I get back to my phone, Carys has sent a photo of a beautiful white sandy beach and a turquoise blue sea. Coconut trees gravitate over string hammocks. I can't help but compare it with my view and the damp patch that is getting worse in the corner of my ceiling. One of us is living their best life and it's certainly not me.

Her photo spurs me on to accept the interview for Calm Air. It feels like a moment of madness as I email back to say I shall be attending the interview. Jane owes me a lieu day from the day of her dental appointment. I still feel like a bit of a traitor though, but try to remember that she could sell the business at the drop of a hat if she decided, and where would I be then?

I message Carys to tell her about my interview but she has gone offline. She is probably sipping a cocktail by now.

The notion of doing something about my life cheers me up immensely. That and the thought of my visit to the dog shelter in the morning. I always feel happier when I visit the Doodle Sanctuary to help walk the beautiful dogs every Wednesday morning. Whether rain or shine, watching those dogs when they spot you getting their leads to walk them is the best feeling in the world. Their little expectant faces never fail to cheer me up.

-

The next morning, I park Dolly up outside the kennels and hear barking as the dogs get excited at the arrival of a car. I wonder if they think it could be someone arriving to pick them up and take them to a new home.

When I walk in, Janet, the owner of the sanctuary, is organising a new delivery of dog food, thanks to a kind dog food sponsor.

47

'Hey Penny, would you be able to take Oreo and Willow out? They came in Sunday night. Their poor owner died, nobody could take them in. The lady had no family. They're sweet enough, shouldn't give you any bother,' says Janet.

Poor little mites. It makes me slightly emotional as I realise I would be in the same situation and why it is probably best I never have a dog of my own, as much as I love them. Oreo and Willow are two gorgeous Labradoodles, one black and one apricot coloured.

I give them a little treat that I keep in my pocket for whenever I have to meet a new dog for the first time, to show them that I am friendly. Sadly, you just don't know what their circumstances were before they arrived. I make a big fuss of them once I can see they're okay with me stroking them and take them on a lovely walk to a nearby wooded area. They run around and play with a ball and I hope their dog mum is looking down and realises that they are being well cared for. I wish I could take them home myself.

When I drop Oreo and Willow back a while later, I see a message from Carys.

> Oh, Penny, I'm so pleased you're applying. I promise you'll love it. I'll send you some interview tips.

> That would be amazing, thank you.

I can't believe I am lucky enough to have someone on the inside who can give me tips. I have looked online and, reading through some of the information, it seems that you have to do group exercises to see how you work with others. I'm not the best at things like that. The introvert and only child in me much prefers to get on with tasks by myself rather than in a group. And what do you even wear to a cabin crew interview? Should it be formal, such as a smart suit? I certainly can't afford anything new. Dolly is getting rustier by the day and needs even more work than I do on her poor ageing body.

I am glad that I have now been able to share my secret with someone. There is no point in upsetting Jane with the news that I am applying for another job when there is a big chance I may never get it. Even though I want this job more than anything, I tell myself that I must leave it to fate. If I am meant to have it then I will. Perhaps my fate was for Carys to walk in that day and give me this idea.

Then I remember my poor hanging baskets. I am such an awful plant mum! I realise I haven't watered them for two days, the poor mites. I am not worthy of plants. I hope they survive. I rush outside with an empty water bottle I find under the sink, since I never thought to invest in a watering can whilst I was at the garden centre. A busload of passengers watch as I try to reach the hanging baskets. I feel my short dressing gown ride up. Oh no. Thankfully the bus soon heads off into the distance and then I notice a big advertisement on the back saying 'Fly now for just £49 from Cardiff to Barcelona'.

Oh, how lovely that would be. I've never been there. Perhaps the bus is also trying to tell me I need to get out a bit more and at that price, I could afford it, although finding someone to go with would be more difficult. But it is as though there are signs everywhere. It is like someone is telling me that it is time for me to travel, just as I wanted to when I was in school and, with the help of Carys, it could finally happen. I am so grateful for this new friendship.

Popping the TV on, I search for something of interest through the channels, but there's nothing. Now that I have the travel bug, I have the urge to watch a holiday programme.

Why can't we still have Judith Chalmers and *Wish you Were Here...*? Even in her eighties, I am sure she would be wonderful. Eventually, I manage to find a cruise programme with Jane McDonald. I wonder if cruise ships employ people over fifty if I fail my interview. It looks like hard work though, being at sea for months on end. I don't have particularly good sea legs either so perhaps it is not the career for me, as fabulous as it does look, sitting here from my motionless sofa.

Once Jane McDonald finishes her rendition of her latest song as the programme ends, I feel a bit flat so I reach for my jar of happiness. This is the pot that I keep all my chocolate Freddos in. Whenever I feel low, I reach in and take out a Freddo and it makes me smile. I notice there are only two left. I seem to have been devoid of much happiness this week, but then again, is anyone truly happy? Perhaps Geraint is now that he is no longer living a lie with me. Carys seems happy too. She isn't in a relationship and is fulfilled in other ways, by travelling the world and enjoying her life. I am happy when I help the doodles, of course. Yet for some reason, I still don't feel fulfilled. It is as though something is missing. People talk of their happy place. I don't even have a happy place. Well, apart from when I am sitting in Dolly, driving somewhere with my music on. I realise that this is what I am missing in life.

Happiness. It has been missing for some time now if I think about it.

I want to make myself happy, and what could make me happier than a job where I lie on the beach in an exotic location after a few hours at work? Getting this job would be life-changing, and as I realise just how important it is to me, I feel a determination from within me start to rise.

I haven't felt this determined since I wrote to the Bros Fan Club asking if I could get the autographs of Matt and Luke Goss. I even sent them my photo, convinced that one of them – if not both – would fall in love with me, possibly even fight over me, if only they saw me and my gorgeous perm.

Of course, I was deluded. I only hope that applying to a world-renowned airline at the age of fifty is not equally deluded.

Chapter 6

On the morning of my interview with Calm Air at their Heathrow office, I am anything but calm. This means so much to me that I don't know what I will do if I am unsuccessful. Now that the idea has been sown in my head, I can't imagine a future without this.

When I see some of the posters of the destinations that Calm Air fly to, I know that this is what I want, even more so than Geraint apologising and saying he made a mistake. This is about me. I am single, independent and have nobody to answer to. What better time could there be for me to travel the world? I missed out when I was younger; I am not missing out on this chance now.

I have worn a suit for the interview today. I found an old trouser suit which is the same light grey colour as the airline uniform. Since the letter arrived, I have splurged and had my highlights done, although they cost a small fortune and it means Dolly won't be having a new exhaust this month. However, I need to look my best today. I figure this could be a lucrative investment and if the salary works out, Dolly could even be fully restored finally.

Waiting for the receptionist to attend to me, I glance around at the posters of Caribbean islands, European cities and Middle Eastern countries. I can't imagine what it must be like to visit all these places.

Whilst the receptionist carries on with a phone call, I notice a sign to the bathrooms and decide to freshen up after my journey up to head office.

I am struck by the fancy bathroom that is full of empowering slogans on the toilet doors, like *It's your day today* and *Don't look back, you're not going that way*, which I would hope would be the case if these toilets are for those who are about to board an aeroplane.

Maybe I should invest in some of these positive affirmation signs that say *I am gorgeous* and *I love myself*. What if I am not happy because I don't have white wooden letters above my fireplace telling me to *Be Happy*?

I check my hair in the mirror, making sure it is still in the neat French plait I managed to get it into this morning. I have put so much spray on that I don't think it could move if I was in a tornado. Then I squirt lots of my favourite English pear and freesia scent all over me to freshen myself up until I smell a bit like the garden centre I visited the other day. I think I may have gone a bit overboard and start to cough and splutter just as two women in uniform walk in.

'It's nothing contagious,' I say, coughing.

They look at me with a sort of smile, as in one of those 'bless, pity for her' types of smiles. Then they continue chatting with each other.

'Did you see that captain on the Barcelona flight? Shame he is a bit of a shit,' says one of them to the other.

What a conversation to have in the toilet in front of a stranger. Don't they realise I can hear everything?

'Yeah, isn't he the one who flew his wife to Amsterdam, then flew on to Marbs and met his girlfriend down-route? She's only a junior as well.'

'Well, that's the thing with those juniors, they haven't been around as long as us. He might be hot, but we all know pilots can be trouble,' says the other one.

'Bloody idiot,' she continues.

My mouth is almost open as I listen to this cabin crew gossip. I know I am already staying well away from the male species of all kinds, but I make a note there and then not to be a gullible 'junior' and ever have anything to do with a pilot if I am successful in today's interview. That's disgraceful behaviour.

I squeeze past them and head back to reception.

The receptionist is now free but, for some reason, I am a little nervous about speaking to her and so I put on what Jane would call a 'posh' voice when I speak to her. I am fully aware that I really shouldn't change for anyone, but it's a nervous thing.

'Hello, I am here for the interview,' I say in my best cut-glass accent.

'Welcome, and good luck today,' says the receptionist with a smile as she reaches for the signing-in book.

I can see immediately that she seems friendly and is not to be feared.

'If you just wait a second, I'll give you your pass,' she says as I sign in. 'Are you from Wales, by the way?' she asks.

'Yes, I am,' I reply. My Cardiff accent obviously shone through after all.

'Oh, amazing. I'm from Llanrumney, thought you weren't from too far away from me,' she says.

My accent suddenly becomes much stronger as I begin to relax.

'Oh, that's brilliant. Small world. How do you manage working here? Did you have to move to Heathrow?' I ask.

'In the end, yes. I used to be crew and decided to come into head office when I had kids. I commuted when I was flying though, it's not too bad from Cardiff.'

'That's good to know,' I say. Although why I should be successful today, I don't know.

Having someone here who comes from not too far away from home puts me at ease and I feel a little more confident about being out of my comfort zone.

I notice that a queue is forming behind me so, although I could chat with her all day, I make my way to the seating area where three friendly women smile at me.

'Ta-ra and, once again, good luck,' says the receptionist.

The other interviewees are immediately friendly too.

'Hi, I'm Alicia,' says a dark-haired woman in her early twenties.

'And I'm Nicole,' says someone similarly aged.

I attempt to confidently introduce myself even though I realise that I'm probably old enough to be their mum. It hits me again that I should have done this years ago and not at my age.

Around ten more interviewees walk across to the three of us one by one and gather around. I notice one guy who is more my age and here for the interview. This makes me feel a lot better about being the eldest here, so I try to walk to the interview room beside him.

'I'm Penny,' I say.

'Greg, how do you do?' he says.

'Great, what made you want to apply for Calm Air?' I ask him. My question makes me feel as though I am interviewing him.

'Always dreamed of it. Hit my fortieth and my wife encouraged me to apply.'

I instantly feel dreadful. Firstly, that I am ten years older than him, I am older than I think I am, and the way he dropped in that he had a wife. I do hope he didn't get the wrong idea that I was trying to flirt with him. I always overthink everything and now I worry I have given him the wrong impression, despite him seeming affable.

'What made you apply?' he asks.

'Oh, need a change of scenery,' I say.

Hopefully that is enough information. I don't want to bring Geraint up or I know I will never stop and go into one of those nervous tirades that I have a habit of getting into.

Fortunately, I don't have to say anything further as two of the recruitment team, Tina and Sam, begin to talk. They seem down to earth.

'Hello, everyone, so lovely you can be with us today. Before we start, we just want to say, please don't be nervous. We don't bite. To show you that we are actually nice people, we're going to start the morning off with some informal fun so that you can all get to know each other. Who knows? You may even make some new friends here today. Sam and I met at our interview and we're still besties, aren't we, Sam?' says Tina.

'We are indeed. Though we didn't have WhatsApp groups in those days, like most of the recruits now put together during their selection days,' says Sam, laughing.

Sam leans behind and grabs a couple of games of Twister. Oh no, do they expect us to play Twister? Can my limbs even do this? I'm not twelve years old any longer. I guess it is one way to see if we will pass the medical, which is the next stage of the process if we get through today.

Sam lays out the Twister mats and puts us into groups of four. Thank goodness I wore trousers today.

I am put into a group with Greg, Nicole and someone I have just been introduced to as Michelle, who I would say is in her thirties. As soon as we get chatting, we realise we have so much in common. Michelle drives a Beetle, albeit a new one, and works in retail. I can see what Tina and Sam meant about making friends. We seem to instantly connect. I even consider that I might bite the bullet and offer to create a WhatsApp group. I have never been the type of person who would do such a bold thing but perhaps it might show me as being assertive to Tina and Sam, even if I am not.

Sam spins off the needle to see where it will land for the Twister game and gets all jumpy and excitable. It's all right for him, he's steady on two feet. I am almost toppling over in the first round. I begin to wonder if they are testing our balance to see if we can withstand turbulence.

It all seems a bit awkward for a minute but after a few more spins, by the time we are all bent around each other, we have no choice but to relax and get along. Sam spins the arrow to red and it is my turn to move. I really don't want to lose the game; who knows how they are marking this exercise. However, if I am to stay in the game, it means my legs are twisted around and it leaves Greg's crotch right in my face.

Oh dear, I look like one of the dogs in the doodle sanctuary when they are sizing up a new member in their kennel. I decide I will have to leave the game; it's far too embarrassing to be in this position with my face in his nether regions like this. So I wobble and fall and am the first one out. I do hope that I am not penalised for losing, and that Sam has some sympathy for the predicament I was in.

Next Michelle is out and then Nicole pushes Greg's leg, falls and topples them both over. She lies on top of Greg and slowly pulls herself off, apologising.

'I hope you all enjoyed that and I am sure anything else you do after that won't be half as embarrassing. That's why we call it an icebreaker,' says Tina, laughing.

By the time we finish the game, we are all laughing and enjoying ourselves. I even begin to forget that this is an interview. Sam and Tina certainly put people at ease.

'Next up, you're going to have some fun. We're going to put you in uniform and you can see what it feels like to be cabin crew with Calm Air. We're also going to give you some pampering with a make-up session for those who would like it. I must point out that we have recently relaxed our grooming regulations so make-up isn't compulsory,' says Tina.

We all look around the room excitedly.

'I'm loving this interview,' says Nicole.

'Me too, I am definitely going to have the make-up session,' I say.

I am so excited when Sam takes us off to the grooming room.

I can't believe what I see when we walk in. It is like an Aladdin's cave or a child's dressing-up room. I can imagine the children who come into Little Darlings would adore this.

There are small Hollywood mirrored dressing tables full of make-up and fancy make-up brushes dotted around. This looks like the type of theatre dressing room celebrities at a West End show would get themselves ready in. Except to one side is a wall full of uniforms. Grey trousers, skirts and jackets are neatly lined up with the pink blouses and shirts that are worn underneath.

A man in uniform introduces himself as Nick and says that he will help us all find our sizes.

He picks out a size ten skirt and a size twelve blouse and jacket for me. I try to tell him I am a size ten top also, but he insists I try the twelve.

'Darling, our sizes can come up small,' he insists. Despite what he says I have a sneaking suspicion that the bigger size is more likely down to my jar of happiness.

I enter the special fitting room and put on the uniform. Looking in the mirror, I feel so glamourous, but then, when I put on the uniform hat, I feel like a million dollars. I look like some kind of genie. I wonder if they would let us take this beautiful uniform home. I could walk around town like this. In fact, I would walk around everywhere like this. The doctors, the library, the supermarket; I don't think I would ever take this uniform off if I got the job. In fact, if it wasn't for my favourite Snoopy pyjamas, I would be tempted to sleep in it.

Nick takes me to the make-up table once I reveal myself from the fitting room and starts doing my make-up.

'Do you prefer a natural look, or heavy?' he asks.

'Oh, I don't mind. You're the expert. I feel as though I'm in safe hands. Whatever you think,' I reply.

'You're very brave. You sure you're ready for this?' he says, laughing.

'Ready as I'll ever be,' I say with a smile.

Ten minutes later he whizzes around my chair to face the mirror.

He pops my hat on and the look is complete.

'Wow. I love it,' I say.

I feel like a completely different person in uniform with my make-up done. Yup, I am definitely assertive enough to offer to create a WhatsApp group in this uniform. Perhaps all I ever needed was a uniform in my life.

Nick has given me a smoky eye which brings out the green fleck in my eyes. My eyebrows that have thinned badly due to the over-zealous plucking of the Eighties have been filled in and I actually have eyebrows for once. I feel like the best version of myself. A new empowered Penny.

I could even tell a passenger to put their seat belt on in this uniform, unlike in the shop when I was too scared to confront a child for trying to break the rocking horse. I am powerful Penny dressed like this. All I need are huge shoulder pads and I would be like Joan Collins in *Dynasty* and able to take on the world.

'Would you be able to write down the make-up colours for me?' I ask. I want to look like this when I get home. Geraint would have a right shock if he saw me now.

'Of course,' he says.

As Nick is about to get a paper and pen for me, a pilot walks in.

I can't help myself; I actually gasp out loud. I don't know that I have ever seen anyone more handsome. I feel as though fireworks have gone off inside me. I'm all jittery. I always had this silly belief that when you saw your soulmate you would know. Of course, over the years, I came to realise that this wasn't true and there is no such thing. It was a silly childish notion that I believed, having been brought up reading fairy tales. Now I am more pessimistic and sometimes think that life is no fairy tale but a heap of disappointments we endure as we trundle through our day-to-day living.

But this man, in this split second... It is as though we have been together in another universe. Is it because of those beautiful deep blue eyes, perhaps? Or is it the tan that makes him look like someone who just stepped off a plane from Monaco? Oh my, he is just gorgeous. So gorgeous that I immediately discard the warning that those women in the toilets said about pilots. I try to calm my nerves as I watch him head towards us. It looks as though he needs to speak to the grooming guy and makes a beeline for him.

'Hi Nick, I need to get a new jacket. Dry cleaning in Jakarta wrecked my spare one. Knew I should have waited till I got back,' he says.

'No worries, Matt. Let me make sure we have your size,' he says.

'Excuse me a moment, won't you,' says Nick.

'Of course,' I say, smiling.

The handsome pilot doesn't seem to notice me and turns around to follow Nick. However, as he does so I manage to fling my arm in a fluster and hit a foundation bottle towards his leg. The open bottle flies in the air, dripping the beige liquid all down his trouser leg, before finally landing with a crash on the floor.

The pilot looks at me with complete disgust and says, 'What the hell are you doing? I'm about to do a Singapore flight. My bloody trousers.'

'I am so sorry, it was an accident,' I say.

I look at the table and notice some tissues and find myself instinctively rubbing at his leg. Of course, as we all know, rubbing foundation in makes it spread further, so why I did this I really don't know and it will be something I will always ask myself furthermore.

'What the hell are you doing? Get off,' he says.

'Sorry, trying to help,' I mutter.

He might be absolutely gorgeous, but he is certainly not very nice. What an obnoxious man. I thought everyone here was lovely until now.

Fortunately, Nick calms him down a bit and provides him with a new pair of trousers and tells him he will pop them in the staff laundry and that they will be ready by the time he returns from Singapore. He seems a bit happier by the time he leaves but still gives me a mean look as he walks out. Thank goodness *he* isn't interviewing me; what a horror bag.

'Don't worry, at least he was in the right place for that to happen,' says Nick.

'I feel such an idiot. Are pilots always that rude?' I ask.

'He's probably just a bit stressed. The airline does tend to over-work some of the pilots, to be honest,' whispers Nick.

'Is that safe?' I ask. Surely that must be dangerous.

'Calm Air knows its limitations and what they can and can't get away with,' says Nick.

'Gosh.'

Nick makes me wonder if the airline has any regard for its employees, but then I guess most big corporations are the same. That is why working with Jane makes things so different.

Looking in the mirror at my glamourous reflection once more makes me want this job, despite the fact I might get over-worked. Even just for a short time, this would be such an adventure, as long as I stay away from moody mean pilots like Matt.

'Right then boys and girls, you're all looking fabulous in here. I know you could probably stay and play in this room forever but I've come to grab you for your one-on-one interviews. You can come in uniform, you don't need to get changed,' says Tina.

The rest of the interviewees look at each other nervously. I don't think any of us want to get out of this uniform; it could be the only chance we ever get to wear it.

'After your interviews, you're free to come back in here and get changed. So if any of you want to swap numbers, maybe now is the time to do it.'

I take a big gulp. I am almost breathless as I say it.

'Shall we make up a WhatsApp group?' I ask. There! I did it.

I am officially the type of person who pulls everyone together and makes up a group chat!

I notice Tina look at me approvingly. It appears that I have done something right. This gives me the validation to continue with the confident, powerful Penny act.

'If we all keep in touch then we'll know who was and who wasn't successful and can be there for each other,' I say.

Everyone gathers around giving me their numbers. I title the group 'Calm Air Recruitment Day, (CARD)'. I have noticed already that the airline seems to like its abbreviations. There are signs around the offices saying things like 'SEP', whatever that is, and I heard one of the crew walking around talking about how she had a 'LAX', which seems to mean an airport code in the US and not an abbreviation for a laxative.

'First up, who will be the lucky one?' says Sam.

'Ooh, it's Penny,' says Tina.

Oh, my goodness, I am a little concerned about being first up as now I won't hear from the others what questions they asked.

All around the room, everyone shouts good luck. I can just feel the comradeship between us already. Walking out of the room to a small office, I feel as though I have all the strength of the team behind me.

Sam and Tina are very lovely. Although, as with Jane, I don't quite let my guard down as sometimes you can be interviewed by someone and they feel like your best friend. That's when things go wrong because you become complacent.

'You look very nice in your uniform, Penny,' says Sam.

'Thank you, it's a gorgeous fit. Don't want to take it off,' I say, smiling.

'Everyone says that, but believe me, you wait until you're on a long flight. It is the best feeling ever to kick off the uniform. And don't talk to me about the tights,' Tina says, giggling.

I wonder what she means by saying 'when I'm on a long flight'. Does that mean I have the job? I tell myself to stop it. It was purely a figure of speech.

Throughout the interview, Tina and Sam both say a lot of positive things. By the time they are done with me, I am on top of the world. I know I will probably come back down to earth with a bang when I get that letter, but at least they have made me feel special for now. Today was exactly what I needed.

I head back to the grooming room and get changed back into my civvies. I could cry as I hand the uniform back to Nick.

'Good luck then, hun. I'm sure I'll be seeing you soon for your real uniform fitting,' says Nick.

'Oh, gosh, I hope so,' I say.

I wish Nick could have a word with Tina and Sam for me. Although perhaps he wouldn't be recommending me after what happened to the foundation bottle.

As I leave the building and say goodbye to the lovely receptionist, I make my way towards the revolving door that is both an entrance and exit. I walk into one section and notice that there is a pilot in the other part of the revolving door. I panic as I realise that it is that Meanie Matt. I have never been a fan of revolving doors and so I push at the glass panel to make it go faster. Only it doesn't. It just sticks. So then I panic further and push it some more. But the more I push it, the more it goes on strike. I am now stuck in a revolving door with Matt and then he turns and looks to see who the moron is that is pushing the door. I put my hand in front of my face to hide as he turns back, giving me the evilest glare.

'You again,' he says through the glass.

I hear the voice of the receptionist shout from the back.

'I've put it on manual, push the door,' she says.

Matt stumbles out first and then me straight after as we are finally ejected from the revolving door from hell.

We both stand on the path outside and he shakes his head at me.

'I'm already late and still have to get the crew bus to the airport. Passengers are waiting for me to fly the plane,' he says.

Please, someone save me. It is at this point that I know I should walk away. Ignore him. But perhaps it is because I have been so hurt by Geraint that I answer back. I can't help myself. Words just tumble out. Harsh ones that I would never say to anyone. I have absolutely no control over them and feel as though I will burst if I don't explode right here on the steps of the Calm Air head office. All my frustration comes out on Meanie Matt the pilot, a total stranger.

'Well, maybe you should try being a bit more punctual, you obnoxious little man. Who do you think you are?' I say, glaring back at him.

'Obnoxious little man? Well, I've never been called that before. Who do I think I am? Well, usually, it's captain. And for your information, I just got called out on standby. The previous captain had to offload himself.'

Why do these airline people talk in such a weird language? 'Offload'? 'Standby'?

'Can't you talk normally? What is it with your special weird language?' I say.

'I beg your pardon? I make announcements on planes, I talk very normally, thank you,' says Matt in an assured captain's voice.

'I admit you do have a beautiful voice, but you're still a jerk, sorry,' I say.

Thankfully he doesn't have time to retort as the crew bus pulls up as he's about to speak.

'Toodle-oo.' I wave as the crew bus drives off with him.

I turn to leave, and as I do so I realise that I have just made the biggest scene outside the Calm Air head office and have probably lost all hope of wearing that uniform ever again. I think it is time I had a little herbal tea to calm down, although I do feel a lot better after having a rant. I just pray it wasn't captured on CCTV.

Chapter 7

The CARD WhatsApp group buzzes away all the next morning. One of the interviewees has received a rejection letter already. How disappointing. We give him our commiserations and then once he has had ten of our messages saying we are sorry to hear this, we get a notification that he 'has left the group'. I can understand; it can't be nice being the first one out. This is suddenly feeling like *Squid Game*.

Back at work, Jane is as bubbly as ever and I try to make sure she doesn't notice my phone seems to be bleeping a lot from my handbag. As I am such a loner, she would wonder what had happened to make me so in demand suddenly. I still don't think she should know about my interview unless I will be resigning for sure. She would probably be incredibly hurt, although part of me wants to believe that Jane will be selling the business and leaving me behind.

We haven't discussed that conversation again, and so it could well be just a pipe dream, but if I think of her swapping Cardiff for the Cayman Islands then I can handle the guilt about going behind her back to an interview a little easier.

'Did you have a nice day off yesterday, Pen? Do anything nice?' she asks.

I don't know where to look. I can't lie but she can't know. She wouldn't believe it if she had seen me in that grooming room looking like a completely different person. The best empowered version of me.

I quickly grab some security tags and press them into the latest stock that has arrived. Focusing on getting the pins through the fabric keeps me busy and means that I don't have to look Jane in the eye. I feel terrible. How are you supposed to lie to the best boss in the world?

'Yes, watered my hanging baskets, chilled a bit,' I say. At least that is the truth – after I got home.

'You need to get out a bit more, Penny,' says Jane.

'Oh, you know me. Boring old Penny,' I say, laughing.

Lying to Jane like this makes me feel like some kind of burlesque dancer that hides her secret pastime from the people at work. In fact, that might be an option if I don't get Calm Air. I may well look into burlesque; that would bring me out of my shell a bit. Quiet and unassuming Penny becomes burlesque dancer extraordinaire; how fun that would be.

'You know, Penny. You might think it's a bit soon, but I have a lovely nephew. He's going through a divorce at the moment. I never did like his wife, to be honest. He's coming down for a break. How about I fix you up? Would you entertain him for me?'

Jane is like one of those aunts who are always trying to matchmake. She thinks everyone should be in a relationship and can't understand why someone would want to be single.

'Thank you for the kind offer, but it's okay. I'm happy being single. I'm re-evaluating my life at the moment so don't need a man to interfere with any of that. I'm sure your nephew is very lovely though, so thanks.'

'Oh, but just think, if you two hit it off we could be related. Then you could take over the business and I'd run off to the sunshine. It's more for me than him,' says Jane, laughing.

There is definitely more to this jetting off joke than she is letting on. I am becoming more convinced that she wants to sell up just as much as I want the job at Calm Air. At least, I convince myself of this for the rest of the day.

Most people needing fancy party or bridesmaids' dresses for summer weddings have them by now. So I hide away with the new stock and the security tagging whilst I think of Jane in the Cayman Islands and me in that gorgeous uniform.

The new children's autumn collection that I am tagging is so pretty. Jane is great at buying stock; she always picks the best. Probably another reason why she is so well thought of by her target customers.

It's hard to believe the autumn clothes are already in. How fast the seasons run away. Before I know it, I will be fifty-one, another year whizzed by. What will I be doing with myself? Will I be sitting at home every night? My one chance of excitement could be blown because of a rant at a captain I have never met before. I curse myself for going through that revolving door at the same time as him. I really shouldn't have lost it like that. The interview day seemed to go well before encountering him.

When I leave the shop and am back in the comfort of Dolly, I catch up with the WhatsApp group. My gosh, there are twenty messages I missed throughout the day.

The first one is from Alicia.

> So upset, popped home lunchtime and the post had been. Must have been late this morning. It's a no :(

> Aww, sorry, gutted for you, big hugs, Nicole x

The next message is from Michelle.

> OMG, OMG, I got in!!!!!! I can't believe it!

Then there is the predictable notification.

> Alicia left the group.

Everyone congratulates Michelle and discusses how the previous theory that we would hear the next day if you were unsuccessful is proven not to be true. We simply can't work out what the response will be by how quickly we hear. We all have to wait for our post and there is nothing else we can do.

Michelle tries to downplay her good news by saying that the job is still dependent on passing a medical and getting references. It seems she is a bit worried about a previous boss who, in her words, 'hated her'.

Greg tells her she will be fine. She has done the hard part.

I try not to bite my nails as I read through the messages. If I got the job, I may decide to wear the company's recommended nail polish, so it is something I need to keep in mind. I bite nervously at the skin around my nails instead. I am so anxious to find out whether I am one of the successful ones that I manage to draw blood.

I attempt to distract myself with social media, which is my lifeline at home. I don't know what people who lived alone did before it came along. I check Facebook and see that Carys has been messaging. My glamourous, globe-trotting, new friend.

> How did it go? Did you meet Nick in grooming? Did you do everything I told you to? Hope it all went okay. Just arriving in Nairobi. X

I can't keep up with her. She is in Africa now. Is there anywhere she doesn't fly to?

I message her back right away. I had planned on telling her how the interview went as soon as I was finished. But after that incident with Miserable Matt, I felt a bit deflated. I consider mentioning him in my reply, but choose not to. You never know, she may have dated him, or they might be good friends. I wouldn't want to upset Carys as well. She has been so kind to me.

> Oh, Nick is just so gorgeous, isn't he? I loved the uniform part, how fabulous we got to try it on. Everyone was so nice.

Apart from Matt, I want to put in brackets.

Carys hasn't been online for quite some time since we messaged. She could be walking around the markets of

Nairobi by now. I make myself a cup of chamomile tea and decide to have an early night. I want the post to come to put me out of my misery so much that I just want to wake up and it be a new day and a new post delivery.

What will tomorrow bring? Is it my destiny to stay here and work with Jane and plod along for the rest of my life, or until Jane decides to sell? Or will I become a flight attendant and see the world? It is anyone's guess right now.

Before closing my eyes, I see Carys has been on Facebook finally. She has posted photos of herself on safari in Kenya and sat around a campfire with some of the other crew who are on her trip to Nairobi. I can't help but feel jealous. Imagine getting paid to do that. It really would be a dream come true.

I reach for the lucky ceramic model of Dolly that I keep beside the bed and kiss it. Please, Dolly, let me get that letter tomorrow.

Chapter 8

As soon as I switch my phone on, the WhatsApp group goes wild. The first message is from Greg.

> I got in. At 40 years old I got my dream job! Wife says she's super proud of me. Can't wait to join you, Michelle. Wonder if we'll be on same AB Initio?

Ab Initio?? Lucy has typed. Lucy is one of the other women in the group but not someone I had much to do with.

Yeah, our course, Greg has written.

Again, it confirms my suspicions that you have to learn a whole new language in the airline industry. I do find that odd, I must say. Why don't they just call it a training course like other businesses would?

> Oh man, just got my letter. It's a NO!!!!

Dan is another of the guys I didn't have much to do with, as he was on the other side of the room.

I get a message from Lucy.

> OMG, getting so nervous now

I respond to her

> Me too. Are we the last ones to know?

The group goes quiet and I start to feel paranoid. Do they not like me, or is it just that they're not online? I click on it to see if anyone has seen the message. Nobody has, so hopefully they're all just busy and getting ready for the day ahead and not purposely ignoring me as my low self-esteem would like me to believe.

Whilst I wait for them to pick up the message and offer me some moral support, I head outside to water my hanging baskets. I have managed to salvage them and they are not looking too shabby. I am starting to feel quite proud, even if my conscientious watering is now more to do with the fact that I keep checking for the postman rather than my green fingers. Perhaps I am a good plant mum after all, to bring them back from the brink like this.

As I pour the last of the water into one of the hanging baskets, I spot the postman's van further along the road. I almost topple off the stool I am standing on to reach my hanging basket. I thought I should be more prepared now, after my incident with the short dressing gown.

With the postman getting closer by, I rush inside so that I don't look too sad hanging around for him. I pace up and down as I try to remain composed. The airline wants candidates to be calm under a crisis? I can't even keep calm when the postman is due!

My phone pings with a message from Lucy.

Yeah, it's just us two waiting to hear now. But guess what?! I just got my letter. I didn't get it, but they said they wanted me to reapply after six months.

Oh no, this is terrible news. Lucy looked perfect for the job and although we didn't speak much, she looked like the type of person in my mind that I thought they would choose. Airlines obviously go for more than looks nowadays then, which is a good thing for me.

I hear a thud on the mat. I am too afraid to look. I can see the usual flyers and junk mail from the hallway. An advert for dentures lies on top today; no thank you. Fortunately, I still have all my own teeth.

Gingerly, I work my way through the mail in my hand. Then I see the letter from Calm Air. Instinctively, my hands start trembling. I want to open it, but at the same time, I am too scared. Will they suggest that I reapply after six months as they did with Lucy? Or will it be a flat no thank you? What if it is a laundry bill from the uniform department for the damage I caused to Miserable Matt's trousers? I am suddenly too scared to open it. I need someone else here to do it for me. But, unlike Greg and his supportive wife, there is nobody. Just me. So I have to be strong and open it myself. I start to tear the top of the envelope open. Then I stop. Oh my gosh, I don't want to open it. But I do. But I don't. Then I think it is like a plaster. Just rip the envelope straight off and get to that letter inside.

I begin to unfold the letter bit by bit. I peek to see the odd random word.

Dear... Pleased... AB Initio... Start Date.

They are all pretty positive words so I read the letter in one go. I scream first, then I jump around and dance about the room. Then I pick up the phone to tell the others.

> I can't believe it. I got it. I am about to join you on the course!!!!

It takes me about half an hour to come back down to earth. I feel as though I am literally flying. Greg and Michelle are thrilled we will all be together and Lucy leaves the group. Only three out of a group of twenty of us were successful, although we still have our medicals to pass and a training course after that. We are still a long way off from reaching the sky.

I consider telling Jane, but Greg and Michelle both agree that none of us should quit our jobs until we have completed our medicals. Apparently, they check your heart, and there are all sorts of blood tests. Eww. I must say, this bit doesn't sound glamourous at all. I don't like going to the doctor as it is, let alone having a full-on medical. I am always terrified they will find something, and I have the most awful health anxiety. As both my parents died of cancer at such an early age, I suppose I do have an excuse for being paranoid that doctors will find something. The fact is that Dolly is all I have left of my family, their ashes having long disappeared into their favourite seaside spot. Dolly was bought by my dad for my mum. I guess you could say it was a kind of birthing present for having me. Geraint never understood that's why I love that car so much and now I have to face my health anxiety by having a full check-up, just as Dolly has her annual service. I hadn't thought about this part of the job before. I was too preoccupied with the interview. I remind myself to stock up on chamomile tea and do my utmost to remain calm. Nerves aren't going to help the ECG.

Despite the hurdles I have to face, I am incredibly excited. They want me to start in six weeks' time. It doesn't give me long to prepare. The first thing I have to do is book the dreaded medical. They have given me a phone number to call for an appointment. Urgh. I suppose the sooner I do that the better, so I decide to call before I head off to help out with the dogs. Unfortunately for me, they can fit me in next Wednesday, which means I will miss next week's dog walk in favour of having probes and needles stuck all over me.

I would certainly prefer to be with lovely Oreo and Willow, who are already waiting for me when I arrive at the kennel today.

'Hello, my gorgeous little ones,' I say, as they wag their tails and wiggle their hips at me. If my life had been different, I could have taken them home and gone on long Sunday walks with them. When I would have a holiday from work, we could stay in a cottage somewhere dog-friendly in the summer. That's what I always dreamed my life would have looked like. The stability of a family, two dogs and a hamster. I have always found them strangely cute. All I have to care for are my new hanging baskets and Dolly. Even poor Dolly is looking worse for wear and I can't pretend I'm not worried about the service due in a few months' time. What if there is something majorly wrong with her?

I confide my concerns with Oreo and Willow. Poor things, they have enough problems of their own, without me dumping my problems on them. However, they seem to brush the weight of my issues off and happily wag their tails. I wish I was more like a dog and could disregard my problems with a run in the woods. Perhaps I need to try it.

I take them back after our lovely walk and feel so much more positive as I get back into the car. I stroke Dolly's steering wheel.

'We're going to be okay, Dolly. We'll both pass our medicals. I'll make sure of it,' I say.

Chapter 9

Like most medical appointments, it comes around too fast and so the week flies by until the dreaded medical examination springs upon me.

I take the train to the medical centre just outside Heathrow as I don't believe Dolly will make the motorway journey. Travelling with Dolly has never been an issue until now as I have always stayed local, but I think the time has come for her to have a big service if I pass the medical and have to travel on the motorway with her. Hopefully, I will soon make enough money, as I have learned that there are additional benefits along with the basic salary, such as flight pay for when you're working, and allowances when away from your base. So, I figure that I should be able to manage better with those along with the full-time salary. Walking through the car park nervously, I spot the most gorgeous camper van. It makes me miss Dolly more than usual.

The pastel blue colour catches my eye immediately. It is the cutest thing ever, apart from Dolly, of course. How gorgeous to drive something like that. I can't help but peek my head through the window. It's got a small hob oven, a sink and looks like a home away from home. It must come in handy if you need to stay close to the airport; what a fantastic idea.

A strip along the top of the window says that the campervan is called Nigella. I'm glad it isn't only my family that names their cars. I go to take a photo of the camper van. I know it's a bit cheeky of me, but I am such a VW enthusiast I can't resist. It is then that I hear a male voice.

'Are you lost?'

'I'm sorry, I was just admiring the van…' I start.

As I look up in front of me I stop talking. I can't believe this.

'You again,' he says, looking at me.

'Me again,' I say.

I want to ask him if there is only one captain in this airline, but I am determined not to get into another fight with him.

'Excuse me,' I say.

He lets me past without a fight as I am sure he is as horrified at seeing me as I am of him.

I end up a few minutes late for the medical, thanks to the distraction of Nigella and Miserable Matt. So I rush straight into the medical building and confirm my identity with reception. A nurse is already searching for me and leads me straight into an examination room.

'We'll start with your blood pressure,' she says.

She places the cuff around my arm and I try to relax.

'Goodness, your blood pressure is alarmingly high,' says the nurse.

'Oh dear,' I respond.

The sight of that man is enough to send anyone's blood pressure skyrocketing.

'Look, can I have a minute and then try again? I just saw someone quite unpleasant out in the car park,' I say.

'Oh goodness, I hope you're okay?' she asks.

'Yes, I'm fine. He just stressed me out a bit. Nothing my chamomile tea won't resolve, or maybe a cider. Not that I have too many units of alcohol a week, of course,' I say.

'Let me get you some water and we'll try again,' she says.

I take some deep breaths, sip the water and try to get him out of my head. Finally, I am ready to give this blood pressure malarky one more shot.

'Perfect, that's much better second time around,' says the nurse.

Yay, I passed the first round.

Next, she does an ECG and then the blood tests. Finally, after feeling dizzy with all the stress of being poked around she tells me I am done. What a relief. I wouldn't want to go through all that again. Although the results scare me even more. The nurse says they will be with me by the end of the week. This means if everything is satisfactory, I will be resigning next Wednesday or Thursday. I don't relish the thought of telling Jane. Perhaps I should take her out to the tapas bar for a bite and some drinks to soften the blow. After all, it seems to be the place to break bad news.

On my way out of the car park, I see that Nigella has gone. What a pity; I'd have liked a proper look without Matt poking around the place.

On the train home, the three of us on the CARD WhatsApp group discuss our medicals.

I even had my prostate checked, complains Greg.

Poor Greg. Well, at least it can't be said they're not thorough with our medical check! Michelle then messages to tell us that she has just had her medical results back in the post. Her iron level was a bit low, so they have told her to check this with her GP, but apart from that, she is fit to fly. She is the first of us to resign from her job in the clothes store. I am so thrilled for her.

Once again, it looks like the hanging baskets will be watered frequently as I stalk the postman for my next important piece of mail.

Back in work, Jane chats excitedly about the spring collection she is about to order. She shows me pictures of the children's wear, asking me for my opinion.

'Shall we plan a fashion show for March?' says Jane.

I gulp, knowing that if everything goes to plan, I won't be here.

'That would be great,' I say, my face burning.

'Fabulous. I wonder if we should start thinking about venues. I tell you what, as we shouldn't be too busy today, do you want to start ringing around and getting prices for me? Then maybe we can book something next week so we can start plans on the invites etc,' says Jane.

'Sure,' I say flatly.

'Are you okay? You usually love planning fashion shows. Still down about Geraint?' says Jane.

I know I have to say something. Give her some warning. I don't want to leave her in the lurch but I also worry about not passing the medical. Then I will have upset her for no reason if I happen to fail. I don't know what I should do for the best. However, I feel like a totally fake friend planning something I am hoping I won't be at, so it seems now might be the time to say something.

'Jane, I'm sorry, but I've got something to tell you. It's nothing confirmed,' I start.

'Oh goodness, you're not ill, are you?' she says.

'No, not at all, well, I hope not. But I'll soon find out,' I say.

'What on earth do you mean, Penny?'

'It's just that… Well, remember I told you about this glamourous woman who came in the other day and she flew for an airline?'

'Yes, and?'

'Well, she told me that her airline accepts people my age. So, I applied and got accepted!'

'Good grief, did you?' I am afraid to look at the expression on Jane's face. I can't tell if her tone is one of shock or annoyance. I have never liked confrontation and whilst Jane isn't particularly confrontational, I am worried about how she will react. She relies on me for a lot of things; what if she gets annoyed with me and it spoils our relationship?

'It was a silly idea, I won't pass the medical they require anyway,' I say.

'Why would you not pass the medical? Of course you will. Look at you. You're a healthy woman. Oh no, I am so disappointed to hear I'll be losing you. What will I do without you?'

'Look, nothing's certain yet,' I say.

'Come on, that medical isn't going to show anything. It's just routine, I'm sure,' says Jane.

'No, even my blood pressure was a bit rocky to start with. Who knows what will show up? I won't be going anywhere. It was silly of me to apply.'

I regret saying anything now. I was only trying to give her a bit of warning in case I passed everything. Now she's practically putting an advert out for my job. Why did I not keep my mouth shut?

'You have to go for it. You haven't much to keep you around here, especially since Geraint. I'm just incredibly

83

sad. I thought I could keep you here forever but that's unfair of me.'

I feel like the most awful person. Perhaps I should have told her from the start. Maybe when we were having lunch and she was telling me about her dreams I should have casually popped this in. She is a friend and not a monster, after all. This is so difficult and unlike a job where the boss doesn't care less. She treats me so well and now I could leave her in the lurch.

Jane reaches over and hugs me and I start to get emotional as the realisation takes hold of quite what a big step it would be to join Calm Air. I begin to realise that I do have a lot to lose if I leave. I lose working with a lovely boss and never having to worry about being out of my comfort zone. I will no longer be able to help out regularly at the Doodle Sanctuary as I won't know my shifts. Poor Willow and Oreo. I begin to get a dreadful fear of the unknown.

What if I pass the medical and it ends up being the biggest mistake of my life? Then what will I do? But a little voice in my head says, *What if it is the best thing you ever do?*

I guess there is only one way to find out. But it is going to mean leaving the best boss in the world behind.

Chapter 10

'Yay, you got accepted,' says the lovely Welsh receptionist at the Calm Air head office on my first day of the training course following my notice period at Little Darlings.

'Yes, can you believe it?' I say. I am still in shock that I have come this far. It has all happened so fast that I still haven't got my head around the fact I have left my comfortable job to work 33,000 feet in the air.

'Aww, I am so chuffed for you. You'll love it,' she says.

I try to smile at her convincingly, attempting not to show the trepidation I am really feeling. I am terrified and at this moment regret letting Greg and Michelle talk me into this when I had my last-minute panic. They were having none of it when I passed my medical and knew that I would be able to start the training. I told them I had changed my mind, that I was too scared to make the move. But they insisted I go for it. I did even consider blocking their numbers at one point.

Last minute nerves, said Michelle.

Meanwhile, Greg said that I would never get an opportunity like this again, especially not at my age. He did say that he didn't mean that in a horrible way; he was forty after all and fifty would hit him in the blink of an eye.

When I told Jane I had passed the medical, and that I was too scared to take the job, she said I must go for it and that she wouldn't let me stay as it was for my own good. I was surprised at how selfless she was. I thought she would offer me a pay rise, or something to make me stay. Perhaps beg me! But she didn't. She told me that she had advertised the position and that she had received an unprecedented number of applications. She interviewed them immediately and offered one of the applicants the job. So that left me temporarily unemployed. I have promised her that if I get through my next challenge of the rigorous training course then I will try and get her a cheap flight as a thank you. Naturally, she said she would appreciate a flight to the Cayman Islands, but I am not sure if we even fly there yet. I haven't seen that on Carys' Facebook list of trips.

In the training room, I am relieved to see the familiar faces of Greg and Michelle and take a seat beside them. Greg excitedly tells me that when someone opened a door, he noticed that our classroom was attached to another room which has a mock-up of a plane; this is where we will practise serving passengers. The passengers will be us newbies and we will take turns at getting served. I am looking forward to this part of the training. I wonder if they will serve the cream teas they offer on long-haul flights. I could do with a scone and a cup of tea right now. My first-day nerves subside a little at the thought.

Just like on the day of the interview, the rest of the group and the Cabin Service Instructors, Yousef and April, are friendly. However, I am definitely out of my comfort zone. I am not one for training courses. I suppose I have never liked stretching myself; I have always taken the easy route in life. Staying in my hometown all my life, secretly knowing that I wanted more of a commitment from Geraint after being together for so long, but too afraid to say anything in case I rocked the boat. For some reason, seeing all these people around me who seem so much more adventurous and assertive than I am, I find myself annoyed for not asserting my demands in life sooner. I recognise that I have always tried to accommodate other people over my own needs for so long. Why would I not rock the boat with Geraint? I had needs in the relationship too. I won't ever allow a relationship to drift along again like that.

Thinking positively about my life makes the morning more enjoyable than I imagined a training course could ever be. I remind myself that this is all part of learning something new and becoming the best version of me.

When we have finished the morning introduction session and know where the fire exits for head office are, we get taken to the cabin mock-up for a look around. This is so exciting. It is identical to any plane you would fly on. You would never guess it was fake, except for the way you step on-board directly from the big room that it is in. Greg gets excited when he sees the big aircraft door and wants to have a go at familiarising himself with it. He is reassured that we will all have our turn to open and close it, but Yousef allows Greg a quick go. He shows him how to pull at the door and then locks it shut with the big bar.

'Go on then, you try it,' says Yousef.

Greg pulls at the door but nothing happens.

'Umm, I can't seem to do it,' he finally admits.

'It's not as easy as people think, is it?' says Yousef.

He shows him how to do it one more time and then Greg manages to pull the door closed. However, he doesn't quite manage to lock it properly with the big heavy handle.

'Heavens, that's harder than it looks. I hope you've got some muscles, girls,' says Greg, sitting down.

His face is red and I begin to wonder if I will be strong enough. Greg is a six-foot Yorkshireman; I would have thought he'd have managed it easier than that.

'I lift weights in the gym. I don't know what went wrong there,' says Greg.

Yousef must pick up on our concerned faces.

'Don't worry, there is a knack. You'll be opening and closing them all day long by the end of the six weeks. I should explain now what the training schedule will be. So, you will have one week of learning first aid procedures, and three weeks of SEP.'

'SEP?' says Arabella, who is one of the young women on the course that I haven't met properly yet. She must be in her twenties. Her skin glows, as though she should be on an advert on the telly trying to sell older women anti-wrinkle creams. I am sure she will look like a china doll in her uniform.

'Sorry, I should have explained properly. It becomes second nature after a while. Safety and Emergency Procedures. This is when you will learn all about evacuating, what to do in the event of a ditching...'

'Ditching?' says Arabella. I am pleased she is so curious as I can't keep up with these terms and abbreviations.

'Sorry, if I am going too fast, please do just stop me, just as Arabella has. Ditching is when an aircraft crash-lands into the sea.'

'Bloody hell,' says Arabella.

'It sounds bad, I agree. But it is very unlikely that any plane would crash into the sea because we would try to divert to the nearest airfield if something untoward happened. And I probably shouldn't say this, but to be honest, the plane would probably crash into bits with the impact if we landed in the ocean, but you never know.'

'Oh my god,' says Michelle. She pulls at her long auburn ponytail and grabs the end, biting at her hair. She doesn't look happy at all.

'Look, we learn all these drills and procedures of what to do, but the chances of survival in such an instance are slim,' adds Yousef.

'Sully did it in that movie,' shouts out one of the recruits called Jonathon. He is a friendly gay guy who doesn't miss a trick. I can already tell that he is going to be great fun on the course.

'Indeed, Sully did a very good job. But if you're in the middle of the Atlantic and you come crashing down, let's face it… Well, let's just hope it never happens. There's no reason for it to. Flying is the safest form of travel, after all,' says Yousef.

Every one of the recruits looks at each other with a petrified face. Now this is definitely out of my comfort zone and not what I signed up for, whether it is the safest form of travel or not.

'Hey, now, as I said… This is seriously unlikely. Not going to happen. You just need to be trained in case, that's all. We will equip you for every eventuality. You'll even know how to deal with sharks in the ocean by the end of your course.'

'Sharks! I didn't sleep after watching *Jaws*,' says Greg.

'Oh, you just smack them on the end of their snout with the paddle from your life raft. But anyway, that's for your SEP trainer to teach you,' says Yousef.

We all look at each other, absolutely horrified. Learning how to deal with sharks doesn't do much to calm our nerves. So, after our first day at training school, ten of us decide we need a stiff drink. I begin to wonder if that's why they built the head office opposite a pub.

Three of the recruits decide they're exhausted after having travelled in last night and want to get back to their hotel. Most of us are staying in local B&Bs that the airline has recommended.

'All right ladies?' says some oik at the bar as we get our drinks.

'Ignore him. Some of these guys only come in here on a Monday because they know the latest recruits for Calm Air come in. Don't say I didn't warn you,' says a lovely member of the bar staff. It seems we are not the only course to need a drink after day one of training then.

I notice a very nice-looking, slightly older guy glancing over at me. For a second it does wonders for my confidence, but then I begin to wonder if he is one of the dodgy guys seeking out the new recruits. I decide it is better to be on my guard and stay away from anyone in here. I look around carefully just to ensure there is no sign of Matt. Knowing my luck, I would spill a drink over him if he was here. Fortunately, there is no sign of him for once. He's probably jetting off to Bangkok or somewhere equally exotic.

'Ah, that tastes lovely,' says Greg, taking a swig of Guinness. 'Going to need to keep my iron levels up if I'm to be closing those aircraft doors,' he jokes.

'It looked so hard,' says someone who still has a sticky label on her blouse with her name, Veronica, on it. Thank goodness we have name labels. It is so hard to remember thirteen people's names.

'All right there, young lady?' says a creepy guy hitting on Arabella. It doesn't come as a surprise that Arabella is the first one to be hit upon.

'Excuse me, I'm having a drink with my friends,' she says, giving him a look that tells him to stay well away.

'All right, all right. Aren't you lot supposed to make people happy?' he says and then shuffles off.

'What a bloody cheek. Is this how it's going to be now? Creeps trying to hit on us because we are cabin crew?' says Veronica.

I begin to feel a little uneasy. I hope that it doesn't continue like this. We are not even in our uniforms yet. This is terrible.

Fortunately, we manage the rest of our drinks in peace. It must be the warning signs we are omitting.

'So, what did you think about Yousef telling us about the ditching? Scary stuff, huh?' says Michelle.

'And the sharks!' says Veronica.

'I must confess I did wonder if this is the job for me after hearing that,' I say.

'Yeah, I think we all did. I have my missus and three kids at home, it's a bit of a worry,' says Greg.

'That's for sure,' says Michelle.

'Well, the missus deffo wouldn't be happy thinking of me fighting sharks with a plastic paddle just to pay the mortgage,' says Greg.

'Yeah, I only recently met the love of my life, I don't want to die in the mouth of a shark. That would be just my luck,' says Michelle.

She takes a sip of her cocktail and makes a concerned face at me. I realise that I could definitely be friends with Michelle and, although the job sounds a little scary, I am glad we are all in this together.

I think of Carys. She's been flying for years and I don't think she has had anything bad happen. She wouldn't be still flying otherwise, surely. I must message her when I get back to the B&B and ask her. I can't believe I didn't think more about this kind of thing before signing up. I suppose I thought more about medical emergencies and helping people, rather than the whole plane falling out of the sky and practically into the mouth of a shark. Surely that can't happen.

'Does anyone know about Calm Air's safety record, any previous crashes?' I ask.

'Great idea, will google now,' says Greg.

We get the next round in as Greg checks their history. Why nobody thought of this before I don't know.

'Oh good god. They've lost two planes. One in Holland that landed on a motorway and then burst into flames!' says Greg in shock.

'And the other?' says Arabella.

'A bomb went off, over the Atlantic,' says Greg dramatically.

'I feel quite faint,' says Arabella.

We clutch our drinks in our hands.

'Cheers, I think we're going to need these drinks,' I say.

'I think so, too,' says Arabella, taking a big swig of her espresso Martini.

'What the hell have we done?' says Greg.

'I think we're all wondering the same thing,' I say.

Chapter 11

When we arrive the next morning at the training centre, there is one empty seat around the conference table.

'Sadly, we have some news to share with you. I am sorry to say that Veronica has left the course. She decided this isn't the career for her,' says April.

Greg and I look at each other. We know full well why she left. She was ashen when Greg read out the stuff on Calm Air that he found. Carys hasn't yet come back to my latest message to her asking about emergencies. She must be flying somewhere. Now I worry if she is even safe! Did her latest flight land okay?

'I know it might have been a shock yesterday when we briefly discussed the ditching scenario, but I promise you, this is not something you can ever expect to happen. I've been flying twenty-five years and I'm still standing to tell the tale,' says Yousef.

'But there have been a few disasters at Calm Air though, haven't there?' says Greg.

Those of us who were in the pub last night nod our heads. Let's see how Yousef deals with this one.

'Oh yeah, like any airline, things do happen. But the chances are very slim. Like winning the lottery,' says Yousef.

'I know which I'd prefer,' says Jonathon.

'Yeah, me too,' agrees Greg.

'Look, you know, we did have a bomb on-board once, but this was pre 9/11. Things changed a lot after that. The world, and the airline industry, became a different place. Before those days anyone could sit in the flight deck. Now things are so much stricter and perhaps we left ourselves vulnerable before,' says April.

'You'll feel a lot better about the safety aspect once you finish your SEP training, I can assure you. Now, moving on we have two of our lovely staff here who are going to show you how to resuscitate someone unconscious. Now, where's Annie?' says April.

'Who's Annie?' whispers Greg to me.

I feel as though I am one of those popular girls in school with all the whispering going on in the classroom with Greg. It is like I finally belong somewhere.

April takes out what looks like a blow-up doll from a zipped bag.

'Oh my god! What the hell do you expect me to do with that?' shrieks Jonathon.

We all laugh so much that we can't take it seriously when April holds it up and says, 'Meet Resusci Annie!'

'Flipping heck, she looks like me when I'm hungover,' laughs Arabella.

'I don't think you'd ever look that bad, Arabella,' says Michelle.

The whole room is in fits of giggles. I don't know that any of us will manage to keep a straight face to blow into Annie's mouth at this point.

Eventually, we do however simmer down and get on with rescuing poor Annie. Who definitely looks very sick.

After a long strenuous day of huffing and puffing, we pass the initial part of our first aid course. We managed to resuscitate Annie! Next up we are being taught the differences between our bandages from our tourniquets.

This is so much fun. We are bandaged and made to wear our arms in slings for the benefit of our fellow trainees to practice on. I am surprised at how beneficial what I learn is. I am so motivated that I now believe that everyone should be trained in first aid. This should certainly be essential learning at school instead of algebra. After all, someone could choke in the school dining room and who would be around to do the Heimlich manoeuvre? What good is knowing the difference between a linear equation and a negative number when someone is choking on the school's lumpy mash potato?

By the end of the week, we all get our first aid certificates. One part of the course is complete.

The next step is the dreaded SEP. For some of the group, like Jonathon and Arabella, they are super excited. The thought of jumping down a massive slide is their idea of hilarious fun and they are treating today like a trip to Alton Towers. To this fifty-year-old woman, it is my idea of hell. Plus, I am not very good with heights. Everyone on the course thinks I am joking. The first thing they asked me was how on earth could I want to be cabin crew when I don't like heights? But there is a difference. When I am in an aeroplane I am sealed in safely. Looking down at the ten-foot drop from the aeroplane door sill to the bottom of the slide feels very different. All I see is a sheer drop and now I am standing on top of what feels like a precipice, looking down in sheer terror at the bottom of the slide with a load of people waiting for me to jump, and wishing I hadn't got this crazy job. This is even worse than when someone is watching me parallel park Dolly. The nerves are off the scale!

'Come on, you can do it,' shouts Arabella.

'I can't. I'm sorry but I just can't.'

We are being trained for the short-haul fleet, so the aircraft isn't as huge as some of them. I can't imagine how big the slide would be on the jumbo-sized planes that Carys flies on.

'I'm afraid you have to if you want me to sign you off,' says Jerry, who is taking us for our safety training. All the trainers have their specialist areas, but I prefer Yousef and April in Cabin Services personally.

'Well, I can't. It's too high,' I say.

'Look, just sit on the top of the slide. You don't have to jump. Just sit and slide down,' says Jerry.

I carefully crouch down and gingerly sit on top of the slide. Urgh, I never liked slides in the park as a child. I much preferred the swings. I really do not want to do this. I look down at the drop below again; it's horrendous.

'Right, now move your bottom. Slide down, come on,' shouts Jerry.

I am now the last person to jump. The sea of faces beneath me cheers me on.

'Come on, Penny. We know you can do it,' says Greg.

'Just pretend I'm Ronan Keating and I'm going to catch you,' shouts Jerry from below.

'I don't care who you are. Tell Ronan I don't want to jump!' I cry.

Michelle climbs back up the steps of the aircraft to sit beside me.

'Come on, I did it. It's not so hard. It looks worse than it is. Don't think about it. How about we go down together? I'll go in front and you come down straight after me?'

'I don't know,' I say.

'Come on, you have to just do this one time. Get it over with. One, two, three... Go!' I watch as Michelle slides down with ease.

I then close my eyes and shuffle my bottom a little further towards the edge of the slide until I have no control over where I am going. There is no turning back.

I scream all the way down.

'Well done! See, was it as bad as you thought?' says Jerry.

'No, worse,' I cry.

'Come on, you did it! Look what you achieved,' says Greg.

One by one everyone on the training course comes over and gives me a hug.

'Thank you, you guys are the best,' I say, when I have finally got over the shock a bit.

Once again, I have that feeling that I belong some-where and, by the end of the day, the relationship between us all has deepened further. We pulled through together and became the closest, most supportive team I have ever known. Despite the moments of anguish, I did it with the support of my team.

'Tomorrow morning, we're fighting fires,' says Jerry, before we head off for the day. 'Don't forget to wear scruffy clothes as we'll be taking you to the fire station. You're going to fight oven fires and then don smoke hoods and fight a fire on an aircraft. A very exciting day tomorrow,' she says.

'Oh no, that doesn't sound like my idea of excitement. I don't like the sound of that, those smoke hoods sound claustrophobic,' says Michelle.

'Don't worry, I'll be there for you. Just as you were there for me,' I promise.

Chapter 12

We arrive early at the fire station. Jerry has already warned us to keep our hands, or should I say safety gloves, off fireman George.

'His name's not really George, but he reminds me of George Clooney, the God of men,' says Jerry, laughing, as we pull up outside the fire station on a bus. She is way more excited to get here than the rest of us.

We are instructed to follow two firemen to an outside area which has five galley ovens on tables. There is no cup of tea before we start, or any niceties; we are just told about the different types of fire extinguishers (one is for electrics and another is a water-filled one for paper and such). Again, there are abbreviations and the fireman keeps calling an extinguisher a BCF. I have no idea what he is on about.

We put on our fire gloves and start spraying the oven with the foamy stuff that comes out of the extinguisher. Ah, that wasn't too difficult. But then for the next part: it is time to enter a smoke-filled cabin and crawl on the floor and find our way out! If we fail this we are finished. I can see that Michelle is visibly shaking. We all have our nemesis, and claustrophobia is to her what heights are to me. I remind her once again that I am there for her and that she doesn't have to do this alone.

'I was stuck in a lift once. Two hours it took to get me out. I've never been the same since,' says Michelle.

'You don't have to explain. I can totally imagine. I hate heights and I don't even know why. There is no reasonable explanation. It's just irrational for me.'

Although phobias can be debilitating, it feels good to be able to compare notes on our fears. I have never been so open about my anxieties until I met Michelle and the rest of the training team. It's as though we can share anything and be so open and honest.

We are split into groups of two and so naturally I go with Michelle. The fireman shows us how to place the sealed smoke hood over our heads. It isn't the best of feelings, that's for sure, and I look like a Ghostbuster with the breathing contraption hanging off my back.

The fireman helps Michelle put her smoke hood on, but immediately she starts to panic. She struggles and pulls at it until the fireman tells her to take it easy.

'Do you know how much these cost?' he complains.

Michelle gasps for breath as she is released from the smoke hood and we let Jonathon and Greg go in before us. I know how it feels to have to mentally prepare yourself for something you find so difficult, so I have every sympathy.

I give her a hug and tell her she'll be okay. If I could get through the slide, she can do this.

The guys are soon out and Michelle still can't face going in. So, we leave it until last, just like I had to do yesterday. It only puts off the inevitable, but it feels better at the time.

The fireman eventually manages to get Michelle a bit more acclimatised to the smoke hood by letting her wear it in the open air for a bit. She manages to calm down enough that we can finally go in.

I am shocked that there is zero visibility. We crawl along the floor and I tell Michelle to follow me by grabbing my leg. I try to follow the emergency lighting that is hardly visible and eventually I can see a spot of light ahead.

Michelle has been screaming things the whole time, but everything is muffled in the smoke hoods.

'We're nearly there!' I shout to Michelle.

She says something but I can't work out what it is. But I can tell Michelle is crying so I move faster to get her out of here.

'Yay! We did it,' I say as we reach the exit.

Michelle practically rips off her smoke hood and sobs.

'I don't ever, ever, want to do that again,' she says.

'Hopefully, you won't have to,' says Jerry.

When she gets over the panic, we board the bus and are told about our next session.

Back in the classroom again, we have to learn where every piece of safety equipment is on-board the plane.

We are given diagrams of the aircraft type we will be flying and told that we have to fill in blank copies of these by tomorrow morning with details of where all the fire extinguishers, baby cots for ditching and emergency beacons are in case we are lost somewhere in the jungle. Once again, I begin to worry about the safety of flying with all of this on-board. And, in reality, who would find you in the jungle? Only a terrifying massive gorilla who would have a field day with all those passengers. Are you better off crashing in the sea or the jungle? I can't quite decide. Yikes.

'Why do we need all of this equipment? Are we going to crash land in the jungle?' asks Arabella.

'It's just in case of an emergency. I'm sure you won't use half of this equipment in your lifetime. Can't believe we didn't get to see George today. Hopefully, he'll be there when I go down with my next group,' says Jerry.

'Never mind George, I want to know more about that emergency beacon and why we need flares in case the plane crashes somewhere,' whispers Michelle.

'I don't think Jerry would be much use in a crisis if her phantom fireman was about,' I reply.

'So, get your homework done tonight and then we have another exciting day tomorrow. Hope you have your swimmers handy. Tomorrow we're training for a ditching. Six thirty a.m., bright-eyed and bushy-tailed, please. I'll have the life raft at the ready. Bring your joggers or pyjamas as you'll have to swim in clothes too. I love a ditching day,' says Jerry.

'I bet she does. She doesn't have to do it,' says Greg, laughing.

Jerry really does remind me of the sadistic school swimming teacher I had in primary school.

'My swimming isn't up to much. What if I fail?' I say to the group.

'You won't, we're all in this together, remember,' says Michelle.

Once again, I am reminded that whether sink or swim, we make the greatest team.

'God, I swear, if anyone dares to call me a Trolley Dolley, after all we have been through in training, I am not responsible for my actions,' says Arabella.

'I think we would all agree with you there,' says Michelle.

Back at the B&B I pop the kettle on in the room and look at the diagram carefully. This is so hard. There are first aid kits to put somewhere, fire extinguishers go somewhere else. We even have emergency torches to put into place. How on earth are you supposed to remember all of this by heart? This training course is the hardest thing I have ever done. I message Carys for help. She was great about the emergencies at Calm Air and told me not to worry; she had never had any serious incidents, only major turbulence over the Bay of Bengal, where one of the crew broke their hip, but apart from that, nothing. I chose to ignore the broken hip part. It's better not to know sometimes.

Carys comes back straight away, thankfully, and explains that there are easy abbreviations to remember things. I may have guessed an abbreviation would be involved since they love them so much at airlines. Basically, she says you can work out a word and try to remember it that way. ELF is one example she gives me.

'It's simple, remember ELF. Extinguisher, light and first aid kit. Just keep making up a name you can remember for each part of the aircraft and you can work it out.'

By using her technique, I find a way to complete all the diagrams from memory. Why didn't Jerry tell us this? If only I could get Carys to do the swimming test for me too.

–

At 6:30 a.m. I am shivering at the local swimming baths. I am dressed in unicorn pyjamas with a black swimsuit underneath, once again wondering what I have signed up for. At least I didn't have to make much of an effort this morning. My hair is scraped back and, with not even the slightest hint of make-up, I feel so much older than the rest of my course mates. The unicorn pyjamas just make me look as though I forgot how old I am. However, I am totally aware that I am fifty and have a penchant for pyjama styles that I should have stopped wearing when I was five. At least I made the right decision by not wearing my favourite Snoopy ones today as they are far too precious.

'Right then, I think we're all here,' says Jerry, doing a headcount.

The public swimming pool is closed to everyone else and so it is just us staring at a huge life raft and thirteen life jackets that are floating around the pool.

'So, the first thing you're going to do is jump in and put on a life jacket while treading water. Then you can swim over to the life raft,' says Jerry enthusiastically.

Oh no, it's a bit too early in the morning for this.

Everyone else makes a leap for it, but I stand there in my pyjamas looking in horror at the swimming pool. I have never trodden water before in my life. Just as I did with the slide, I stand on the side not wanting to jump. I can't do it. It's that idea of falling again. Taking that leap into the unknown.

'Come on, Penny,' shouts Michelle.

'You can do it,' says Greg.

By now they have their life jackets on and are making their way to the life raft.

'I don't want to,' I say.

'Here we go again,' mutters Jerry.

I feel so pathetic standing there in my faded pyjamas with Jerry rolling her eyes, that suddenly I jump. I will not have Jerry underestimate me, as so many people have done in my life. Geraint underestimated me; he thought I would never make it without him, and look at me now. As I plummet to the bottom of the pool and try to make my way back up, I realise that even I underestimated myself.

I don't think I ever believed that I was capable of making such a leap.

Determined, I splash back up to the surface, coughing and spluttering. The chlorine stings my eyes and I regret the decision of not investing in some goggles.

Then my determination falters as I struggle to swim.

'Urgh, argh, I'm sinking,' I scream.

I spot Arabella heading towards me with a life jacket.

'Here, put this on,' she says.

'That's cheating, Arabella. Let her put her own life jacket on,' shouts the sadistic Jerry.

'Sorry, just trying to help. Look at poor Penny, you can see she's struggling,' says Arabella.

She swims off and leaves me as instructed and I manage to tie the life jacket around me and get my breath. Finally composing myself, I swim to the life raft.

Getting onto the life raft isn't much easier than the swimming test. I slip and slide all over the place as I attempt to hoist myself up. Fortunately, Michelle reaches out her arm to help me. I should have remembered that Michelle is never far away with a helping hand.

I have hardly caught my breath when we are instructed by Jerry to remove our life jackets on the life raft and swim back to the poolside unaided. My energy is already depleted and I don't feel as though I have anything left in me to get back out. Can I not lie on this life raft a while longer and pretend I am on a huge inflatable flamingo in the Mediterranean?

I slide off the life raft and manage to lose my unicorn trousers. Thank goodness I have a swimsuit underneath. My trousers expand full of water in the pool like a bloated whale and make me look like I have the biggest backside ever.

Luckily Greg grabs them for me and throws them to the side of the pool. Again, I am grateful for how we pull together in every crisis and mortifying moment. I begin to wonder if this is what the recruitment team saw when we were interviewed. Did they see something in us that we didn't even know about? Do we have some kind of teamwork superpower?

Finally, I reach the edge of the pool. I cling on for dear life and climb out. It makes me realise once again that if I had all this trouble in the local swimming baths, I would never manage a ditching in the wild seas of the Atlantic. I'd be gone with the first wave.

Fortunately, we get the rest of the day off after the swimming test as tomorrow we have our big SEP training exam. We have the afternoon to sort ourselves out and get on with revising. Once we pass this, we are on the home run. I am so glad the safety bit is mostly over with. With this part over, we can concentrate on the nicer parts, like getting measured up for our uniforms and working with the cabin services department on how to make cocktails mid-air and learning all about where the wines come from that we offer with the meals. Apparently, they're mostly from a place in France called Alsace. Michelle and I couldn't resist having a peek at an empty bottle they use to practise with. I hope we get to taste some too and they're not all empty.

There is no time for wine tonight though; as much as I could do with something to put my pre-exam nerves to rest, I have to revise like I never have before. This is my big moment to show Jerry I can do this and she should never roll her eyes at me again.

Chapter 13

We all pile nervously into the exam room for our SEP theory test. I haven't felt like this since I did my GCSEs at school. The papers are laid out upside down and we have an allotted time to complete them. We take our seats; you could have heard a pin drop.

I take my lucky unicorn pen out and hope that it has magical powers to help me pass. The more I studied overnight, the more confused I became. I can't even remember the name of the fire extinguisher now and keep wanting to call it a BCG, but that was a vaccine I had in school. Oh my goodness.

'You can turn your papers over. Your time starts… Now,' says Jerry.

I turn the paper over and have a quick scan through the questions as we were advised to do. The first section is multiple choice. I thought that was the easy part. But most of the choices could apply to the question. I gasp as I read one of the questions.

'Quiet please,' Jerry reminds me.

I read over the question again.

What is tundra?

I want to answer that it is some kind of jeep, but that isn't one of the multiple-choice answers. I decide to leave the first question and come back to it. We have to get over 90 per cent, so I only hope I find something I am able to answer.

I look over to Michelle to see how she is doing. However, like everyone else, she has her head down and seems to be ticking boxes and concentrating. Damn, nobody seems to be finding it as difficult as I am. Or are they filling in the wrong answers?

Focus, Penny, I tell myself. This isn't about how everyone else is doing.

I turn my attention to the aeroplane diagrams and start to fill in where the safety equipment is throughout the plane. I still can't remember the name of the extinguisher though. My mind is blank and the more I try to remember, the more it confuses me. So, I fill every slot where there should be an extinguisher with the abbreviation 'BCG' and hope that they understand what I mean. Surely they won't take points off me for a slight spelling mistake?

'You have five minutes remaining,' says Jerry.

I look up and notice that Greg has his pen down already. What a smarty pants he is. I wish I was like that. I remind myself this is not a race. What is important is the pass mark.

I frantically go back to the first question and tick the option 'A place on the moon'. Perhaps they think we are budding astronauts. I hope we don't fly that high though.

'Papers, please. If you could hand them to the person in front of you and I will collect them from the front, here,' says Jerry. She seems to be loving her role as an invigilator. I really do think she should have worked in a school and not an airline.

'Right then, I'll mark these and call you in one by one once I'm done,' says Jerry, piling up the papers. 'You can take a break now. Head for brunch, whatever you want. I'll be about an hour or so,' she says.

'What the heck is tundra?' I ask Greg as soon as we are outside the room.

'It's like a large area of ground. With rock and moss and stuff,' he explains.

'Why on earth would we need to know that?' I ask.

'Well, I suppose if we crash land in the Arctic Circle, we can tell the rescue services that we're in an area of tundra and they'll find us,' says Michelle, laughing.

'Ridiculous, some of those questions were. I think I need some caffeine,' I say.

'We need something stronger than that, I think. Drinks to celebrate finishing SEP?' says Arabella.

'Deffo, we'll go over the Rose and Crown, yeah? We so deserve it,' says Michelle.

'Sounds like a great plan,' I say.

We decide to have an early lunch to line our stomachs for this afternoon's shenanigans to celebrate the end of SEP. I am so glad to see the back of it. The only problem is that we have to do what they call rechecks every year, so it means we haven't seen the back of Jerry and our aircraft diagrams whatsoever. Every year, we will have to have a refresher course, we have been informed. I just hope I don't have to go down the slide or do the swimming test every year, or I may have to quit by next year's rechecks. Right now, I can't face going through this ever again. I am assured it is all worthwhile once we get our wings though.

I take a sip of my coffee. It feels so good. I didn't realise how dry my mouth was. The pressure was really on in there. It reminds me yet again about being calm under pressure and this is something about myself that I haven't seen at all. I'm not sure where the recruitment team felt I had that essential quality for the job. Perhaps they know me better than I know myself. I did get through it, after all.

I treat myself to a lasagne in the staff canteen to line my stomach. I think this afternoon could be a messy one, with us all being so relieved to finish. I have to say, we totally deserve it, too.

–

Arabella is the first one that Jerry calls in for the exam results. She is only with her for two minutes and comes out with a big smile on her face.

'Yay, I'll head over to the pub, yeah?' she says.

Greg asks her to order him a pint as he's next and won't be a tick.

He then comes out of the room with Jerry, moments later with a big thumbs up.

'See you in a moment,' says Greg, smiling.

'Yeah, order me a cider please,' I say, as it is my turn next.

I enter the room with Jerry and she tells me to take a seat. I can see she has my paper in front of her, but it has big red biro marks all over it. I begin to get a terrible feeling.

'I'm afraid you have failed,' says Jerry. I look for signs of empathy but I am not sure I see any. At least she did have the compassion not to roll her eyes, though.

'What?' I say in disbelief. Why I should be shocked, I don't know. Let's face it, I struggled, despite all the revision I put in. It reminds me I need to consider HRT. So many celebrities swear by it to help with their hormonal brain fog. Perhaps that's what went wrong here and the reason everyone else has passed except me.

Jerry starts going through the paper with me. It appears that I didn't do much right, really.

'You couldn't even remember the name of the BCF. Imagine being on-board and suddenly there's a fire and you're shouting, "Can someone give me a BCG?"' says Jerry.

'Okay, point taken. I know how badly I've done. What happens now?' I ask. There's no need for her to make things worse. I feel rubbish enough about myself as it is!

'Well, you'll need to resit it tomorrow. It shouldn't take long. Come here at ten and I'll be here with your exam paper ready for you,' says Jerry.

'I studied so hard though.' Passing this meant so much to me. I revised until eleven p.m. last night. I don't know what more I can do.

'Well, you obviously need to study some more. Take more blank aircraft diagrams home tonight and study, study, study. It's the only way,' says Jerry.

I walk out of the room in a daze, clutching the diagrams I will have to work on this evening.

Jerry calls Michelle in once she is done with me. I am sure she will have fared much better than I did.

'Can you order me in a gin and pink lemonade?' asks Michelle.

I nod my head. I don't have the energy to tell her what happened in there and that I won't be going to the pub. She will find out soon enough. I make my way out of the building and cry. I don't think I am cut out for this at all and feel incredibly disappointed.

By the time I get back to the B&B the WhatsApp group is bleeping and ringing, but I can't answer. I don't want to speak to anyone, not even my lovely training cohorts or Carys, who could probably help. I am so embarrassed; I don't want anyone to know. I switch my phone off and clutch my pillow to my chest. So much for my lucky unicorn pen.

Chapter 14

After a few hours' sleep, I am a little less emotional. It has sunk in now that I have failed and the more I think about it, it isn't surprising. I set the alarm for 5:30 a.m. so I can cram everything into my head at the last minute. Perhaps this is what I should have done yesterday instead of forgetting everything overnight. I am going to give this one last shot. Nothing much throughout this course has been easy so far, so why should the exam be?

When I switch my phone on, the group is going bonkers trying to find me. Their concern warms my heart.

Michelle sends me a private message.

> We're getting really worried now. Are you okay?

I message her back, finally admitting the truth

> Sorry, I couldn't face telling anyone yesterday.

Michelle messages back once she is awake and tells me to meet her for breakfast where she will test me on what she remembered from yesterday's exam. It was supposed to be our day off today and we were all planning on going into town for a browse. But Michelle wants to make sure I pass so that I can meet them all later. I am still not confident and feel such a fool for being the only person to fail such an important part of the course.

When I walk outside to meet Michelle, I see that it is the most gorgeous day. Far too nice to be resitting an exam. It must be the best part of twenty-three degrees. People are already walking around in shorts and floaty summer dresses, and smiling at the heatwave we are having.

Michelle is already sitting down with her latte and croissant by the time I reach the coffee shop we have planned to meet at.

'Hi, sorry I'm late, it took me ages to get sorted. I'm in such a tizz,' I explain.

'Don't be silly, it gave me time to start on my breakfast anyway. I'm starving. We stayed out so late last night celebrating… Oh, I'm sorry. That was so insensitive of me.'

'No, it's okay. It's not your fault I failed. It was all down to me. I take full responsibility. I just went blank,' I say.

'Look, let's go through this with you now. It'll be different today. You know what to expect on the paper this time,' she says.

She asks me questions as if I were a contestant on *Mastermind*, only my specialist subject most definitely isn't safety procedures, that's for sure. Why can't they ask about Volkswagen Beetles through the ages? That's more my area of expertise.

I skip breakfast and stick to drinking my coffee. I am far too nervous to eat.

'Well, at least you know what tundra is now, anyhow,' says Michelle.

'Yes, I won't forget that one,' I agree.

'And what is the fire extinguisher called again?' says Michelle.

'A BCF,' I say.

'Yay! Well done,' says Michelle, giving me a high five. 'You can do it. I have every confidence in you. Just calm down in there, and don't let nerves get the better of you. That's what I did yesterday. I gave myself a good talking to before I started the paper.'

'Yup, you're right. It's just my head goes as soon as I look at that paper,' I say.

'Well, we're out of practice doing exams as we get older. It's not surprising.' Michelle bites into the last of her croissant and looks at her watch.

'Have you seen the time? Now, go, break a leg, or whatever they say for luck in the airline industry,' says Michelle.

'I feel sick,' I say, looking at her nervously.

'Come on, go!' she says, smiling.

'You've seen what the paper looks like, we've tried to memorise it. It'll be easy this time,' Michelle reminds me.

When I arrive at head office, I see the lovely Welsh receptionist I now know is called Joanne.

'Hello, you back again? Can't stay away from the place, hey?' she says.

I give her a nervous laugh that comes out more like a squeak. I don't want lovely Joanne to know how incompetent I am too. Luckily, I no longer have to sign in since I now have my own ID badge, which could be taken off me today if I fail again.

It feels like déjà vu as I sit down in the exam room. However, this time there is just one lone exam paper and it's all for me. Jerry quickly hides her phone away as soon as she sees me. Always the consummate professional – unless, of course, George the fireman is about.

'Okay, are we ready, Penny?' says Jerry.

'Yes.' I try to smile.

I turn the paper over after her instruction and prepare to fill in the first question about the tundra. But it's not there. I want to ask Jerry, *Where's the question about the tundra?*

I look through the other questions and see that they too are different. I feel so silly as it registers that this is a different paper. Of course; why would they give you the same paper when you know all the questions? I start to panic slightly. I am unprepared for this. I sit back for a moment to calm my racing thoughts.

'Everything okay, Penny?' says Jerry.

'It's a different paper,' I say.

'Well, yes, of course, it is. You didn't expect the same one, did you?' she says. She looks at me as if I am from a different planet.

It takes me a few minutes to gather myself together and then I think about how much I have got through these past few weeks. *Come on, Penny, this is your last hurdle.*

Slowly, I read the questions and, one by one, do my best to answer them. After I have calmed down a bit, I realise that this paper feels easier somehow. Not so many trick questions, or perhaps it is because I revised this morning. I can't quite decide, but I think I am doing okay.

Finally, I finish and hand the paper to Jerry.

'Thank you. If you'll sit outside, I'll call you in when it's all marked,' says Jerry.

I run to the toilet at least four times before Jerry eventually comes out and gets me.

'Right, sit down,' she says. She seems quite stern with me.

'You've passed. But only just. I suggest you read through the safety manual we've given you a few more times before you start flying. You really do need to be tip-top with the procedures. Remember, it's not up to your superiors to save you in an emergency. Everyone could be incapacitated and it would be up to you to save all the passengers.'

Once again, I feel that Jerry is really not selling me this job. But I agree and promise to study the manual further.

Jerry then shakes my hand and says congratulations through gritted teeth. I get the impression I wasn't her favourite of pupils. What matters though is that I have passed. I did it! I got through one of the hardest challenges I have ever had in my life and it gives me a huge sense of achievement and satisfaction.

This time I am smiling when I get outside. I punch the air. It has been such a challenge but I have eventually managed it, even if at first I didn't succeed. I am learning so much about myself throughout this course.

As I walk around the corner, I see Michelle.

'Hey, why aren't you in town with everyone?' I ask.

'Never mind about that. How did it go?' she says.

'I did it, I did it, I did it!' I scream.

'Yayyyyyy,' I hear.

I look around and see that the whole group are standing behind Michelle.

'You lot! What are you up to?' I say.

'We wanted to be here for you. But we were also worried if you failed then you may not want to see all of us. We weren't quite sure what to do. So, I came out first just in case it was bad news. Not that I ever doubted you for a moment. We all knew you could do it. We're so proud of you,' says Michelle.

'Yeah, we are,' says Arabella, hugging me.

'You're like one big family to me. You know that?' I say.

'That's exactly what we are,' says Greg.

'Yup, you have a load of sisters now that you never knew you needed,' says Michelle.

'And brothers,' chirps in Greg.

'You're the best,' I say with a smile.

'Well, I think it's time to celebrate again. Drinks are on me,' says Greg.

'Urgh, how can you face more alcohol again? It's only twelve o'clock,' says Michelle.

'Come on, you can have a squash, you lightweight. Penny here has been studying all night. I think she deserves a round being bought, don't you?'

'That does sound good, but I may need some lunch to go with it. Not eaten yet,' I say.

We grab a big round table and pull another one close to accommodate us all. At the pub I am the only one to eat and feel a bit greedy as I scoff at the spaghetti bolognese special that was on the menu. I am ravenous though and I think all the stress of the course has hit me. I realise that until now I haven't eaten that much these past few weeks.

I am fighting with a piece of spaghetti when two men walk towards our tables. It's a bit early for the usual sleazy guys in here. I hope they're not going to give us a hard time again. I suck on my spaghetti and make a popping noise as I look up and recognise one of them. Oh no. Not him. Again! And he is staring right at me.

'Arabella, how's things?' the other man says to her.

'Great, just finished SEP. Cabin services next,' she says.

'Not long now till you get your wings, then,' he says.

Eventually, the man realises that we are all staring at him.

'Hi all, I'm Neil. This is Matt,' he says to us, introducing us to his companion.

'Apologies, we're both flight deck. I know, I know,' says Neil.

We all laugh as it looks as though we are expected to. However, I don't think any of us are quite sure why he's apologising at this stage in our careers. There appears to be some kind of in-house joke that pilots have to apologise for being one.

'What you up to then?' says Arabella.

'Just across the way doing a conversion course, thought we'd pop in for a quick bite,' says Neil.

'Conversion course?' says Greg.

'Yeah, we moved to short haul, like you, Arabella. Used to fly the big birds but they're getting rid of the last ones now. It was either this or they might send us on our merry ways,' explains Neil.

Short haul; I wonder if that means Matt is flying that too. He hasn't said anything so far and has let Neil do all the talking.

'Well, I'd better get this lunch order in. Got to be back by two. Good to meet you all. Hope to fly with you soon, yeah, Arabella?'

I notice a twinkle in his eye as he says this. Goodness, Arabella is a dark horse! I didn't know she had been chatting to any flight deck whilst we were training.

Matt finally nods his head and says goodbye to everyone. As he passes me, he leans down and hands me a napkin that was laying on the dark oak table.

'Splodge of sauce on your chin, thought you should know,' he says, laughing as he walks off.

'Oh my god, I *hate* that man,' I say.

'Do you know him?' asks Michelle.

'Not really, kind of. I suppose you could say we've had a few encounters.'

I look at the back of his annoying head and that dark wavy hair. Then I glance at his white linen shirt and those smart navy chinos that he probably insisted his wife iron to perfection.

'I really, really hate him,' I say.

As he steps out of sight, I pray that is the last I will ever see of him.

'Oh really? I thought he was rather nice. Quite easy on the eye too,' says Michelle.

Chapter 15

On our first day back with April and Yousef in Cabin Services, they take us to see Nick to pick up our uniforms.

'Hello, so happy you made it,' says Nick when he sees me.

'Oh, you remember me,' I say.

'Well, you did make quite the splash with that foundation,' says Nick, laughing.

'I'm so mortified. That captain was very annoyed with me,' I say.

'Matt's all right really. No harm done. He was just a bit stressed because he was late and already had one uniform ruined by the dry cleaners. You know, if he'd missed that slot to fly out, it would cost the airline a fortune. There's a lot of pressure on these guys,' says Nick.

'Oh, right, well, I still find him quite rude,' I say.

Nick laughs.

'You've seen nothing. Just wait till you start flying. Matt's one of the good ones.'

I can't imagine that but I let Nick have the last word. After the spectacle I made of myself last time, I figure it's best to stay quiet.

'Anyway, if you can sign here to say you've had all your uniform,' says Nick.

I check off the list. Three uniform skirts, four blouses, two jackets, two scarves, gloves, coat, handbag, cabin holdall and uniform shoes. There is so much designer gear here, I feel as though I have spent the morning in Harrods. The best thing is, I didn't spend a penny. This whole experience is like nothing else.

For the following two weeks of cabin service training, we wear our uniforms with pride. Then, finally, when we have eaten our fair share of plastic tray meals and learned about the wines – who knew there were so many varieties and not all of them come in a box? – we are ready for our final day of training before we officially get our 'wings'. The wings are a gold-plated badge with the airline logo in the middle of two wings either side. I can't wait to flash my wings about in the way some women flash their engagement rings. 'Who needs rings when you can have wings' is one of Arabella's favourite quotes.

Our very last afternoon of training is spent in meetings with April and Yousef to discuss our progress and what we need to work further on as we begin our careers. It is like an appraisal, just as Jane would sometimes give me. However, this is a lot more formal and not over a glass of wine at lunch in a brasserie.

'So, Penny,' starts April, as I sit down for my private meeting. 'We know you found the SEP side of things difficult. We have Jerry's notes here, but you did a lot better on the cabin services training. Well done. You seem to be quite a people person, do you agree?'

'Well, I suppose you could say that. I mean, I try to be friendly at work,' I say.

'Yes, that's the only thing, Penny,' says Yousef. 'I would be careful about the amount you speak to people. You could get stuck down the aisle with passengers if you engage in conversation too much. There could be 365 passengers in economy, depending on the aircraft you're working on, and a very limited time to do the service. You need to be fast and efficient.'

'Yes, serve the passengers. Ask them, chicken or beef, tea or coffee, await their response and move to the next passenger. Don't ask them where they're going on holiday like you did with Arabella in the mock-up. You know where they're going on holiday. They're on your flight,' says April.

'Yes, but they could be going on somewhere from there,' I suggest.

'Okay, but just try not to get too involved in small talk. But apart from that, you've done brilliantly. Well done, Penny. You should be very proud of yourself. See you at the wings ceremony this evening,' says Yousef, shaking my hand.

The wings ceremony is taking place at a local posh hotel. I am pleased I had my meeting early as it gives me more time to get ready.

I stop at a small cosmetic shop and treat myself to a new lipstick, before rushing back to the B&B to start on my pampering so I look my best this evening. Tonight will be the first time we will wear our uniform with its wings. Until now we have had a blank space where the wings should sit, which sets us apart from the rest of the crew that mill about the head office and was what made us stand out as complete rookies. In a few hours that will all change.

Back in the B&B I take a moment to digest what I have managed to achieve these last few weeks. I have dealt with so many of my fears and, at times, doubted my ability, but I came through the adversity. I am proud of myself for not quitting. It would have been so easy to walk away some days. However, with the help of my course mates, we all got through the hard parts. What a team we have made. Despite normally keeping myself to myself, I am beginning to trust others, all thanks to the support of Arabella, Greg and Michelle. Even though we lead different lives – Arabella being a party animal, Greg married with children and Michelle having settled down with the love of her life – we have formed an unbreakable bond. Our training brought us so close together and even if we all left Calm Air tomorrow, I know we would remain the best of friends. I don't think this will ever change and certainly hope that it doesn't.

As I am getting ready for the evening ahead, applying the last coat of my nail polish, I receive an email notification. I have been on pins and needles since this morning, as we were told that the rostering department would be emailing our first roster over at some point today. This means we will finally learn where we fly for our very first flight. Will it be Frankfurt, Paris, Malaga, Larnaca or Rome? I quite fancy Larnaca as that is a slightly longer flight and, due to the way they roster us with a hop over to Beirut, we get a twenty-four-hour stopover in a hotel on the beach in Cyprus.

I open the email and see that it is the message I have been waiting for. My first flight will be to Geneva. Okay, that's not bad, an easy flight to Geneva with a stopover. Should be fine. I look at the rest of the roster and am disappointed to see that the remainder of the month is either days off or standby. That means I have to hang around for eight hours every day waiting for a phone call in case I am needed for a flight that someone calls in sick for at the last minute. I might not even be called out and only have one flight in the month if I don't get a call. That would also mean I wouldn't have any flight pay to bump up my basic salary. I do hope that doesn't happen. April did explain that you normally get called out early on though; there is usually someone who rings in sick.

Everyone must receive their roster at the same time as suddenly the WhatsApp group goes crazy.

> I got a Larnaca. Look out Arabella is going to hit the beeeeaaacch. Woohoo.

> Brilliant, I got a Paris. Wish we already had our cheap flights and didn't have to wait a few months, I'd take the missus otherwise

We still don't know Greg's wife's name. It is always 'the missus'.

> Woohoo, Paris, Larnaca and I got a Rome

> Great stuff, Michelle! I have Geneva, and then all standbys

Arabella responds.

> Oof, that's a toughie. Hopefully, you get called out on the first one and then it will knock it all out of sync

I tap out a reply.

Yes, hope so. Don't fancy a month of
hanging around Heathrow

Right. Off to shower, the missus should be
here any moment

Yeah, my boyfriend's already arrived

I sit on the bed and consider how lucky Greg and Michelle
are. I didn't have anyone to invite to my wings. I assumed
Jane wouldn't be interested. In hindsight, she probably
would have come but I would have felt awkward asking
her when she has already done enough for me. It is like
going to a wedding party; you have to spend a fortune to
attend. I didn't want her to have to pay for travelling up
here and then an overnight stay. That would be far too
much to ask of her.

So, although my cohorts may be like family, I do feel
a little left out. It's not like I could have asked if I could
bring Dolly along. Although, I am wearing my mother's
bracelet. I touch it fondly as if I am touching her arm.
I always feel as though it gives me strength, like one of
Wonder Woman's golden cuffs. It is as though when I
touch it, the small quartz stone in it releases its mystical
energies into me.

–

It's amazing how quickly time passes when you are getting
ready for an event; soon it's time to leave for the wings

party celebrations. This is the first time I have been at an event with such pomp and ceremony.

I see Arabella as soon as I walk into the conference room of the hotel. She is standing talking to a glamourous lady. It strikes me that this is her mother and she must be practically my age. Until now I didn't feel old enough to be her mum, but I guess, once again, I forget how old I am.

Next, I see Greg who looks pleased as punch with his children by his side and his wife. She looks proud of him and they are all giggling and happy. One of the boys pulls at Greg's shirt.

'Oi, stop it, I have to look smart,' teases Greg.

I feel like an outsider as I walk about by myself. A waiter offers me a Buck's Fizz, which I gladly accept. I need something to fill my hands with. I feel like I am at a loose end as I walk about the room alone, looking for someone to make eye contact with. But they are all too busy chatting to the guests they have invited.

Finally, Michelle spots me.

'Penny! Come here, come and meet my family,' she says.

I am so pleased to see her.

'Hi there,' I say, smiling.

I can see that Michelle looks like her dad and brothers, with their identical mousy coloured hair. They are all extremely bubbly too, just like Michelle. They make me feel at ease.

'This is Pete, isn't he gorgeous?' says Michelle, introducing me to her partner. 'I think he looks a bit like that captain in the pub, don't you? You know, that one with Arabella's favourite pilot. What was his name? Matt, that's it. We should have invited him as your plus one.'

My cheeks burn up at the mention of his name. How on earth does she have such a good memory? I can't remember what day it is, let alone a random man in a pub's name. Except for Matt. How can I forget *that* name?

I change the topic and turn to the excitement of our first flight when Yousef makes an announcement.

'Hello everyone, good evening and welcome. Would you please take your seats, so that we can make a start.'

He garners everyone's attention and all the family and guests take their seats as us new cabin crew move to the front row, which have been reserved especially for us.

One by one we are called up to get our wings and a certificate confirming that we are now Junior Cabin Crew. At my age, it does feel a little strange to be called 'junior', but we have to start somewhere before we can work our way up.

Families clap as their loved ones go up to Yousef to get their certificates and, as my name is called, I fear that there will be nobody there to cheer me on. But thankfully, the group gives me the biggest cheer and Greg lets out a huge whistle, practically deafening the room. I have a big grin on my face as I walk back to my seat. They really are my family. I love these guys.

Once everyone has had their wings and certificates, and has shaken the airline CEO's hand, we are free to dance and be merry. I am unable to have any more drinks as I have my first flight in the morning and we have been warned that we are not allowed to drink before a flight. Technically, I probably shouldn't even have had the one Buck's Fizz.

I only stay for a couple of dances with the group and then head off as the slow songs begin and people start to dance with their partners. For a moment, the image of me dancing with Matt pops into my head, but I sharply admonish myself. Why am I even thinking about him? Why does he get under my skin? I am glad of the excuse that I have to leave due to my early start in the morning.

As I bid everyone goodbye, it feels slightly daunting. This is it. After the safety of the training school walls, we are all off on our own.

Like birds leaving the nest, it is time to make our own way flying around the big wide world we live in. Well, Europe for now, anyway.

Chapter 16

My first flight as cabin crew departs at 7:15 a.m. and I have to be in the briefing room a couple of hours before. It was hardly worth me going to bed as I had to set my alarm for three a.m. and it was only at two a.m. that I started to get sleepy. Nervousness and excitability made sure I wasn't going to sleep. I just hope all this nervous energy will see me through the long shift I have ahead of me. We have to shuttle back and forth to Geneva four times before we are given a night's stay in the city on the last leg. I am already bleary-eyed; I can't imagine how I will be at the end of the day. I pack a chocolate Freddo into my cabin bag in case it's needed to keep me going.

Finally, my big moment arrives. My stomach is full of butterflies as I reach the Calm Air briefing room where the purser in charge of the flight sits at the head of the table. It is almost like a board meeting as everyone sits around waiting for her to speak. This is definitely the hardest first day in a new job I have ever had. In training they told us to expect the purser to go around one by one asking us safety questions before we are allowed to board the flight. If we can't answer the question, we could get kicked off the flight. I seem to be living on the edge of my nerves at the moment. What if I freeze and can't answer and I get what they call 'offloaded'?

'Hello, I'm Christine for those of you who haven't flown with me before. I think I know most of you here,' says the purser.

'Yeah, we won't talk about that time we got lost down the backstreets of Bangkok, will we?' a woman seated to the side of her asks, laughing.

'Yeah, less said the better,' says Christine.

I shuffle in my seat and feel a little left out at this private joke they have between them.

'Anyway, so, we have someone on her first flight today. Say hello to Penny Thomas.'

All eyes turn to look at me.

'Hello,' I say meekly. I feel my cheeks go crimson, despite all the make-up I have on to try and make me look human at this ungodly hour. You'd think I would have stopped blushing by the age of fifty, but it seems worse than ever.

Everyone says hello and gives me a friendly smile.

'Don't worry, we'll take it easy on you,' says a male flight attendant sitting next to Christine.

The crew give me a sympathetic smile and we move on to the safety briefing.

Fortunately, Christine asks the others the safety questions before me. I listen carefully, trying to remember everything she says. She asks things like how many doors are on the type of aircraft, how many seconds it takes for an evacuation slide to inflate and what to do if it doesn't inflate. Crikey, so many things to remember all the time. Eventually, it's my turn to answer a question. I concentrate on Christine's lips so that I don't miss a word of it.

'In the event of an emergency, what would the brace command be?'

Brace command? It takes a while to sink in and then I realise this is what we say to passengers to get them to move into the position for a crash landing. I hope I don't ever have to do this in real life.

'Brace, brace, heads down, hold your ankles, stay down till we stop,' I say sternly.

'Excellent, and what do we shout when we have had the evacuation command from the captain?' she asks.

I recall the number of times I had to go over this in the classroom. It's an easy one.

'Evacuate, evacuate, evacuate,' I say proudly.

'Great stuff. Okay. So, we have a full flight this morning. Special meals will be loaded in the back galley. Ten vegans, five gluten free, one kosher and two diabetic meals. Penny, you'll be R3 position so you'll be in charge of allocating the special meals.'

We were taught in training school the different positions and what we would be responsible for but suddenly I worry about all these special meals. What if I give the wrong one to the wrong person? I think Christine can read my thoughts.

'Don't worry, Gavin is the economy supervisor today and will help you. We all remember our first flight, don't we guys?' she says.

'We do indeed,' says Gavin. Is it my imagination or do they all seem to be in on a joke? I do hope they are not going to make me do any initiation like I have heard some new recruits have. Everyone giggles and Christine smiles and says, 'Behave, you lot! Now, come on, let's get on-board.'

I was looking forward to walking through the airport in my uniform, like I have seen the crew doing when I have been on holiday with Geraint. I planned on holding my head up high with my airline regulatory wheelie bag behind me and my hat firmly positioned on my head. However, it doesn't work like that in British airports. Instead, a crew bus takes us to a separate security area and we have to walk up the steep staircase outside the aircraft that the ground staff use. My heels almost stick in the slats of the steps. I am not sure the grooming department thought this bit out responsibly. Thankfully, after a few steps I master the heels.

It is strange seeing a plane empty and freshly cleaned ready for us. Usually, there are people with socks and feet up everywhere, their headphones on listening to music or watching the latest movie by the time I board.

Gavin takes me to the back galley and shows me where to store my cabin bag. I place it with the blankets we keep in the overhead storage. It is an odd first day in a new job as there is no desk to sit at and be told what is what. Everything is all over the place. I look at the carts that are full of miniature vodkas, beers and wine bottles that are sat next to carts full of meal trays. We are only doing a short service today since it is a quick flight. But we still have to serve them and clear everything in before we land. It's going to be busy trying to serve all this stuff. I can understand now why Yousef and April warned me I mustn't chat with the passengers too much.

Before I can finish counting the meals and checking everything we need is on-board, Christine makes an announcement for us to stand at our boarding stations. This means I am to stand at the back of the economy cabin near the toilet as the passengers are on their way. My tummy is doing somersaults at the sight of them all streaming down the aisles with their carry-on luggage. I wonder where they think we will fit all those items on the plane.

A lady asks me to help her place a wheelie bag in the hat-rack. I try to keep a smile on my face as I struggle with its weight. I am definitely going to have some impressive muscles after a few weeks in this job.

A cute family come towards me and take their seats together. I can't help but be a little envious of them. They look like the perfect family. I bet they don't even have arguments in their household.

'Good morning,' I say, smiling professionally.

'Morning, would you be able to put this up there?' says the mother, holding a teddy and pointing at the hat-rack.

She hands over the huge brown teddy with a bright blue bow.

'Ooh, we had better take care of this, hadn't we? Is this yours?' I say, looking at the little boy who must be around five.

He nods shyly as I try to stuff one leg of teddy in against jackets and overnight bags. I feel a little bad as I grab teddy's bottom and squash him in, but space is getting super tight now.

'In you go little fella,' I say, praying they haven't noticed my unavoidable slight manhandling of him.

I hear the dad say something and then finally the little boy speaks.

'Can I see the captain?' he asks quietly. He looks so like his father, who has a cashmere jumper thrown insouciantly over his shoulders.

'Ah, I'm afraid nobody is allowed into the flight deck, but I can ask if we can do anything once we land.' I smile.

'Can I get a water?' asks the mother.

'Umm, yes, sure,' I say.

'Excuse me, do you have somewhere I can hang this coat?' says a gentleman to my left.

'Where is this seat?' asks a lady poking me with her boarding card.

We haven't even taken off yet and there are so many questions. I try not to get into a tizz but I am definitely thrown into the deep end. These passengers have no idea it's my first day on the job and I have to look as though I have been doing this for years.

I feel as though my head is spinning. How can I deal with all these demands in one go?

Fortunately, Gavin comes up behind me.

'Do you want to get the water and I'll deal with the other requests,' he says kindly.

I am pleased to hide in the galley to catch my breath. I pour the water and as I head back into the cabin, Christine makes the next announcement.

'Boarding complete. Doors to manual and crosscheck.'

I quickly hand the passenger the water and run to the back right door of the plane. I stare at the door trying to remember how we engage the emergency slides and life raft ready for departure.

The crew on my opposite side has already armed her door for departure and wants to check I have done mine. Oh, my goodness, so many things to do. I feel in a bit of a panic.

I take a deep breath and recall how I worked the door in training. Eventually, it comes back to me and a red flag appears on the door showing that it is now armed with a slide. If anyone opens this door now, a huge slide will inflate and cost the airline thousands of pounds. I look at the door with satisfaction. I did it! I remembered everything that Jerry taught me. Perhaps she wasn't such a bad instructor after all.

Then there is another announcement.

'Cabin crew to safety demonstration positions, please,' says Christine.

I rush for my demonstration kit with its fake life jacket and seat belt and run into my position. I am the last one in place. It feels as though I am on the stage as all the passengers stare at me as I puff and pant while smoothing down my uniform grey skirt. This is my moment to shine. Not for a moment did I ever think I would actually be standing here. What a dream come true.

As I lift my arms to point to the passengers where their nearest exit is I notice an extraordinarily handsome guy watching me closely. Oh no, do we have to have a handsome passenger watch the every move of my first ever safety demonstration? This is not at all what I imagined.

I clip in the seatbelt and unclip it, almost missing the slot as I am now trembling so badly. I avert my eyes from the male passenger and focus on a kind-looking older lady. And then it is soon over and I put all my paraphernalia back into its pouch. I have completed my first safety demonstration, just like you see in aeroplane movies. Let's just hope there are no disasters. I suddenly feel protective of these passengers who depend on me and the other crew members to lead them to safety if anything untoward was to happen. I look around and want to tell them they are all in safe hands, especially the one lady who looks like a very nervous flyer.

I notice the handsome passenger smile at me as I walk past. Oh no, I am going to have to serve him after take-off. This thought makes me feel even more nervous and I wonder if I should quickly open the door and jump down the slide rather than serve him. I feel slightly intimidated dealing with someone so handsome when I am such a newbie at my job. But I strap myself into my harness and sit on the stiff crew seat. I am facing backwards, which is such a strange feeling as we lift off into the air with me facing the back of the plane. I focus on keeping my feet on the ground as we were taught. Jerry told us that we shouldn't cross our legs on take-off and landing and to sit upright and straight with our feet firmly on the floor in case of any sudden need to brace. I really am quite impressed how she drilled all of this into my head when my memory isn't the best.

We are still on quite an incline when there is a double *bing* noise, which means we can now get up and start the service. How on earth we are supposed to pull the carts up at that angle I don't know, but I am soon to find out. I quickly prepare my cart and am told by Gavin that I have forgotten to put the tomato juice on the top. I knew there was something missing. The pressure is starting to get to me. All the things that I have to remember seemed so much easier during training sessions with a list of instructions in front of me and a trainer giving constant reminders.

We quickly take the carts into the aisles and I am thankful that Gavin is on the other side of the cart with me as he helps me push it uphill.

Asking the first passenger, a young male, what he'd like to drink is nerve-racking, but I soon get the hang of it as I work my way down the cabin and get more confident the further I go. Until I come to seat 23A. I wish Gavin could serve him.

The good-looking passenger gives me another of his gorgeous smiles.

'Umm, yes, would you like anything to drink?' I say.

'Orange juice, *s'il vous plaît.*'

I notice his heavy French accent and want to melt.

His grey eyes seem to see right through me, and I blush again.

I pour the juice just as we hit a bit of turbulence and it splashes up onto my pink shirt sleeve. Did we have to have turbulence in front of this gorgeous guy? I am just grateful that I didn't land on my bottom.

I hand the drink over and move on as fast as I can.

'*Merci,*' he says, giving me another smile.

'Think you've a fan there,' says Gavin as soon as we are out of earshot of the passenger.

'Oh, I don't think so,' I say, blushing.

'Just be careful, you don't know who you meet on flights,' he warns.

'Oh no, of course. I'm not interested anyway. I'm just here to do my job,' I insist.

I have already heard about pilots; now it seems passengers are off limits too.

'All I want is to keep my head down and save Dolly,' I say with a smile.

'Dolly?' asks Gavin.

'My VW Beetle,' I explain.

'Ah, how cute. I flew with a pilot recently who was mad in love with old Volkswagens. If you ever find yourself on the same trip, I'm sure you'd have a lot to talk about. To be honest, I found him quite boring going on about his camper van,' he says, laughing.

'Excuse me, do you have any sick bags? My husband doesn't feel well,' interrupts a passenger.

'Oh, gosh, yes, I'll bring it right to you,' I say.

I run and find a sick bag and give it to the couple who are sitting right in front of the handsome French guy. I am certainly not looking very glamorous now with my big splodge of orange juice and a sick bag in my left hand.

'Excuse me,' the male passenger says as I head back towards the galley.

'Yes,' I say, smiling. Oh my gosh, he is so good-looking. Those eyes, that fair longish hair. He looks like he would live in a penthouse in Monte Carlo, although I suspect he doesn't since he is sat in economy.

'I give you this,' he says, handing me a napkin.

'Oh, thanks,' I say. Can he not wait until we clear all the rubbish in? Goodness, these passengers are impatient!

I rush back to the galley and throw the paper in the trash cart. But then I notice some writing on the back as it flies in upside down. Curious, I reach in to get it back out. A used tea bag bursts all over my hand.

I read the napkin.

Call me, Pierre 00973 998670 x

Is that his phone number? Was that meant for me or someone else? Surely he didn't just give me his number! Perhaps he wrote it down for someone else and now he's given it to me to throw, so I chuck it in the bin.

By the time we clear in the rubbish we are told that we have only twenty minutes until landing and have to secure the cabin again. This has got to be the fastest flight ever.

Passing Pierre for the last time, he makes a gesture to me with his hand. He holds his hand up like a phone beside his ear and says, 'Call me, yes?'

I just smile, blush again and rush off. As I take my seat for landing, my feet already starting to throb, I am in shock that at fifty years old, a handsome French passenger has asked me out on my very first flight. The things this uniform does to people!

Chapter 17

We go through the same procedures four times before we finally land in Geneva for the last time that day. How different I feel by the final flight. Gone are the nerves and I am starting to remember what needs to go where. I suppose practice makes perfect and nothing at training school can prepare you for the real deal.

Although I am now feeling a lot more confident than earlier this morning, I am beyond exhausted and that is possibly why I am practically hallucinating about chocolate Freddos.

I must look as though I am starting to wilt as Gavin is keen to get me off the plane.

'Come on, you. Let's get off this plane. I've got some of this for the crew bus,' says Gavin, waving about a water bottle full of a dodgy-looking brown substance.

'What on earth is that?' I ask.

'Brown cow. Just you wait. You haven't lived until you've had some brown cow on the crew bus,' he says, smiling.

Gavin grabs some plastic glasses off the aircraft, and we get through the airport together with the rest of the crew and onto the crew bus.

'Cheers,' says Gavin, handing me a glass of brown cow. 'So, how did you find your first flight?'

'Absolutely loved it. Nerve-racking, but I loved it,' I say.

I take a sip of the brown cow. It is certainly an acquired taste.

'Yup, you'll soon settle into it all,' he says.

I watch as the rest of the crew soon top up their drinks again before we arrive at the hotel. One glass of brown cow on top of a chocolate Freddo is definitely enough for me though.

The bus slows down and I look out the window to see the most gorgeous hotel near Lake Geneva.

'Oh my, is that our hotel?' I ask.

I worry that Gavin might say no and point to something teeny next door as this surely can't be where the airline puts us up.

'It is indeed. The airline has an agreement with the hotel, so this one is particularly nice. They're not all like this, so be warned,' says Gavin.

'Oh no, they're definitely not all like this one. Remember when that guy came out from under my bed in the San Fran hotel? Thankfully we stopped staying there after that,' says Christine.

'Yeah, hun. Word of advice, always check under the bed and inside the wardrobes when you arrive at a hotel,' says Gavin.

'Oh yeah, definitely. Make sure the shower curtain is pulled back too. You never know, someone could hide in there,' says Christine.

I feel very unworldly. I had no idea this type of thing could happen. What if this hotel isn't safe? I mean, it looks fantastic but now I am freaked out.

'Drinks in the bar in ten minutes?' says Christine before we get off the bus.

Although I am exhausted, I am quite glad of the opportunity of drinks with the crew. It will be nice to unwind after those busy flights. Besides, if I don't turn up, they will think someone was hiding under my bed and raise the alarm.

I feel like a princess as I walk into the beautiful hotel in my designer uniform. There is the biggest chandelier I think I have ever seen in the lobby. The reception desk is almost taller than me and the receptionist smiles with our keys in her hand ready for us. She gives them out, along with an envelope to each of the crew. I am the last to receive my key and envelope. I sign a paper to say I have received it. We seem to have to sign lots of things in this business.

Once I am in my room, I open the envelope to see my cash allowance inside for me to spend in the hotel. Goodness, this airline is incredibly generous. I have a bedroom with sweeping curtains, a big mahogany desk and an en suite marble bathroom. It is like a palace, and then I even have an envelope stuffed with cash to buy food whilst I am here. This truly is the best job in the world. Carys was right.

I check the wardrobe and all the crevices in the room but, fortunately, find nothing that shouldn't be there, so I throw my uniform on the chair and quickly change to meet everyone for drinks.

It's funny how everyone looks so different out of uniform. If it wasn't for Christine's Scottish accent that I hear as soon as I walk into the bar, I wouldn't recognise her.

The bar is busy with businessmen in suits. Some look as though they are enjoying themselves socially, some seem to be doing serious business over a scotch. A piano plays in the corner, but nobody takes any notice; they are all too busy chatting amongst themselves.

'Hey, how did you like your room?' says Gavin as he spots me.

'It's gorgeous, isn't it?' I say.

'Yeah, some of the rooms have a jacuzzi. Although I'm convinced it's always the flight deck who get those, isn't that right, Tom?' says Gavin.

Tom, the first officer, is cradling a pint of something and looking very relaxed. He seems to be distracted by the group of five females sitting around a table to the left of us. They are all sipping on what looks like champagne.

I order a half cider and realise that there isn't going to be much change from my allowance at this rate. The price of the drink makes my eyes water. It makes me wonder what the ladies on the table do to afford to drink champagne in a place like this.

We chat amongst ourselves as Tom carries on not listening to a word we are saying. What is it with him and those women? He is starting to look a bit creepy now as he tries his best to get their attention.

'They're with the royal flight,' says Gavin, pointing over at them.

'Royal flight?' I ask.

Tom finally pricks his ears up.

'Yup, my dream job. Flight deck on a private jet. None of the nonsense we have to put up with, passengers going missing in duty-free and stuff,' says Tom.

'Ah, but a mate of mine was crew on a private jet and the owner calls all the shots. He packed for four days in Europe, two weeks later he was still in Frankfurt with the same pair of pants. He left in the end. Didn't have a life,' says Gavin.

'I don't have a life anyway,' says Tom, laughing.

'Who's coming to the Irish bar?' interrupts Christine.

'Me. Not paying these prices,' says Gavin.

I am pleased to leave the hotel bar or I would have had to start paying out more than I earned all day just for drinks, so I gladly accept the invitation.

Although the evening is mild, the fresh air hits me as I walk outside. I can already feel the effects of the brown cow and cider. I probably should have said I would head to bed instead, but I wanted to be social, particularly as I am finding my feet with this new job.

The Irish bar is packed and seems to have some special offer on shots. Gavin thinks it's a great idea to buy me some shots to celebrate a successful first flight. This is the moment I know I should leave, but I don't know my way back to the hotel so I stay with Gavin and Christine until they are ready to head back.

'We still have an hour before we legally have to stop drinking for the flight back,' says Christine.

I can't believe what a party animal Christine is. She and Gavin dance about and as soon as we finish one round of shots, Christine calls for more. I am feeling woozier and woozier. I know I should say that I have had enough but it feels like pressure from your new boss to keep up with them. I want to impress them and show that I am like they are, even if I know in my heart this is a bad idea. I really don't fancy flying back with a hangover, and since I reached forty-five those are getting worse and worse.

The next round of drinks is black velvet; Gavin tells me that it's Prosecco and Guinness and that if we were on the private jets, like those other women we saw earlier, then we might have been able to swap the Prosecco for Dom Perignon.

'At Calm Air, we're more Prosecco than Perignon,' he says, laughing.

'Well, that's good enough for me,' I say.

I can almost feel the headache I will have when I wake up.

'Cheers,' says Christine. I notice how fast she takes down her drink. I really can't keep up with these two.

I manage to avoid the next round by pretending I want to check something out in the bar. Between the tiredness and the drinks, I am very tipsy and the beginning of nausea is creeping in. Still though, I don't refuse the next drink when Gavin tells me we are having one for the road.

'Or one for the runway, I should say, bahahahah,' says Gavin with a laugh.

The way he says it seems incredibly funny, but I think it's more our intake of alcohol than his actual sense of humour that makes us laugh so hard.

As we finish the drinks, Christine switches back to purser mode.

'Ooh, time's up. We're about to turn into pumpkins,' says Christine, noticing the time.

She grabs my arm as we walk back to the hotel and Gavin grabs my other arm and we run up the road, arm in arm, in what I am assured is the direction of the hotel. Christine and Gavin giggle and mess about all the way back to the hotel. I don't though, as I am feeling more nauseous than ever. I cannot be sick in front of my new bosses.

Walking back into the hotel, Christine and Gavin decide to check if Tom is still in the hotel bar, leaving me to run for the lift before I am sick. I press the buttons violently for the lift to come. *Please, please come quickly.* I see the lift reach the third floor, then the second and then first. As it reaches the first floor I can take no more. I vomit all over the lobby floor just as the lift doors open. *Please let the ground swallow me up.* This is such a posh hotel. This is horrific.

I don't look up at the person who comes out of the lift, instead keeping my head down. If I can't see them then maybe they can't see me. But I hear a voice.

'First flight? Word of advice, stay off the brown cow,' says the voice.

I look at the shiny black shoes, the black flight deck uniform trousers, then I lift my head up further to see four stripes on the cuff of a jacket. I can tell that it's a captain from Calm Air. But I don't need to look to see which one it is, as I recognise that patronising sickly voice.

–

I try to keep my head up high the next morning as I walk through the airport, but I am mortified. Matt! Of all people, he had to be there right at that moment, didn't he? What is it with that man?

Fortunately, none of the passengers realise the state I was in last night and as we are boarding the passengers to fly back, a little girl comes up to me.

'You look like a doll,' she says.

Despite the horrendous headache I am struggling with, I smile at the mum and daughter and say thank you. What a lovely little girl.

I have certainly learned my lesson to never get carried away or give into peer pressure again. I have hardly been able to look at Gavin and the rest of the crew.

'You all right, chick? You seem a bit quiet,' says Gavin as we are getting meals out of the oven for the service.

'Not really, a bit embarrassed about last night,' I say.

'We've all done it. What goes on down-route, stays down-route. Forget it. Believe me, some crew have made us lose hotel contracts, their behaviour's been so bad. Being sick in the middle of a hotel lobby is the least of the airline's worries,' says Gavin, laughing.

'Oh no,' I say. It makes me feel terrible as he says it out loud like that.

'Don't blame yourself. It was all those shots, cocktails and then, of course, it was your first time trying brown cow, to be fair,' says Gavin sympathetically.

'Don't remind me. Urgh. What was in it anyway?' I ask.

'Tia Maria, brandy, milk. I don't know, whatever dregs I managed to find off the aircraft. I may have put some vodka in. I just mixed it all up,' says Gavin.

No wonder I was so ill.

'Well, I don't think I'll ever touch the stuff again,' I say.

'You'll get used to it,' he says, smiling.

Somehow, I manage to get through the flight. I don't know if things seem easier on this flight as I have had more practice, or if it is just because I am feeling so rubbish that I don't overthink everything, as I have a tendency to do. Still, the plane can't land fast enough for me to get off.

When we land and all the passengers have disembarked, I say goodbye to Gavin, Christine and the rest of the crew. Despite my misadventure, they have been great to fly with. So friendly and, more importantly, so forgiving.

'Hope to fly with you again soon,' says Christine as we sign out at head office.

'You too,' I say with a smile. Although, if truth be told, I don't think I would be able to keep up with her again. I think I would insist that at least I eat next time and not just go for drinks.

As soon as I reach home, I breathe a sigh of relief. I survived my first flight and worked through a horrendous hangover.

I make myself some tea and lie on the sofa with a blanket. I am happy to be back with Dolly; thank goodness I have a day off tomorrow before I await the instructions for my next flight.

I have promised to visit the dog shelter and I am looking forward to helping out with Oreo and Willow. Perhaps I should ask if they have any paid jobs and I could be a kennel maid. At least I wouldn't get carried away in a fancy city and the dogs wouldn't judge me if I did make a mistake, unlike that horrible Matt. Whatever happens, I pray that I never see him in a hotel lobby again, or, god forbid, fly with him. Surely life wouldn't be that cruel to me?

Chapter 18

I have been on standby for two days with no call out for any flights. I just had to hang around and be ready to shoot to the airport if the call came, but it didn't. Until now, and I have finally been called out for a Paris night stop. Paris! When the man in rostering called me and told me, I was over the moon and wanted to pinch myself for landing such a dream job. Who on earth would go sick for a Paris trip? They must have been very ill. The moment I have always dreamed of has come true. Penny Thomas is off to Paris and, what's more, I am being paid to go!

Fortunately, I had an overnight bag packed with pyjamas and a few bits just in case, so it takes me no time to get to the airport. I manage to rush to the briefing and meet the new crew that I will be working with for this trip and off we go to the aircraft. Today I am working in the middle of the economy cabin.

We have just finished boarding when the captain makes an announcement.

'Good morning, everyone, this is Captain Garcia speaking. We are expecting a smooth flight to Paris today where the weather is just perfect. You'll also be pleased to know that you have a wonderful crew looking after you today. You're in very good hands, so please relax and enjoy your flight with us.'

My confidence is building with each flight and, with Captain Garcia's belief in his crew, it makes me feel even more self-assured. I smile at the passengers and feel as though I am floating down the aisle. I was born to do this job.

The flight is so short, it whizzes by. Then we fly back to London again, then back to Paris for our stopover. Captain Garcia makes the same announcement on each flight. He sounds gorgeous each time. I remind myself that I must remember the flight deck rule.

Finally, we land in Paris for the last time and grab our bags to leave the plane. I have arrived in my dream city.

'Bonsoir,' I say to the passengers as they disembark. How I wish I had paid more attention to Mrs Edwards, the French teacher in secondary school.

'Welcome to Paris,' says a French passenger.

'Merci,' I say, giggling.

'Are you coming for drinks with us after? A few of us are heading to a bar near the hotel that does the best Chambord cocktails,' says my supervisor, Karen, as we head towards customs.

I remember my last drinking session, but I am in Paris so how could I not make the most of every moment?

'Absolutely,' I say.

'Don't drink too much then,' a voice says.

I look behind me and see a captain's uniform and a body wearing it that looks familiar. There are those customary four stripes, those shoes. Matt is Captain Garcia? How can this even be possible? He must put on a different voice for his announcements as I certainly didn't suspect it was him for a moment.

'Madame, we need to see your bag,' says a customs officer, pulling me over.

No, no, no. This can't be happening. Not with Matt behind me, please.

'You have some liquids?' he says. I am highly aware that Matt is listening to everything.

The customs officer starts unzipping my bag and pulls out a liquid syringe-looking thing.

'Madame, what is this?' he says, holding it up.

At this point, I am not sure whether to say a syringe for a non-existent drug habit or be honest, as the truth is going to be extremely embarrassing with Matt in such close proximity.

'It's my corn pen,' I say.

'Pardon?' says the customs officer.

'Corn pen,' I say.

'Explain?'

I lift my foot up and try and balance on one leg as I explain how I have a very uncomfortable corn on my left foot and this is a pen that is supposed to contain some kind of acid stuff to burn it off.

I hear Matt laugh behind me. Can someone please not call him forward?

'Do you not have a crew bus to the hotel to catch?' I say.

'I'm in command of the aircraft. I have to make sure all the crew get through customs,' he says, winking.

I feel like squirting my corn solution in his eye, but obviously that would be a criminal thing to do.

I take a deep breath and sigh. This man drives me mad!

The customs officer seems content with my graphic explanation and continues to rummage through my bag, pulling out my pyjamas.

'Are those Snoopy pyjamas?' says Matt.

'No,' I say.

'They look like them to me,' he says, laughing.

What an obnoxious little man.

How dare he mock my Snoopy pyjamas? They're very comfortable. What does he sleep in? *Nothing*, my head says to me. My cheeks turn red at this thought. I just thank goodness he can't read my mind.

I watch as his muscular little bottom shuffles away in his uniform trousers as he finally makes his way through the arrival doors and the customs officer zips my bag back up. I make a note to not have any further thoughts of what Matt wears to bed. The sooner we finish this trip, the better!

I don't go anywhere near Matt on the crew bus or at the hotel. When Karen comes over to tell me where everyone is meeting to go out, I apologise and tell her I have a sudden migraine. I must not be in the company of annoying Matt and I can't be sure that he isn't going for drinks. As silly as it seems, I make the decision to go it alone in Paris. I should have gone with the rest of the crew and enjoyed myself, but I can't face seeing him. So, I go for a walk outside the hotel when I know that the crew will have already left for drinks. I soon realise this was a ridiculous idea as I don't know my way around Paris at all. I immediately curse myself for being so obstinate.

I walk out with no idea which direction I should be heading, a dead phone battery and no handy travel guide-book for help. It is starting to get dark and I foolishly thought that the Eiffel Tower would guide me through the city, but I can't see it from where I am standing.

I look across the street towards a boulangerie, which has already closed for the evening. Deciding that I might be better on that side of the pavement, I step out onto the road. As I do so, a horn beeps angrily at me and I see the glint of a black metal car bonnet. I realise I have almost been run over by a man driving an old Renault 5. My mistake for forgetting that cars drive on the other side of the road in France.

'*Tu es imbécile!*' shouts the older man out of his window.

I stumble back onto the pavement and, when someone pushes past me, almost bruising my arm with their big bag, I burst into tears. I should have stayed with the crew and not tried to make a point.

I choose to head back to the hotel, shaken up with my tail between my legs. I am sure there will be other Paris flights where I can explore further than the streets near our hotel. Next time I won't make the same mistake and will stay with the crew.

I get to my room, don my Snoopy pyjamas and order room service. I decide that bingeing on Netflix is preferable to risking getting lost down the backstreets of Paris.

I tuck into a delicious croque-monsieur and am frustrated with myself when the thought of Matt pops into my head again. Perhaps that is another reason I was so distracted on the road. *Leave me alone, Matt.* What is wrong with me? Why can't I stop thinking about him? He is like this annoying little mosquito that's buzzing around my head. *He did sound hot doing the pilot announcements though*, my brain reminds me.

By the time we have to leave for our flight back home, I am refreshed, even if I did have a dream that I was pulling Matt's trousers down. Goodness me. Luckily, I woke up with a start at that point or I don't know what would have happened next. I don't know how I am going to look at Matt after that dream. Whilst this hasn't been quite how I planned my trip, at least I managed to watch a whole series of *Emily in Paris*. So, in some ways, I still got to see the sights of the city. It doesn't get any more authentic than watching *Emily in Paris* in Paris itself!

As we head to the airport, I notice Matt looking over at me a few times. Is he psychic and knows I dreamed of him last night? I hope not. What does he want with me? Why can't he leave me alone? I continue ignoring him. I figure that the best thing is not to give him any attention. That's what we do with the dogs in the sanctuary when they are playing up.

When we board the aircraft to leave Paris, Matt heads to the left of the plane with the quiet first officer and the rest of the crew turn to the right. I am so grateful this trip is almost over. I almost want to hurry the passengers along as they start boarding so we can take-off immediately.

Finally, all the passengers are on-board. We close the doors and are almost ready to push back the aircraft. I breathe a sigh of relief but then there is a call for the purser to go to the flight deck. I don't think too much of it at first; Captain Garcia is probably demanding a coffee before take-off or something. However, then there is an announcement from him personally and he isn't quite as jovial as on the way over.

'Good afternoon, this is Captain Garcia. I'm afraid that, as we have prepared to push back, a light has come on in the flight deck. We have a slight technical issue but hope to get this sorted within the next few minutes. Engineers are back on their way to resolve this and we hope we will be pushing back again shortly.'

Everyone groans around the cabin and people start asking for water.

We have to be delayed when Matt is captain, don't we? He probably pressed the wrong button or something. I bet this is all his fault.

I can see the flight engineers are busy from the window. They seem to be looking inside the left engine. A passenger pulls me to one side.

'I don't want to fly if there's an engine problem, I don't like to fly. Please, I want to get off.'

I don't quite know how to deal with the lady so I ask Karen if she can have a word with her. I am usually quite good with nervous passengers, but that is because there is no reason for them to be afraid. With Captain Garcia in charge of those engines, goodness knows what could happen.

Karen is trying to reassure the passenger when there is another announcement calling for the purser. Perhaps things have been resolved.

Five minutes later Captain Garcia is back making yet another announcement.

'Ladies and gentlemen, I do apologise. It seems we have a problem with one of our engines and cannot safely take this aircraft back to London today. We need a special part, which is not readily available. The ground staff will help you with alternative flights or accommodation where necessary. Please accept our sincere apologies from everyone at Calm Air. I can assure you that this is highly unusual and we pride ourselves on getting our passengers to where they want to be on time. We are deeply sorry for the inconvenience.'

There is a lot of swearing and shouting around the cabin as passengers clamber to get their bags back out of the overhead lockers. I want to hide from them. I want to get home as much as they do; I don't want to get stuck down-route with Matt. This is my worst nightmare. I feel like telling the passengers I am coming with them. Could

I get an alternative flight too? No wonder someone went sick for this flight. Perhaps they had a premonition.

Eventually, all the passengers leave the plane and the ground staff are left to deal with the fraying tempers. You can hear the shouting from the arrivals hall. Unlike the crew, the passengers will now have to liaise with the Calm Air ground staff about all their options.

Karen tells us how Matt has already spoken to our operations team at head office who have quickly arranged for a crew bus to take us back to the hotel that we have just left.

On the way over to the hotel, I pretend I am not listening to Matt as he tells Karen how he thinks it might be two nights before we can get out of here. I roll my eyes behind the sunglasses I am wearing. I can't believe I am stuck in Paris for two nights with Matt. However, I decide that I am not going to hide this time. I will simply ignore and avoid him. Perhaps this is my opportunity to see Paris properly.

Sue, one of the senior crew, is on annual leave starting tonight, and I listen to her complain as she tells me that she is due to fly to the Seychelles on a cheap ticket in the morning. However, the rest of the crew are much more positive and decide that we should make the best of a bad situation and plan lunch at Montemarte. My stomach is rumbling and I would love to find a good place to eat, so, I agree. We have to meet in the lobby in ten minutes.

I don't even know that I have the clothes for two nights here. I only have a pair of jeans, a sweatshirt and some trainers. I feel so scruffy as I think that Matt will be there, all perfect as usual. Why am I thinking of Matt? Who cares what he thinks? I get that annoying mosquito feeling again and want to swat him.

I decide to stick with Karen and the other crew in economy and stay well away from Matt on our lunch. Since there is a crowd of us, surely I can manage to keep my distance from him.

Although ten of us set out from the hotel, it is impossible to keep tight together as we juggle the busy Paris pavements. I try to stay beside Karen but I end up on the kerb where mopeds whizz past me and an old Citroen struggles up the hill. It makes me think of Dolly. I take an artistic black and white photo of the street with its bistros and the Citroen heading out of sight, using a filter on my charged-up phone. Perhaps I could get more Instagram followers if I become a little more artistic. I think the creative atmosphere must be rubbing off on me.

–

The square at Place Du Tertre is certainly making me fall in love with art. I stop and watch a local artist paint the scenery of cobbled streets and pavement cafes. A couple of tourists ask the artist how much it will be to get a painting done of themselves. So I move away with Karen and notice another artist beside us who is doing caricatures. I would never be brave enough to have a caricature; imagine what the artist would do with my pointy chin! I decide I might need to make a quick exit from him.

I walk along with the others for a while and we end up on the busy Rue Lepic.

'See that place there? That's the cafe Amélie worked at in the movie of the same name,' says Karen, pointing to a cafe with a red canopy and plastic chairs.

'Cafe des Deux Moulins,' she says in her best French accent.

'Oh wow, can we not go there to eat?' I say.

'No, Matt knows a fab place. Let's follow the leader,' says Karen.

With the thought of French movies in mind, I get carried away in the atmosphere and decide that I need to look as though I belong in Paris. There is an important accessory I need if I want to make myself look French. I am delighted to see a shop selling souvenirs and postcards of the Eiffel Tower also selling berets! I can't resist it. I tell Karen I will catch her up and put a navy beret on my head, hoping that I look sophisticated and that it changes my casual, scruffy look into Parisian chic. It probably doesn't and I look like an absolute tourist, but it makes me feel confident and chic anyhow. Although I am sure I have seen these exact berets for sale in H&M for much less than I paid here.

Fortunately, I am not too far behind and run to catch up with the rest of the crew who are heading to a pretty bistro that is on the other side of the cobbles. Matt leads them all to a table. As a captain, it makes me wonder if he ever gives up being in charge. I bet he's even got to be in charge in the bedroom. *Now, Penny. Stop that now!*

Because I have trailed behind, by the time I reach the table there is only one seat left. It seems nobody wants to sit beside Matt. I begin to regret my beret purchase. I should have picked it up on the way back, but I was worried I wouldn't find the shop again. Why couldn't someone have saved me a seat next to them? I really don't want to sit next to him.

I pick up the menu that is sitting on the table and busy myself so that I don't have to speak to him.

'They do a nice spaghetti bolognese here, rather messy though,' he says, leaning into me.

Does this man remember everything? At this point I want to smack him over the head with the menu. My goodness, he really brings out the violent side in me! I decide to ignore him.

'Although, when in Paris, you should really have something a bit more authentic than spag bol,' he says, laughing.

He picks up the menu and points to something in French.

'These are excellent here. I wholly recommend the frogs' legs,' he says.

I couldn't think of anything worse than frogs' legs. I feel guilty enough eating a chocolate Freddo!

'Mademoiselle, what would you like?' asks the waiter. I can see Matt watching me. I want to order the fries with some ketchup, but I just can't say it.

'Escargot, *s'il vous plaît*,' I say, pointing to the first thing I see on the menu.

The waiter answers me in French and speaks super-fast. I don't understand any of it. Matt has obviously picked up on me not getting what the waiter has said.

'He's asking if you want garlic butter with the escargot?' he says.

'*Oui, s'il vous plaît*,' I say, ignoring Matt. My French is really coming along now.

The waiter seems to understand me and then rushes off to get some wine that Matt has ordered for us all.

Goodness, I am a proper Parisian now, with a beret on my head, drinking wine at lunchtime and speaking practically fluent French. What a difference to that nervous tourist I was less than twenty-four hours ago.

When the waiter arrives with the wine, I take a sip and I hate to admit it but Matt ordered well. He does seem to know his stuff. I suppose it's because he is so well-travelled and, apparently, half Spanish. I heard Karen call him Matteo when she was teasing him about something. When I asked her about it, she said his dad was from Madrid, but he was brought up in England.

As I sip my wine I watch the people go by. Tourists and couples holding hands look around at the beguiling street we are on. They will have paid to come here and I still can't get over the fact that this is my job. I'm being paid to be here! Whilst others work in a dark office, with artificial lighting, I am here sipping lovely French wine on a pavement cafe with a beret on my head. I am living the dream and it is Geraint getting Alex pregnant and my chance encounter with Carys that made this happen. Perhaps freedom was the best present Geraint could have given me.

I focus on the conversation as I overhear Matt telling Karen about some fantastic bookshop that he goes to every time he is in Paris.

'It has the most interesting books, some you can't find in other places. You can't come to Paris and not have a wander around,' says Matt.

It sounds fantastic, not that I would ever let on that I am interested. I will make sure I visit it once we all split up later today. Dolly was once in a book about VW Beetles and I have tried everywhere to find it. It is a long shot, but if they do have some different types of books, you never know, it could be there.

I put the name into my phone and check on google maps. It isn't too far away. I will certainly visit it later today.

The waiter returns and I am horrified to see that someone has ordered snails. How could anyone be so cruel? Probably Matt; he's such a show-off. However, the waiter puts a burger and chips in front of him.

'Escargot, *mademoiselle*,' says the waiter. He puts the snails down in front of me. '*Bon appetit*,' he says and walks away.

I am speechless and almost drool at Matt's burger.

'Excellent choice, *bon appetit*,' says Matt. Then he takes a big bite out of his juicy burger. I want to say that I think there has been a mix-up and grab the burger from his smug little hands. Why does this man make me feel such extreme emotions?

I sit and stare at the snails. Perhaps Matt won't notice if I leave them untouched. If I turn the shells upside down, you won't be able to see that they're not empty.

'Well, tuck in, then. How are they?' says Matt, staring straight at me.

He grabs a skinny French fry and bites into it. I am so hungry and I think how I could murder him for his chips, except that we need someone to fly the plane back.

'Go on then, tell me what they are like,' says Matt. He won't take his eyes off me and waits for me to take a bite.

I pick up the special instrument I have been given to eat my snail with and want to die. I am almost waiting for Ant and Dec to come out and tell me that I don't have to do it, that I am not in the jungle now. How could I order so spectacularly wrong?

After taking a swig of wine, I grab the snail out of the shell. Oh my god. I can't believe what this man drives me to do.

I throw it in my mouth and swallow it quickly.

'Yes, delicious,' I manage.

'Oh good. I'm not that keen on snails myself. I prefer a burger,' says Matt and starts laughing. I am now wondering what the penalty for murder is in Paris and if a replacement captain can be found to fly everyone home.

'Excuse me, I am just going to the bathroom,' I say.

I walk into the bathroom and scream into the mirror.

'Argh, I hate him, hate him, hate him!' I say to my reflection. When I stop screaming I notice the beret has slipped and is not nonchalantly perched on my head like I thought it was. I look more like that legendary comic, Frank Spencer.

I remove the unflattering beret and head back downstairs. I take a deep breath to compose myself before having to sit next to Matt again.

'All right? I ordered you some French fries, thought they'd go with your escargot,' says Matt as I sit down. I look at the place mat in front of me to see a beautiful bowl of steaming hot fries sitting next to the mostly untouched escargot.

'Thank you,' I say. Perhaps I won't murder Matt after all. He has redeemed himself.

I devour my delicious chips and drink more wine until I begin to feel a little tipsy. I stop Matt from pouring any more wine into my glass. I am not going to make a spectacle of myself on my second trip; plus, now I have relaxed a bit I am ready to see the sights of Paris. My mood towards him has improved; amazing what a bowl of fries can do to me. I put my beret back on before I leave the table for a day of sightseeing and wonder if Matt is coming too.

Two of the crew decide they want to visit the Sacré Coeur and I agree to tag along. I can see it in the distance and it looks incredible, even from here.

We arrange to meet the rest of the crew for dinner on a river cruise on the Seine early evening and the three of us make our way in the direction of the Sacré Coeur. Then I hear a voice.

'Hey, wait for me. I think I'll come along to the Sacré Coeur after all,' says Matt, catching us up.

Even though I remain grateful for the fries, something in the pit of my stomach tells me that this is not a good idea.

Chapter 19

Getting up closer to the Sacré Coeur with its white travertine stone exterior is quite amazing. The Basilica is so commandeering that it reminds me of Carys' Taj Mahal photos. Only now it is me that is visiting somewhere majestic and I am definitely going to take photos of this for Instagram.

Matt walks up the long trail of 222 steps from the lawns of Square Louise Michel beside me. For a moment, I think I might have a heart attack. Between his charming looks and the fact that he won't stop talking I feel like I may pass out! I normally have to choose between walking up steps or talking. I don't have the cardiovascular capacity to do both, let alone beside an undeniably gorgeous man who, for some reason, seems to make my heart beat faster. So, I try to answer his questions as succinctly as possible.

'What were you doing before you joined Calm Air?' asks Matt.

'Clothes shop,' I say.

'Interesting, so do you own a boutique?' he says.

'Nope,' I answer, taking a deep breath as I struggle up what must be approximately step number 192. 'It was a friend's,' I add.

'Oh right. So, are you married?' he asks.

I almost choke. Did he just ask me if I'm married? Why does he want to know that? Unfortunately, I don't have the oxygen levels to question him as to why he is asking me this, so I just say no.

'You?' I say. I don't know why I ask that but I figure if I put a question back in his court then it gives me time to reach the top step before he fires any further questions at me.

'Yes, married,' he says. For some unknown reason, I feel disappointed. How can I be disappointed that the captain I have been trying to avoid this whole time is married?

'Well, actually, it's a long story. My wife, she…' starts Matt. Ah, every captain has a wife with a long story if those crew at the interview were to be believed.

'Hey, are you guys in line for the queue?' asks an American tourist.

'Umm, yes,' I say as I realise that at last we have reached the magnificent entrance. Excellent timing.

I make my excuses and ensure I avoid Matt for the rest of the tour around the Sacré Coeur. I want nothing to do with him if he is married and possibly trying to flirt. I try to focus on the grand pipe organ in the Basilica that is in need of restoration, instead of thinking of Matt and his vital organs, which I imagine need no restoration.

I have spent enough time hanging around Matt, much more than I planned, so once the visit to the Sacré Coeur is over, I decide to get away from the crew in case he decides to tag along again. I find him really unsettling to be around and I want to try and make the most of my time in Paris without constantly thinking about him.

Perhaps I am being dramatic as I realise I shouldn't have been so independent as it now means I have to visit the Eiffel Tower alone, but I have got my bearings a little more now. On my walk through the Champ de Mars park, I see families having picnics and couples kissing. An antique-looking carousel catches my attention. It reminds me of the funfair my parents used to take me to when I was young. How long ago that was and a world away from my life today. A couple of children laugh and excitedly run into a puppet theatre. I smile at their innocence and think how much I would have loved to have taken my child to a puppet theatre or on a carousel. I wonder if Matt has perfect children who look just like him.

Finally, I reach the Eiffel Tower, which is every bit as spectacular as I thought it would be. It most certainly does not look like a giant electrical pylon as Geraint had described it to me when I told him I wanted to go there so badly. It takes my breath away finally seeing it like this. I made it to the Eiffel Tower – my dream has come true. It is so emotional to see it up close that it gives me goosebumps, although that could be the wind that is picking up too. I hold onto my beret in case it blows away whilst I watch a young lad propose in front of the Eiffel Tower to a beautiful girl. Oh, how romantic. Their whole lives are ahead of them. I hope they don't waste them, fretting and thinking too much about everything as I have. What a lucky couple. I smile at them, but they are oblivious to me. They are too wrapped up in each other to notice the people around them. I look at the other couples around me. Goodness, there is so much kissing going on. This big tower is responsible for so much romance.

After an afternoon at the Eiffel Tower, I am reminded that the only love of my life is Dolly and decide to check out the bookshop next to see if I can find the book I want so badly. I hail a taxi and head to the banks of the river Seine. At least I will be in the right direction for tonight's meetup.

As we get closer to my destination the taxi driver points out the Notre Dame, which still isn't open since the devastating fire. The driver tells me it should reopen in the next year or so. It is quite sad to see the building work, with the scaffolding and boarding around the building. Although on the other hand, a little bit like me, the 'Lady of Paris' is being rebuilt and will hopefully come out better than ever.

'Here is your bookshop,' says the taxi driver, slowing down.

I open the car door to step out towards the most magical bookshop. The sign above the store reads 'Shakespeare and Company'. What a city this is! I almost smack straight into the tree in front of the shop as I am so mesmerised by the frontage of the beguiling bookstore. It is so quaint with its green painted wood and a sign says that they sell new and rare books. Exactly what I am looking for! I can't wait to get in and smell all those books.

I am grinning to myself as I step inside. This is like heaven, a treasure trove of fascinating books. I could spend all day in here.

But then I recognise a certain person paying for something at the till. My grin drops and my heart beats faster.

Oh no, Matt said he was going to visit here today. I thought I would be safe as I had spent so much time at the Eiffel Tower and the park. I assumed he would be long gone by now. I don't want him to see me in here as it was he who mentioned the bookstore. I don't want him knowing I was eavesdropping and thinking that I secretly take note of his every word. I have to be cool and so I hide in one of the alcoves in the bookshop and bury my nose in a book. When I see his feet go past, I know I am safe. Phew, he didn't spot me.

I rummage through the mammoth selection of books. Surely they will have my special book here. I can't find anything on the shelves though, so have to ask. I pray they speak English as I am never going to manage to describe the book on Dolly in French.

'Do you speak English?' I ask nervously.

. 'Yes, sure,' says a friendly lady.

'Oh, phew. That's great.'

I explain about the book I am searching for and am surprised that she seems to be familiar with it. I didn't think anyone would know about it.

'You wouldn't believe it, but we just sold our last copy,' says the helpful assistant.

'Oh no, what bad timing,' I say.

'Yes, the gentleman just left with it. If only you'd been here five minutes earlier,' she says helpfully.

The only man I saw walk out with a book in the last five minutes was Matt. How could he possibly buy the same book I wanted? What would he want a book with Dolly in anyway? Aeroplanes perhaps, but does he really need a book on Volkswagen Beetles?

Disappointed, I take a seat in the cafe. I order myself a coffee and watch everyone go by. I stir the spoon around as I think of Matt. Why does he get under my skin so much and why did he have to buy the one copy of the book I wanted?

Looking at my watch, I realise I have just forty-five minutes until I must meet the crew for dinner and see him once again. I have a good mind not to show up, but I didn't eat much for lunch following the 'snail-gate' incident and I really want to see the rest of the Seine on the cruise.

How the day has flown by. I was hoping I could fit in the Louvre also. Perhaps if we have more time here tomorrow, I can finally visit. I will see what everyone's plans are later and make sure that Matt isn't listening. I don't want him popping up in front of a famous portrait of Napoleon and distracting me.

Arriving at our planned meeting point, I can see a few of the crew standing at the departure point for the glass canopied boat that will take us down the river Seine this evening. Thankfully Matt isn't here yet. Hopefully, he won't show up and, if he does, I am going to make sure I sit next to Karen and nowhere near him. I wouldn't want to have the urge to jump off the boat to escape him and these conflicting feelings I am having. Every time I see him it is like having a cream cake in front of me. You know it's not good for you, you know you should stay clear of it, but you can't help but reach out for it. I remind myself he is completely off limits. No matter what the circumstances, I would never be interested in another woman's man.

The boat opens up for the dinner cruise and we take a table in front of the panoramic glass. The views are going to be fantastic. I am so excited about this cruise, but then Matt comes rushing along.

'Is this seat taken?' he says, plonking himself down beside me.

'Yes, it is,' I say.

'By who? The invisible man?' He laughs.

I stare at him.

'Don't make faces; if the wind changes, your face will get stuck like that. It's a very windy evening,' says Matt.

I think I am going to have to move seats in a minute. I look around, but the boat is completely full. I take the glass of wine that is included in the on-board three-course meal and head to the deck to cool down all the thoughts I am having.

I lean over the side, looking into the water with the lights reflecting back on it.

'Are you okay? Have I done something to upset you?'

I look back and see Matt has followed me out here. I really don't want to speak to him. I am afraid of what I might say.

'I'm sorry but I have a dry sense of humour. Not everyone appreciates it. I do hope I haven't offended you,' he says.

'Well, you have actually,' I say.

'Oh, what did I do? Was it my joke about the invisible man? I know there's no such thing, obviously.'

'Nope, it's everything. First of all, you're a married man trying to pull the new recruit, then you buy the book I wanted in the shop. My car is in that book. It's so special. Why do you have to have it?' I rant.

I am so angry at him and want to push him away from me as far as possible.

'Firstly, I can assure you that I am not trying to *pull* anyone – and how do you know about the book?' he says.

I really shouldn't have said that. He hasn't actually done anything untoward, although he did ask if I was married. Perhaps he was just trying to make small talk and would then tell me about his wife. Did I jump the gun a little? I admit that I could have got the wrong end of the stick.

I calm down as I realise I might have been a bit too hard on him. There is no romantic idea here. It is all above board and he is just trying to be friendly. So I explain that I went to buy the book and tell him all about Dolly.

'No way? You have a Beetle called Dolly. You don't even want me to start talking about Nigella. You'll never shut me up,' says Matt.

'Nigella? That was your campervan I saw you near at the medical centre? I had a sneaking suspicion it was,' I say.

I think of how he caught me looking into the windows of the campervan. Oh no, I really shouldn't have been so nosy.

'Well, she is a beauty all right,' I say.

'Just like you,' says Matt. He leans towards me and pushes my fringe to one side.

Butterflies take over my whole body as his words sink in and his touch sends shivers down my spine. I am amazed he thinks I am a beauty after seeing my corn pen and Snoopy pyjamas. What is it with this man? Perhaps he needs new glasses. I hope he can see well enough to fly us home safely. Or maybe he is simply a serial playboy who is after anyone he meets. Surely no man has a penchant for a woman with Snoopy pyjamas over sexy lingerie in their overnight bag; and besides, he is married!

'Sorry, the wind. It was in your eyes,' he says.

'Hey, here you guys are. Food's on the table for you,' says Karen, coming out to find us.

As we walk back inside, I notice that we are passing the Eiffel Tower. Thank goodness Karen came along when she did as I don't want to be in a romantic place alone with Matt. I can now see why being airline crew can be a dangerous vocation and why so many crew end up in compromising situations that they shouldn't be. Not that I agree with it, and would never dream of giving into a married man.

We sit down and eat in silence. It all feels strange between us. Something changed out there. We should be chatting about our Volkswagens but we are not. Instead, there is some unfinished business between us and we both know this is not the time or place to discuss it. One minute I think we could be the best of friends and then he says I am beautiful and I worry he might be looking for some kind of torrid affair.

'Better than the snails earlier?' says Matt as I finish off a piece of gateaux from the three-course dinner.

'Yes, most definitely.'

'Ooh, look, we're passing the Louvre. You want to go outside and take a look?' says Matt.

My head is telling me that the last thing I should do is be left alone with Matt for even a second. But my body doesn't react like that. I start moving my chair out and get on my feet. It is as though I am in a trance and I just follow him onto the deck.

'Don't you just love Paris,' says Matt, his eyes piercing right into my heart.

I try to look away. He has a wife with a long story, I remind myself. I start to wonder what the story is, but remind myself that it doesn't matter what it is; he has a wife! To avoid looking at him I look down at the floor and notice that he has a bag from the bookshop at his feet. Matt lifts the bag up and hands it to me.

'Here, you take the book, you deserve it,' he says.

'No, no, first come, first served,' I say.

'Don't be silly, your Dolly is in here, it's much more important you have it,' he insists.

'Are you sure?' I ask.

'Absolutely,' he says.

Matt passes me the bag and our hands touch. I can feel the softness of his hands even from that small physical contact. I feel all quivery as I stand there. I know I should just walk away but somehow can't bring myself to.

When Matt leans over to kiss me on my cheek, a bolt of electricity zaps right through me. My head reminds me that I need to run away as fast as I can.

Chapter 20

'Goodness, it is so much smaller than I imagined,' I say to Matt the next morning.

'Oh, I hope you're not too disappointed?' he says, as he puts his hand on the small of my back.

'No, it's just a bit of a surprise, that's all,' I say.

I never imagined some of these famous paintings were so teeny. It is funny how you imagine something and when you see it in the flesh it is so different to what you thought it would be. I suppose Matt is a bit like that. The image in my head of him is so very different to the person he actually is when you get to know him better. He has such a dry sense of humour; it could be mistaken for rudeness. Perhaps we can be good friends, if nothing more.

I am pleased the rest of the crew wanted to visit the Louvre with us. Being left alone with Matt would be difficult given the insane attraction between us. Why does he have a wife with a long story? Of course, I haven't asked him. But I don't care what the 'story' is, I am not going to be another airline statistic and have an affair with a married pilot. So, as much as my spine tingles as Matt touches my back, I move away from him. It was a lovely way to see the *Mona Lisa* though; if only things were different.

Having seen Gericault's *The Raft of the Medusa* and David's painting of Napoleon's coronation, we eventually make our way out as we are expecting the aircraft to be ready later today. Some of the crew are going shopping before we leave and others plan on heading to the hotel to chill before we get our call out. But before we split up to do different things, Matt stops me.

'Fancy lunch?' he says.

The thought of having lunch alone with Matt in Paris is so tempting, but I have no choice but to decline. The feeling I had in the Louvre was far too nice. I am going to hibernate in my hotel room until that spare part for the engine arrives and we can all leave in one piece before we do anything terrible together.

I spend the afternoon back in my room catching up with the rest of my course mates on the WhatsApp group while waiting for the call that the plane is ready. We have been so busy flying to different places and having various schedules that we haven't spoken so much this past week. Greg has been to Rome and Arabella has been sick after catching some virus on her first flight.

Hazards of the job, she says.

At least it isn't as bad as the story Carys told me about one of the crew getting malaria when they flew to Zanzibar. She warned me to always drink tonic water if I ever go to a country where malaria could be present. It is all down to the quinine, apparently. Then there is dengue fever in other places we fly – those mosquitoes have a lot to answer for.

After ordering a hot chocolate from room service, I grab the bag from the bookshop and start flicking through my new beloved book. I did offer Matt the money for it, but he insisted it was a gift. I thought this was very generous of him but I suppose that's how married men get around women. Woo them with gifts and the like. I can't deny it is the most precious gift I have ever received though, apart from Dolly, of course.

I am dozing on the bed when the crew call comes through. The aircraft is finally ready and we can go to the airport. I am relieved, as I am ready to return now – as wonderful as the trip has been. I think it is a good idea for both of us that it ends now.

Four hours later we are on-board the flight back to the UK.

Some of the passengers were on our original flight that was cancelled and aren't happy.

'I'm never flying Calm Air again,' says a disgruntled passenger.

'I'm sorry, I know it's been such an inconvenience. Please do write a complaint to our head office,' I tell her.

However, she seems to hold me personally responsible. Any further aggression and we will be needing the restraint straps for her. Ah, the restraint straps that are kept in the flight deck. That would mean going into the flight deck and seeing Matt. The thought of restraining him feels like a better idea right now. I burst out laughing to myself as I think about Matt being strapped up and me being in charge of letting him go. I must stop such impetuous thoughts!

'Are you laughing at me?' says the passenger.

'Oh, my goodness, no. I am so sorry, I am not laughing at all,' I say.

'I want to speak to the person in charge. I'm not happy. Bring me the captain,' she says.

'I'm sorry but the captain has to fly the plane, he can't leave the flight deck at the moment. I'll get the purser for you,' I say.

I go and find Karen who is now in the front cabin. I notice Matt is in the galley getting a quick coffee after take-off. I am surprised he can't wait until we land, it is such a short flight.

'Hey,' he says.

'Hi,' I manage. I look down at my apron that already has a big splodge of cola on even though it's such a short flight. I wish he wasn't seeing me like this. I self-consciously wipe at it.

'How's it going down the back? Passengers okay?' asks Matt.

'No, not really. A few people kicking off because of the delay. One lady in particular,' I say.

'Ah, okay. I'll make an announcement and try and appease them,' he says.

'That would be great, thanks.'

I lead Karen to the disgruntled passenger and Matt makes his mellifluous announcement which seems to placate a few of the economy crowd.

I reach down the back galley when the intercom rings. I notice it has a different colour light which means it is a call from the flight deck. Oh no, I hope there isn't an emergency after the engines were supposedly fixed.

'Hi, L3,' I say.

L3 is my position on the aircraft today; each time it can be different.

'Hellooo L3,' says the familiar voice.

'Hello Captain,' I say. I try to sound professional and hope that my voice doesn't give away the fact that I wanted to restrain him five minutes ago.

'I'm going to put the seat belt sign on now, stop the passengers giving you a hard time. Just wanted you to know,' says Matt.

'Umm, thanks.'

The second I put the phone down the seatbelt sign comes on. I thought Matt was the consummate professional and I do wonder if he has another side to him that can be a bit naughty.

We secure the cabin quickly for landing and I am so happy to sit in my jump seat. It wasn't the most pleasant of flights, but I suppose that is to be expected, given what the passengers have had to put up with.

As I sign off back at base, I notice Matt hanging around the building.

I try to ignore him, but he clearly wants my attention.

'Great trip,' he says.

'It was indeed. Thanks again for the lovely book. I will treasure it,' I say.

'No worries. It was meant for you. I'd love to meet Dolly one day,' he says.

Yeah, that's not going to happen.

'Sorry, I have to go. I'm in a bit of a rush,' I say.

'Look, umm, could we keep in touch? You know, to talk about cars and things? Could I get your number?' asks Matt.

'It's probably best we don't,' I say. I don't wait for his response.

I quickly walk away and make sure I don't look back.

Chapter 21

It is a few months before I see Matt again. I can't lie and say that every time I checked in for a flight I didn't look around, hoping to catch a glimpse of him shooting off somewhere. Each flight I have looked at the crew list and seen a name that is not his and felt a wave of disappointment. I had almost given up seeing him despite all our prior coincidences. I assumed the aeroplane gods of love wanted to keep us apart as it wasn't wise putting us together on the same Airbus.

Then, today, as I arrive at the briefing for another flight to Paris, I see his name on the crew sheet. Paris in the spring with Matt at the helm. Despite my resolutions and good intentions, I can't help my heart from skipping a beat as I realise I will be in Paris, in the springtime, with him. What if he is single by now? I scan over the crew list one more time to be sure. It definitely says Captain Matt Garcia. My heart skips quite a few beats I can tell you! What are the chances of getting another Paris together? I wonder if he has noticed my name on the list. Perhaps my name means nothing.

I don't see any sign of him at briefing and he isn't on the bus to the aircraft with the rest of the crew. Perhaps he is running late like the first time we met.

Then, finally, I hear his voice when he does an announcement. Oh, that voice! He does a spiel about the economy cabin having very special crew today. Does he know I am working in the cabin? I forget to serve a passenger in seat 25A as I am distracted by this thought.

There is no reason for me to visit the flight deck during the flight, so I have no excuse to pop in and say hello. I remind myself that this is for the best. I have to remember his wife and her long story.

It is only at passport control as we queue at the special crew gate, which we are all gathered around, that I finally see him. He is right at the front, talking to the first officer. From his side profile, I can see that he looks a little more tired than the last time I saw him. The rostering department must have worn him down. I did wonder if he would look back, if he realises I am on the crew and might look out for me. He doesn't though and I feel silly for even thinking such a thing. Who on earth do I think I am? Why would he think of Penny – 'Snoopy Pyjamas' – when he saw that crew list this morning, and why would that announcement be about me? He must have done it so that the economy passengers felt as important as those who have paid a fortune to fly first class.

It is only on the crew bus that we finally come face to face.

'Hi,' I say as I rush past to find a seat.

I guess he is quite good at flirting and manipulating women into falling for his charms as he smiles and gives me that glint in his eye that is so attractive. His smooth captain's voice says hello and goosebumps rush all over me from my head to my feet. I think I am getting palpitations! Thank goodness the airline's medical examiner isn't here.

I am pleased that our purser, Josh, is sitting behind Matt so I don't have the opportunity of sitting near him and making a fool of myself. I take a seat right at the back of the bus instead, as far away as possible.

'Brown cow?' says Josh, getting a bottle out of his cabin bag. He passes cups down the bus ready for us to fill.

I notice Matt laughing at the mention of the drink and it brings back awful memories of our encounter in Geneva once again. I decide to pass on the brown cow.

As I now know my way around Paris quite well, I make the decision to go around on my own this trip. I will visit the bookshop and spend more time in there than my first visit. It will be nice to have some 'me' time alone.

As much as I have wanted to see Matt, looking at him on the bus makes me realise how besotted I am with him. Why is even the back of his head so perfect? It really annoys me. I tell myself that he is the type of man who makes a noise eating his toast in the morning. Yes, he can't possibly be that fabulous.

At the hotel reception Josh asks if I will be joining the rest of them, but I tell a white lie that I have to meet someone so won't be able to tag along to the Arc de Triumph. The crew take their keys and begin to head off to their respective rooms in order to meet back downstairs shortly. However, just as I pick up my bag, I feel a tap on the shoulder.

'Umm, before you head off, could I have a word? Do you think we can get a coffee, just the two of us? I really need to clear the air,' says Matt.

I suppose it is a bit awkward after he asked for my number last time. I will have a hot drink and then tell him straight that I am not interested in hearing his wife's long story. I only hope he can't see how hard my heart is beating.

I want to get out of my uniform, but Matt doesn't seem to want to wait and we find a quiet corner in the hotel coffee shop. I suppose it's better we get this over with.

'Did something go wrong between us after the Louvre?' says Matt.

'What do you mean? No,' I say.

'It's just I thought we got along well and then you just went cold. It was as though I had done something wrong.'

I put my hand in my hair and play nervously with my ponytail. I don't normally like confrontation but I am going to have to spit it out and hope that I don't get this wrong.

'Look, Matt. We can't deny there is an attraction between us. That's for certain. But I am not interested in hanging out with a married man.'

'Who said I was married?' he says.

'Umm, you did,' I say.

'When did I say that?'

'Oooh, let me think. Precisely, I would say it was on the second but last step before we reached the entrance of the Sacré Coeur. Yup, about then.'

I sit back and await his response. My mouth is dry and I realise that I care a lot about what he is going to say. I take a sip of the coffee he has charged to his room.

'Oh, you took it literally. I did say it was a long story, since you remember so much,' says Matt.

'Yeah, but I am not really interested in the story. You're either married or you're not. The circumstances are irrespective,' I explain.

'So, I am married. Was married. I…' he starts. 'She died. In a helicopter accident. She was a pilot. We met at a flight school in Oxford many years ago,' says Matt.

'Oh, I'm so sorry.'

Why do I always seem to misunderstand this man? I am so taken aback that I am unsure what to say next. We sit in silence and I watch as the rest of the crew start to gather around reception for their excursion about the city.

'If you'd have waited for the long story, you'd have known this,' says Matt eventually.

'Yeah, well, a long story is usually "my wife doesn't understand me" or some rubbish. I'm really sorry. How long ago did she have the... you know... accident?'

'Two years ago. It's been very hard. That's why I may have overreacted in the grooming room. The day of your interview. I wasn't in the best of moods.'

'Oh gosh. I am so incredibly sorry. I completely got the wrong end of the stick here. Something that happens with me often,' I say, smiling.

'Well, I'm glad we've straightened things out. If I didn't have the dogs to visit on my days off, I don't know how I'd have got through it all.'

'The dogs?' I say.

'I help out at a Labrador sanctuary. I don't know, does that sound a bit soft?'

'Oh, not at all. That's lovely. I also help out at a sanctuary. It's amazing how therapeutic it is.'

This beautiful man loves dogs and helps out where he can. I really have got him completely wrong.

'Volkswagens, dogs, we have an awful lot in common,' says Matt.

'Yes, we do,' I agree.

'Anyway, how about we do Paris differently this time? Would you be my date?' asks Matt. But then he remembers the little fib I made. 'Oh, but you're meeting your friend, aren't you? You have plans, sorry. I forgot.'

'Oh, umm, you know what, it's fine. Amazingly, she has just messaged to say that she can't make it. Something came up at work, a meeting,' I say.

'Oh dear. That's a shame for your friend. Where does she work?' he asks.

Oh no. Why did I lie?

'In an, umm, office, yup. All very boring. Anyhow, I would love to be your date,' I say with a smile.

'How about I pick you up from your room at 6:30 p.m.?'

'It's a date,' I say.

I curse myself for not packing differently and, as I finally head to my room to change, wonder if I could find a fancy boutique in town. But I doubt I could quite manage Paris prices as I have one hundred pounds left to save so that I can get Dolly completely refurbished. I would love to treat myself to something fancy, but I must think of Dolly. Besides, Matt will just have to accept me for who I am. He has seen my pyjamas, after all. This is the real unsophisticated me. I have never been a chic Parisian and never will be.

I spend ages in the hotel bathroom with its small shower cubicle getting primped and preened for my date. The Paris hotel isn't quite as fabulous as where we stay in Geneva. It is down one of the backstreets and can be a little noisy at night, but it has some of the charms of the city's old buildings with its Parisian Juliet balcony and people outside day and night shouting to each other.

At 6:30 p.m. there is a knock on the door. I am even more nervous than when I went for my airline interview. I hope he doesn't try to grab a sweaty palm as we walk along.

'You look wonderful, *mon cherie*,' says Matt.

'*Merci, monsieur*,' I say, giggling.

Matt pecks me on the cheek and that electrical surge runs straight through me again. I begin to wonder if he is full of static from all those electrical storms he flies through.

'You know, when I saw you on our last flight together, it was like an atom bomb had gone off inside me,' says Matt.

An atom bomb doesn't sound very romantic and I am unsure what he is getting at.

'Oh, is that a good thing or a bad thing?' I ask.

'Good. Very good,' says Matt.

Our eyes meet and he stares straight through me. It's as though he can see into my soul and I can see into his. Could this be what the stuff of soulmates is all about? They say there is a thin line between love and hate and I am starting to believe it.

Once we have managed to stop looking into each other's eyes we head out onto the street and he tells me that he is taking me to a bistro on the Champs-Élysées.

'It's one of my favourites. Gérard Depardieu was in here the last time I came,' he tells me.

The venue he has chosen is absolutely gorgeous. Outside is a big red and gold canopy, which looks so opulent. Inside is just as classy with its candlelit tables and red tablecloths. It's the epitome of all things Parisian!

The waiter is dressed smartly in his dickie bow and before he even puts down the menu, I can see that this isn't going to be a cheap dining experience.

'May I recommend you don't have the escargot,' says Matt, laughing.

'Oh no, am I ever going to live that down?' I say.

Looking at the menu I can see it is all in French. Matt's French is so much better than mine but I don't want to admit how I am struggling to understand it.

'I don't normally do this, but I think I'll leave the ordering to you. I trust you. Order whatever you recommend,' I say.

Matt orders something in French and I sit there swooning at the way he speaks. My goodness, there goes that gorgeous captain's voice again, but in French! Can it possibly get any better?

The wine arrives and, as usual, Matt has ordered well. He seems to know so much about so many things. You can talk to him about everything. I don't know that I have ever met anyone like him before. I just hope my meal is as well selected as the wine he has picked. It is absolutely divine.

The waiter arrives with a trolley in front of us.

'Chateaubriand,' says the waiter.

It seems I can trust Matt to order well. I am in heaven with such delightful food and company.

'Oh, this is superb, and the duchess potatoes. Wow,' I say.

'It's nice to see you so happy, Penny. You always seem like you're somewhere else. As if something is on your mind,' says Matt.

'I guess I'm always busy plotting how I can save Dolly. As you know, it means so much to me that she stays on the road,' I explain.

'Sure, our babies aren't cheap are they? The restoration of Nigella cost a small fortune. I should be saving for retirement.'

'No, you certainly don't look old enough to worry about that,' I say.

I realise we have never discussed our ages. With all the chemistry between us, age doesn't seem to come into it.

'I'll be fifty-eight in December. The big sixty is looming. I guess I am older than I feel,' says Matt.

Do any of us feel our age, I wonder?

'Wow, you certainly don't look that. I thought you were around my age, fifty.'

'It's all this good food down-route,' says Matt, laughing, as he tucks into the rest of his chateaubriand.

'It certainly seems to suit you,' I say, smiling. Then we look into each other's eyes again and there it goes. The atom bomb, fireworks, static electricity, or whatever it is that is going on between us.

After dinner, we take a walk around the streets of Paris. Matt grabs my hand and I hold on tight.

When we have a typical Paris springtime shower, Matt removes his jacket and covers us both overhead, using it as a canopy. He suggests we stop in a bar for a nightcap to escape the shower and I happily agree. Luckily, we are near a lovely Parisian wine bar he knows with exposed brick walls and a huge wine selection. He knows all the best places.

'I am so glad you let me explain myself,' says Matt as we sit down. 'Imagine us missing out on such a wonderful evening.'

'Yup, perhaps it is a lesson I should learn. I need to listen to the facts sometimes and not be too fast to jump to conclusions.'

Matt orders a vintage bottle of red wine. I am really not sure I can drink much more, so I take my time and let Matt have most of it. He seems to be able to handle it better than I do. I just hope he doesn't fall asleep. However, when we eventually get back to the hotel, he seems to be quite awake.

'Thank you. I've had the time of my life,' says Matt as we reach my hotel room.

'Me too,' I say.

Matt leans in to kiss me and I feel like my heart will explode. Oh wow, why does he feel as though he is my soulmate? I don't even know him. It's impossible.

Then, because we seem to have this undeniable connection and some kind of animal instinct attraction, I do something very much out of character. I hold him close and pull him inside my room. I close the hotel room door and pray that none of the crew spots us going into my room. I don't want to be the talk of the crew yet again.

–

In the morning we are woken by the crew call. Matt is curled right into me and I stroke his beautiful dark hair. It's smooth as silk and I nestle my nose into it. He smells of musk.

When he wakes up, Matt gives me the loveliest of smiles. He is so different to Geraint, who would need four coffees before he could communicate in the morning. This man seems truly perfect. There has to be a catch, surely? He is a wonderful conversationalist, something I respect more as I get older. There's a lot to be said for a man who can talk about anything and everything. I have just discovered that he is amazing between the sheets. Perhaps he has a split personality? We didn't get off to the best start. Maybe that is what is wrong with him. He has a mean bad-tempered side. Let's face it, I have seen that side of him. I can't let myself get hurt again. I can't take another heartbreak; it would be too much. I must protect myself. Last night was amazing, but we are in Paris; it is all so romantic and I know what those crew said about flight deck. Don't they have a woman on every flight? I must keep my feet on the ground and not get carried away during such a romantic moment. This isn't what happens to people like me.

I get up and jump in the shower to clear my head. The water is so warm against my skin that was caressed so lovingly last night. I then wrap myself in one of the hotel's big fluffy towels and decide to ask Matt what he thinks will happen next between us.

However, when I come out of the bathroom, he has gone. I knew it was too good to be true.

Chapter 22

I am hurt, humiliated and feel like the biggest fool when I get downstairs and reach the reception. It is as though I am doing the 'walk of shame' with my puffy cried-out eyes. Amazing what forty minutes of tears does to your skin.

I hope nobody says anything to me. Does everyone know what happened last night? I am convinced people are staring at me; from the receptionists to the little old lady waiting for someone in the lobby. Then there's the rest of the crew, do they know? They are chatting and laughing and I can't help but feel paranoid that they are laughing about me. I can almost hear them talking amongst themselves that I fell for that age-old trap. I slept with the captain and he didn't even say goodbye to me the next morning. I wasn't the first and I won't be the last. Those silly junior cabin crew. What a cliché!

How can one man make me feel on top of the world one moment and then bring me smashing right back down to the ground the next? It must be a pilot thing. Up, up and away and then the most terrible crash landing.

'Fun time in Paris?' says Josh.

I rub my eyes, pretending I have a foreign body in there, as an excuse for the redness. I am convinced he knows. What if Matt has already told everyone? What if they even had a bet? Every worst possible scenario starts running through my head.

'Yeah, all good, thanks,' I say.

If he does know and they have all been laughing about Matt's conquest then I don't want to show how hurt I am.

'That's good you had a nice time together,' says Josh.

'Together?' I say.

'Yes, the friend you were meeting. Oh look, the bus is here,' he says.

Perhaps my imagination has run riot after all. But after the shock of this morning, I am so confused I don't know anything any more. After all, I thought Geraint was faithful and loving and look what happened.

I see that Matt is on the bus already. He hasn't waited inside with the rest of the crew but seems to have stayed out of the way. It is obvious he is avoiding me. I decide to ignore him as I walk past him on the crew bus and don't even glance in his direction. I think I hear a hello from him, but don't return the greeting. It is hard to believe this is the same man who was so passionate last night. He filled me with so much hope and I was the happiest I have been for a long time. It felt like he actually cherished me – and now he has utterly discarded me. How could someone be so cruel?

I can't make a scene in front of all the crew, so I pretend to read a book to ensure I make no eye contact with him, even though I can't concentrate on anything apart from revisiting the moment I walked out of the bathroom to find Matt gone.

Thank goodness there are no incidents on-board our flight back, because I am not focused on my job at all. I am so glad that I know what I am doing and can almost do things automatically at this stage.

I don't see Matt again until we are back at our base.

However, once again, he hangs around outside head office as we sign out from our trip. I try to ignore him as I think about the two days off I have to fill. I am looking forward to spending tomorrow with Willow and Oreo at the shelter. I focus on my life back home, back at the kennels and driving Dolly there. I must also pop into the shop to see Jane tomorrow. I haven't seen her since I left and I feel as though I should at least go in and tell her how my new job is going. So far, we have only texted short snippets of what has been happening in our lives. Jane said she had some exciting news in her last message and wanted to tell me what it was face to face. Perhaps she is having another grandchild.

Then I hear that voice again and see Matt facing me.

'It was the first time I had sex with anyone since my wife. Her name was Francesca,' says Matt.

I look around, my face burning, conscious that the crew are within earshot, and see Josh with his mouth open.

'Ooh, you dark horse. You did have a good trip by the sounds of it,' says Josh, grinning.

'No, I didn't actually,' I say, looking at both of them. 'Shh, people can hear you,' I hiss at Matt. I can't believe he said that out loud.

'Then come and chat to me. I want to explain why I left this morning. I'm sorry, but I panicked.'

As we have to take the same bus to the crew parking lot, I don't put up much of a fight as he plonks himself down beside me.

'I didn't know what to do next, if I'm honest. I have only been with my wife for the past twenty years. I was a coward and walked off when you weren't in the room.

I felt awkward, guilty. I don't know, I had a range of emotions, I guess. I didn't know what to say. I didn't plan any of this; my feelings for you have taken me by surprise.'

'I understand it's difficult for you, but imagine how I felt?' I say. I haven't told him about Geraint and what he did to me. We were having far too good a time to discuss exes up until now. But perhaps we should have opened up a bit and then neither of us would feel the way we do right now. He should have told me how he felt instead of blanking me like that.

Despite his tragic circumstances, I stand up for myself. I am not going to be treated badly. I felt like the lowest of the low when he left my room without saying anything. I won't be treated like this again. Geraint already did what he wanted for far too long. I always considered what he wanted and look where it got me. This time I have to make myself a priority and if he doesn't like it then tough.

'I really like you though, you know? I just need to deal with some of my feelings, but I would like us to go out again. I shouldn't have walked away. I'm not used to this dating stuff. I'm out of practice. I also shouldn't have said that we had sex in front of Josh. I didn't realise he was behind me; I was far too busy looking at you. I'm sorry for making such a mess of things,' Matt says with a smile.

The genuine smile on his face makes me soften slightly and so I agree. I will meet him again, but on my terms. This time I will take things much slower. I don't know why I slept with him like that and I regret that moment. I should have closed my door and gone to bed by myself and not been such a fool. This is one lesson I have definitely learned the hard way.

We both get out our rosters and check when we can meet up. However, it seems our schedules collide and when he is off, I am flying and vice versa. So much for the aeroplane gods of love.

'Well, at least give me your phone number this time,' says Matt.

We swap phone numbers and I see the group Whats-App has been busy. I will catch up on it all when I get home.

Matt pecks me on the cheek as we leave each other and I feel that tingle yet again. What on earth is it between us? I shiver and walk towards Dolly, hoping she will start after being left out in the rain for the last twenty-four hours. She starts first time and I tell her what an amazing old girl she is, hoping nobody overhears me talking to the car. I drive out and Matt pulls up beside me at the barrier of the car park.

'Nice car,' he says, laughing. I look over at him in that gorgeous blue camper van. It is in much better condition than Dolly. It must be that captain's salary. It won't be long before Dolly gets the overhaul she needs though, now that I have saved my flight pay and overtime.

'Ditto,' I say, grinning.

Then we drive off in our different directions. Something I think the distance between us may always cause us to do.

When I arrive home, I put my Snoopy pyjamas on and think about Matt. The feelings I have for him are so confusing. Part of me wants to be so close to him, but half of me still tells me to stay away. It feels as though there are red flags everywhere. I have to keep that guard up, as I am not leaving myself vulnerable and allowing myself to get hurt again.

Chatting with the group on WhatsApp is just the tonic I need. Arabella tells us how she is now seeing Neil, who had walked in with Matt that time when we were training. We are all happy for her. Then she tells us how she had a bit of a passionate moment in the first-class toilet with him on a flight and walked back down the aisle with her uniform skirt tucked into her knickers and tights. She says that the worst thing was that it was the start of the flight and so she had to then go and face all the passengers. We are all crying with laughter, although I am a bit shocked they got away with it. That is definitely a sackable offence.

Despite Arabella's wild side, my group are such wonderful people. I don't believe they would ever let anyone down. Cabin crew friendships are so different to other friendships. We might technically be work colleagues, but due to the nature of the job, you need complete faith in each other. Trust is so important when all the lives on-board could be at stake.

Just as I am tempted to tell the WhatsApp group about what happened with Matt, a message from him comes through.

> Hey, I miss you already. Thanks for a
> beautiful time in Paris

He misses me, but just this morning he walked out on me. Are we moving too fast here? I have always thought that moving too fast is a red flag; isn't that what they teach you in magazines? What if Matt has gone from blanking me to love bombing? Perhaps that is what the atom bomb thing was all about.

He is off to Frankfurt in the morning and I consider the possibility that he will now move on to the next newest crew member on the flight.

Even though I had a busy time in Paris, I don't sleep well. My brain fights with all the different feelings I have. Disappointment in people letting me down, or leaving me, conflicts in my head with the need for closeness with someone. Both emotions are as strong as the other.

When I wake up in the morning, there is a lovely message from Matt that feels like an Elastoplast soothing my turmoil. Goodness, how long has it been since someone messaged me first thing? I am flattered to switch on my phone to a *Good morning, beautiful* message.

Stay safe on your FRA flight, I type. I realise that I have automatically become one of those airline crew who are now talking in code like the rest of them.

Don't you have another Paris coming up? I'll try and do a swap. Hope to see you soon. Xx

The thought of being in Paris again with Matt sounds perfect, but it could also bring me closer to him and therefore closer to me being hurt. What if he still hasn't figured out what he wants? I can't be a practice run for a new relationship for him.

I pop into the shop before heading to the doodle sanctuary and am excited when I open the door to surprise Jane. The window display looks great with its turquoise pastel colour scheme and I almost feel a pang of envy that Jane's new assistant, Sophia, has obviously got an eye for detail. Perhaps she is better than I was at her job. I was never the most creative at merchandising. The shop looks immaculate and I see who I guess must be Sophia at the till.

'Hi, anything in particular you are looking for?' says Sophia. She seems warm and welcoming and is exactly what Jane would have wanted for the store. I eye up the leaflet announcing the latest fashion show for the new collection. Everything has moved on without me.

'I'm looking for Jane. I wanted to surprise her,' I say.

'Oh, she's on a buying trip today. In London. Can I take a message for her?'

'No, it's fine. I'll send her a message,' I say.

I bid Sophia goodbye and head to the sanctuary. At least the doggies will be there for me to visit.

A day out with the doodles is very much needed. It is astonishing how I can clear my head on an hour-long walk with my favourite pups.

When I arrive at the kennels, I see the dog warden on duty. I have seen her a few times before but we have never really spoken, so she doesn't know of my fondness for Oreo and Willow.

'Hey, I'm here to take Oreo and Willow out for their walk,' I explain. I can't wait to see their excited little faces. They are like doggie psychiatrists and I do feel rather guilty for pouring out my problems to them, but I hope they enjoy their walkies with me anyway. I have some treats in my pocket that I picked up on the way over. They're going to be so happy, wagging their long bushy tails as they do.

'Oreo and Willow have gone,' she says.

'Oh… Umm. Gone where?' I ask.

'They have a lovely new owner.'

'Ah, I should have expected two beauties like that wouldn't be here for long,' I say.

'No, exactly. Every one finds the right home eventually,' she says.

As she says this my phone bleeps with a photo of Matt from the flight deck.

'Not as good as my last flight. Crew are far less entertaining.'

The question is, have I found my home? Or should I run away? Even Oreo and Willow left when a better home came along, just like Geraint did. How can I expect Matt not to do the same when faced with a beautiful young flight attendant?

Chapter 23

Whilst our schedules clash, Matt and I talk every single day. When he rings me, it is like we have known each other all our lives.

One evening, when I am sitting in my lonely hotel room on a stopover in Dublin, Matt tells me how he had an argument with air traffic control when he saw another plane getting too close on the radar. It was still thousands of miles away from his, but he argued there was a risk of a mid-air collision. I am seriously impressed that he was so strong and astute, and I tell him so. He says he was just doing his job but, in my mind, he is a bit of a hero. A man who keeps hundreds of passengers safe every time they fly; how easy it would be to fall in love with him.

We grow so close over the phone that when our rosters come out, the first thing we do is send them to each other so we know where we both are. It is nice to know what time zone he is in, and I still check the crew list at every briefing, just in case he has swapped and wanted to surprise me. Matt told me that he didn't manage to swap for the Paris trip when I asked him. But when I check in for my next flight to Paris, as usual, the first thing I do is check the crew list.

Captain Matt Garcia is on the list. My heart goes crazy. What a lovely surprise!

I can hardly think when I am asked about the safety procedures at briefing. Even though I have done this so many times before, when the purser asks me a simple question, 'How many doors are there on the A320neo?', I can't think and almost get offloaded for not being able to answer my safety questions. I try and get my head together or I won't be flying with Matt at all at this rate.

'Four main doors and two emergency doors over the wings,' I eventually manage to say.

Because I was so hesitant, the purser picks me out to answer further questions. She even saves the hardest one of all for me.

'What is tundra?' Phew. Thank goodness I will never forget that one.

I finally manage to answer everything satisfactorily and off we go to the aircraft. I still don't spot Matt, even though I am looking out for him.

On-board I keep waiting for Matt to say his usual announcement, or something about the economy cabin, but there is nothing. I notice it is the first officer who makes the flight deck announcements today. How strange.

We fly back and forth to Paris all day until it is the last leg of the journey. They have all been full flights and so I haven't had a chance to get up to the flight deck.

Joanne, my supervisor in economy, makes up some brown cow and tells me to pack up some plastic glasses for the bus. It is a bit of a trek into the city from the airport so we can be stuck on the crew bus for an hour and a half after a long day of flying. I take a miniature off for myself as I am still not into drinking the brown cow. I am glad of the cabin crew rule that you're allowed to take two miniatures with you, although a lot of the time

I don't bother. However, with Matt on the crew, it feels like a party.

As sometimes happens, it is only when we are on the bus that I see Matt. As we greet each other he smiles and doesn't say anything. He simply greets me as he would any other cabin crew he had flown with before. The seats around him are full so I move along the bus towards the back. I sort of hope that Matt may move and come and sit with me but I suppose he doesn't want tongues wagging, and that would be a bit too obvious, but he must have swapped with another captain to get on this flight. I wonder what he told him. *My girlfriend is on the flight.* Probably not!

As we enter the outskirts of the centre of Paris, everyone starts to make plans for the stopover. I don't commit to anything as I am unsure what Matt will want to do. When we get our room keys at reception, I soon find out.

'Give it five minutes. Let everyone go off and come and stay in my room with me. I've got a suite,' says Matt.

I decline the offer. Although the idea of a suite is lovely – the rooms the flight attendants get here are rather pokey – I don't like the way he wants us to hide from the rest of the crew. If something is going on between us, why is he so reticent?

When I have changed out of my uniform, Matt messages me asking if I am okay. I tell him it's nothing, I am just a bit tired.

Let's have dinner then and an early night? says Matt.

I agree to dinner but then he arranges for us to meet up outside the hotel. I find that odd when usually we meet at reception. I begin to think he may have dated someone on the crew and he doesn't want them to know about me. I mentally go through everyone on the crew but I don't know that anyone would fit the profile that I would expect.

As I am waiting for him to arrive outside, my head is in a spin with the conversation I want with him. I go over all the things I want to say; the first question I want to ask is if he is ashamed of me. Why can't we be open in front of the crew about going for dinner? Two of the crew go together for dinner all the time and nobody bats an eyelid. What's wrong with us doing it?

When Matt arrives looking so perfectly handsome, my heart thumps again. Oh my, he is a fine man for sure. He wears dark jeans and a pullover. His hair is still a bit damp from the shower. Just looking at him takes my breath away.

But I remind myself that it doesn't matter what he looks like. I want to know why he is being so coy in front of the crew.

'Hi,' says Matt, giving me a kiss on the cheek.

'Hi, what's up? Why did you say to meet outside?' I ask.

'Oh, I don't know. I just thought there's no point hanging around inside on a nice Paris evening,' says Matt, shrugging his shoulders nonchalantly. Perhaps I believe him, but it still doesn't answer why he ignored me on the crew bus and seems to want us to hide.

'And the crew bus? You seemed quiet. Why didn't you come and sit with me?' I ask. The question didn't quite come out as I had rehearsed in my head, but at least I got out what I wanted.

'I was sat with my First Officer. I couldn't just get up and walk away from him when we were already sat down. What is it with all the questions?'

'It's just after last time we were here and you walked out on me, I guess I am a little paranoid.'

'As I said before, I am so sorry about that. It's just that my head is a bit mixed up. Come here.'

Matt grabs hold of me and gives me a hug. It feels as nice as ever to be so close to him, even though I remind myself, yet again, that I cannot allow myself to get hurt.

'Come on, how about a *galette*?' says Matt.

A what? I want to ask. But I am embarrassed that I have never heard of the word. This man has such a rich vocabulary!

'Sure, sounds great,' I say. I just have to pray that it doesn't involve heights or skinny-dipping in a local swimming pool.

Matt walks along the outside of the pavement as if to protect me from the busy cars that beep along the way. When he takes my hand, I feel that electrical zap again. What is this man made of?

When we get to the venue that Matt wants to take me to, I am pleased to discover that there is no height to reach or water and nakedness involved. We are at a patisserie-type of place with long coarse wooden tables and a blackboard with a chalked-out menu. It is quite casual here, but it seems Matt has good taste. The *galette* is a sort of crepe. We can choose anything from salmon gravlax, ham and Emmenthal cheese and even sardines. I am not sure how I feel about sardines in a crepe, so I opt for the ham and cheese, whilst Matt goes for the salmon. We wash the tasty *galettes* down with cider that the lovely staff recommend.

Over our food Matt talks about work, and the rumours that Calm Air is going to force some of the older flight deck to retire.

'So, do you think you could lose your job?' I ask. I start to wonder if this is why he doesn't want anyone to know about what has happened between us down-route. Perhaps he wants to keep his reputation and his nose clean so he isn't targeted.

'Hopefully not. It's one of the reasons I moved fleet. I loved flying long haul, but I put myself forward for the conversion so I wouldn't be one of the captains they plucked out. Now they're talking about retiring some of the short-haul flight deck too. It's worrying.'

I grab his hand and stroke it. I would hate for Matt to lose his job. I would never get to fly with him if he retired. I look around at the gorgeous place we are in and think how much I would hate for this to end. His company is so delightful. He is always so reassuring and calm and for once I can see that he is worried about the prospect of retirement. I see him as a vulnerable human being.

When we leave the creperie we head for a walk along the Rives de Seine Park. A crowd is gathered around a busker in a beret and blue and white striped T-shirt, wearing rollerblades, dancing to music coming from his stereo. He reminds me of the time I saw Andrew Lloyd-Webber's musical *Starlight Express* just before it finished. People throw money onto the blanket in front of the man and Matt throws him ten euros.

A little further along the way a couple kiss in front of us. It is as though this city has some kind of magical love dust blowing onto everyone. You can see why it is called the City of Love.

Taking his cue from the loved-up couple, Matt pulls me closer. He does that thing again where he looks me in the eyes and I melt like the Emmenthal cheese in my *galette*.

'*Mon cherie*,' he says, smiling.

Then we kiss and I am on fire.

'Shall we go back to the suite?' says Matt.

'Yup,' I say, grinning. Shivers rush around my body as I fight hard not to fall in love with this man.

–

When we wake up in his suite, Matt is sitting on the sofa. He looks thoughtful and I can't work out what he is thinking. Is he worrying about his job? Or is he worried about us getting carried away again last night?

'Is everything okay?' I ask.

'Sure,' he says. But somehow I don't believe him.

Something tells me this is all going to end in tears and I can already tell that they won't be his.

Chapter 24

Before we leave Paris the next morning, Matt seems to have that wall up around him again. He smiles at me, but his eyes don't quite respond as warmly. My stomach does a sad little somersault. Am I imagining something? Overthinking? I can't quite decide.

Back in London, Matt promises me we will see each other again soon. I have a day off after this trip and Matt has two days off. Yet he says he is busy. Perhaps I am expecting too much for him to want to see me immediately. I mean, he has only just seen me and I did think it might be wise to take things slowly. Still, I can't help but feel a bit disappointed. This would have been the ideal opportunity for me to go over to his house and see where he lives, or do something together, but he seems to want to do his own thing.

Home alone in the evening, I google his name. I don't know what makes me want to do this, but it makes me feel closer to him. He hasn't told me exactly where his home is, but it doesn't take long to find out since his wife's accident is online. It says that she lived near Oxford. As always, when you find out the smallest bit of information on the internet, it quickly snowballs. So, I google the town to try and find out more about where he lives. It is a beautiful chocolate-box type place. I notice that there is an announcement in the local news about a Volkswagen

Festival close to where he is from. My goodness, what if Matt doesn't know about it? He never mentioned it. Perhaps he was flying when the article came out and he missed it.

I am so excited that I message Matt to tell him. Of course, I don't show him that I know it isn't far from where he lives, but I casually send him a screenshot of the event. I notice from the date that it is tomorrow. The timing makes me think it's the aeroplane gods of love that have fixed this, or perhaps there are even Volkswagen gods of love. Matt responds.

> Ah, yes. It's an annual event. Shame I can't make it this year. It's a bit far for you too, I suppose

No Volkswagen event is ever too far for me, but I don't argue. I decide I will go by myself. I am used to going to things alone; another event won't make any difference.

So, in the morning, I head off bright and early for the festival. I get Dolly washed on the way so that she looks her part in the car parking on the grounds of the big mansion that it is being held at. I have enough money now for her full restoration so I am determined to go so that I can find someone who can do the job. Although Matt has given me the number of his restorer, it will be interesting to check some of the others in case they are more competitively priced. There are always lots of interesting exhibitors at these events. I went to something similar in Northamptonshire once. The atmosphere is fantastic as all the like-minded Volkswagen fans gather together.

I don't have to worry about my satnav as I get closer to my destination. All I have to do is follow all the other

Beetles that are slowing everyone down on the motorway. I stay behind them and dawdle along, annoying everyone behind us. The good thing about driving a Beetle is that I never have to worry about getting a speeding ticket. Dolly won't let me go past fifty miles per hour. Something I may ask the restorer to rectify when she goes in for refurbishment. Now I am spending more time on the motorway it does hold me back a little.

Two hours later, I arrive at the Great Hall and the marshal directs me to park up alongside the other Volkswagens on the grass. The event looks busy already. Everyone is friendly and we all smile and compliment each other on our cars. Dolly looks tired compared to the bright orange heavily restored Beetle next to me and I worry that I may have tired her further with all my driving back and forth to the airport. But then I remind myself it is like having a lot of plastic surgery and that the car next to me is fake and full of filler. Dolly is a natural ageing beauty. Still, sometimes we all need a nip and tuck here and there.

As I walk through the grounds deciding which stall to visit first, I become distracted by the smell of food from a van selling breakfast buns. A bacon sandwich is just what I could do with. I grab the ketchup bottle to smear it all over my bap, but nothing comes out. I tap it some more and then it all comes out at once, splashing all over my white T-shirt. I look like someone tried to murder me.

Thankfully, there is a T-shirt stand close by and I rush up to the stall so that I can quickly change. I find a cute little pink T-shirt with a photo of a white Beetle on it. That will do. I am paying for it when I spot a lovely navy-blue T-shirt that I can't help but think would suit Matt. It has a picture of a Beetle on it and it says, 'You can't squash an old bug'. I shouldn't really be thinking of buying him something but I can't resist it. I will give it to him when I see him next, whenever that will be.

Once I am changed, I check out the part where all the Beetle restorers are. I look at the leaflets showing rusted-out Beetles and camper vans and the 'after' photos of when they have miraculously turned into dazzling show pieces. It is amazing what you can do with enough money.

One of the guys tells me it will cost around seven thousand pounds to restore Dolly fully so I tell him I will think about it. Goodness, these cars are expensive to maintain.

I head towards an area where some noise is being generated and see crowds gathering near a stage. A guy on a mic says that a band I have never heard of are about to come on stage. I am edging closer when a random man steps on my foot.

'Sorry, mate,' he says.

'It's okay,' I say, even though my little toe starts to throb.

When I stop hopping about, I see a familiar sight.

'Matt!' I shout.

Oh my goodness, he did come after all! What if he messaged to tell me he was here and I didn't hear it with the noise of the festival? I look at my phone in case I have missed a message but there is nothing.

'Matt!' I shout again. It's no use; he'll never hear me with all this noise. So I try to follow him in the direction he is going. However, as a crowd of guys in shorts and T-shirts push in front of me, I manage to lose him.

I find a nearby stallholder selling tea and cakes and stand by their tall drinks table to ring him, but there is no answer. He probably can't hear his phone with all the noise.

By the time I finish my drink, Matt still hasn't called me back since my missed call. So I walk around a bit more in case I can find him somewhere. It is just as I am walking past a balloon stand selling helium-filled ladybirds that I catch sight of him once again.

'Matt!' I shout. Unsurprisingly, he doesn't hear me through the noise so I try to follow him as closely as I can. Despite a huge ladybird balloon obscuring my sight, I can just about see that lovely dark hair of his. I bop the balloon out of the way and give chase. I shout again as I get closer but he still doesn't hear me. So I pick up my phone to ring him again. *Please let him hear it ring.* It rings out and I watch as he grabs his phone from his pocket. Thank goodness!

Matt looks at his phone and puts it away again as a tall blonde lady and a young girl in her twenties come from nowhere. The girl hands him an ice cream and the blonde lady places her hand on his shoulder. He doesn't give his phone a second glance as he walks off with his ice cream and the perfect family. I am so upset that I drop the T-shirt I bought him on the floor.

'Hey, love, you dropped this,' says a stallholder.

'You have it, it looks about your size,' I say.

I never thought I would run from a Volkswagen festival, but I do. I run back to Dolly and start her up. She starts first time.

'Oh, Dolly, you're the only one I can trust not to let me down,' I say as I wipe the tears away.

Chapter 25

Driving home is a blur and it is only when a man in a flashy new car flicks the V sign up at me on the motorway that I concentrate on the road a little better. I don't know what I did to make him do that. I can only hope it is because I am driving slowly and not that I did something dangerous.

All the way home I think about it. Who on earth was that woman with Matt? I know he was telling me the truth about his wife dying – I saw the newspaper article online about it. But I never asked him if he was seeing anyone. Perhaps he has a girlfriend for when he is back home and junior flight attendants for when he flies! Although I deserve an explanation, I decide not to mention it at this stage and see if he tells me anything voluntarily. He clearly didn't spot me there so I am desperate to see what he will say. Will he lie?

When I arrive in the driveway, I soon find out. I pull my phone out to see there is a message from him.

> Hello, how was your day? Hope you're having a lovely weekend.

I quickly message back.

> Yes, all good. Did you do anything nice today?

> No, nothing. Just a bit of gardening. You?

> Nothing, just watered the hanging baskets

It makes me feel as bad as him with my lies.

> Did you see anyone today? It's so boring hanging around on your own, I find

Let's see what he says to that!

> No, just me and the plants. I talk to them. It makes a difference, you know. People think it doesn't help them grow, but it does. That's one of the reasons I have a nice garden. Everyone who comes to the house loves my garden, but it's because I talk kindly to my plants.

I can't help but think how I am amazed anyone is allowed to his house; I am clearly not.

There is nothing else to say to him without blurting out what I saw earlier so I don't say anything further for now. I am still coming to terms with what I saw.

Later he messages again to tell me he is helping out with the Labradors tomorrow.

I'll send you a photo of Lawrence, a beautiful black lab. You'll love him.

Sure.

Are you okay?

This question seems to bounce between us all the time. *No, I am not! I saw you with a beautiful blonde. Does she fly for Calm Air? Is she a gorgeous new recruit that is allowed in your house?* I have so many questions for him.

I decide not to respond. I am in no mood for lies. Fortunately, I fly to Rome tomorrow so I can get away from Matt and his fake gardening stories. Next, he will tell me he was out buying gnomes!

Seeing him with the mystery blonde plays on my mind so much that when I arrive at briefing for my flight to Rome the following morning, I carefully look at any blonde crew member I see. However, none of them are the mystery woman. I have heard of flights where cabin crew have gotten into a physical fight over some guy in the airline that they are both seeing. I would never do that, but I would certainly try and find out more if I was to fly with this woman.

The flight is quiet today, which comes as a nice surprise. I am happy it isn't as frenetic as some of the flights as I am still reeling from yesterday.

As we are not in as much of a rush it gives me more time to spend chatting with the passengers, which is my favourite thing. I try to talk to as many as I can today to take my mind off Matt. I believe that every passenger has a story.

Today's passenger tells me he is heading to Rome for his mother's ninetieth birthday. He is so nice that I try and go above and beyond and ask in business class if I could give him one of the miniature champagne bottles as a present for his mother from the crew at Calm Air. The supervisor gladly obliges and I take it down to him.

'Bellisimo, that's so sweet of you,' he says.

'You're very welcome. It's not every day your mum is ninety,' I say, smiling.

I think of my own mum who didn't even make it to forty. Reaching that age is definitely something to celebrate.

'Please, how can I say thank you? Will you let me take you for dinner when I get back?' he asks.

It stops me in my tracks. I look at him sitting there with his kind smile. He seems like a nice guy. I recall seeing Matt with that woman. I don't really owe him anything.

'You know what, I'd love to,' I say.

His name is Luca and he passes his phone number to me. For the first time since I started flying, I take a passenger's number and also give him mine in return.

'Give your mama our love,' I say as he disembarks.

'*Ciao, bella,*' he says.

I watch him walk off and it makes me realise that there are plenty more fish in the sea. Who needs capricious Matt when you have a Gino D'Campo lookalike on-board your aircraft?

Switching my phone back on when I get back to base that evening, I plan on saving Luca's number. Then I see that Matt has been messaging and calling me.

> Are you ignoring me?

His last message asks.

I scroll through all the messages. The cute photo of Lawrence is one of them, as he promised. I can't ignore a dog photo, so I finally message back.

> I'm fine. Did a Rome turnaround, busy

> Cool. Who was the flight deck?

> Oh, don't remember. Sorry.

My answers are quite curt with him and so after a few messages back and forth I am not surprised he calls me.

'Hi,' I answer. I am sure he can tell that I don't answer his call with my usual level of enthusiasm.

'Hey, thought I'd call you as you don't seem yourself,' he says.

'I'm okay.'

'No, you're not. Something's wrong. Are you going to tell me, or do I have to drive all the way to Cardiff to find out?' he says.

'Ha, like you would. How long have I known you now? You've never been to my home and I've never been to yours. You're like a different person in this country,' I say.

'I don't understand what you mean. I call you and message you, don't I?'

215

'Yes, but you don't see me. Why could you not go with me to the VW festival?'

'I told you. I was busy.' Matt laughs as though he is starting to get nervous.

'Busy. Hmm.' I don't think I can keep quiet a moment longer. I have to say what is on my mind. 'I went there and I saw you, Matt. I saw you with that blonde lady and a young woman eating ice cream. I even rang you and you saw I was calling and didn't pick up. That's an awful way to treat someone.'

There is silence down the phone for a bit.

'Look, I can explain. It's a family member. It's nothing untoward, if that's what you're thinking. I can promise you.'

'Well, if you've nothing to hide, why would you not answer your phone, or let me come with you?' I ask.

'I don't know. You don't deserve me. I'm sorry. You'd be better off without me,' says Matt. 'This is why I never wanted a relationship,' he adds.

'You never wanted a relationship, yet didn't think twice about sleeping with me. Oh my god!' I say.

'Wait, sorry. I didn't mean it like that. Oh, I am not the best at these sorts of conversations. I…'

I put the phone down on him. Well, now I know. He never wanted a relationship with me. He just slept with me and that's it. I only wish I felt the same. There is nothing more to say. I have heard quite enough.

Chapter 26

My next flight is to Dublin again. When Luca messages me to ask if I will go for dinner, I tell him that I will message him when I return tomorrow and confirm. He has invited me to an authentic Italian restaurant. It sounds lovely but I am truly devastated about Matt. Why did I ignore all the warning signs? I should have cut my losses the day he walked out on me in Paris. I should have realised that something was wrong. Plus, he said himself that he doesn't want a relationship. So, he just wants to sleep around, in other words. I wish I had never met him as I don't think my heart can take much more. I thought we had something special, but it is obvious he was never honest with me and we were definitely not on the same page.

Therefore, I am really annoyed when I get to briefing and Matt is checking in for a different flight beside me. I console myself with the fact that at least he isn't going to Dublin. I try to avoid him, but he won't let me escape.

'Can I have a word, please?' he says.

'Nope,' I say.

'Please. I need to explain properly. Face to face. It's useless trying to explain on the phone.'

'There's nothing to say. What on earth could you say that would make up for the fact that you slept with me but don't want a relationship? Then I catch you playing happy families with a blonde at the festival. You used me.'

'Good grief, I most definitely didn't use you. Far from it. You're so beautiful and lovely. I do want a relationship, but I have a problem.'

'You have a problem?' I laugh bitterly. 'Like lying?'

'Now, come on. Don't be like that,' he says.

'Look, I have a flight to catch and so have you. I don't need this now.'

I try to leave but he pulls me back.

'I need you to sit down, please,' he says.

'I don't have time to sit down. I'll be late for briefing.'

'It's just… I have a daughter. Becky. That's who you saw with me at the event. I didn't know how to tell you.'

'Why would it be so hard to tell me you have a daughter? I am not an ogre,' I say. I am astonished as to why he couldn't tell me something so simple. I can't understand why he didn't feel comfortable sharing this with me.

'Well, she lost her mum. She's getting married soon and she still misses her mother terribly, it's an emotional time for her. I didn't want her to get wind that I was seeing someone.'

It isn't the daughter that I am worried about, though; it is the attractive blonde.

'Can I ask who the lady was that you were with?'

Matt looks away and I feel as though I have hit a nerve.

'I don't really want to talk about her right here. I have a lot of respect for the woman.'

'Fine then, don't,' I say. Shame he doesn't have the same level of respect for me.

I walk away and Matt shouts behind me.

'Don't be like that, please! I'm sorry I am such a mess.'

Thankfully, I can see the door to the briefing room and the purser is calling everyone in. By the time briefing is finished, there is no sign of Matt.

I message Luca before I change my mind.

> I'd love to have dinner with you tomorrow.

The trip to Dublin is uneventful and we have the usual drinks and dinner as a crew before flying back to London the next day. I try not to eat too much though as I have noticed I am piling on the pounds, what with all these meals and drinks down-route. I don't want to end up having to get a new uniform skirt like Michelle said she did recently. They say you gain a stone when you start flying. I am definitely on the way to it.

In Dublin, I pick up a new top that I can wear with jeans for dinner with Luca. When I get back to London, I try everything I can to build up some enthusiasm about my dinner-date. I have even arranged to stay over in Heathrow for our night out after my trip as Luca lives close by. We have agreed to meet at the restaurant he suggested. It is down an alleyway, and I don't feel comfortable as I walk down it alone. Why would I arrange to have dinner with a complete stranger? Gavin's words about not knowing whom we have on-board are like an alarm going off in my head.

The restaurant looks okay from the outside, with wooden chairs and twinkling lights. I can see Luca already sitting at a table by the window.

'Ah! I didn't recognise you with your clothes on,' says Luca when he sees me.

'Oh,' I say.

'Joke, you know? Because I only saw you in uniform. Your hair was up, you look different,' he says.

'Ah, yes. I see. So, how was your mum?' I ask.

'Ah, it was brilliant. Maria and Gino came, Mario brought little Giovanni and then he told us that Alfonso was going to Sicily. It was a great time,' he says.

I have no idea who his family are but they all sound great. It must be lovely to have a big family all around you and I can see in his eyes how enthusiastic he is. But I realise that we have nothing in common as I tell him about my next flight and how we got delayed out of Verona last week.

As nice as Luca is, we both live in very different worlds. Perhaps this is why Carys is single. Flying and relationships don't seem to work. We live such different lives that it is difficult for those on the ground to understand sometimes, and vice versa.

After me talking about delayed aircraft, which was obviously of no interest to Luca, the whole night falls flat. Perhaps it is my attitude too as I am not in the right frame of mind. All I can think is how I wish I was talking airline stuff with Matt. It makes me realise how much the job has engulfed me. But more than that, how much the thought of Matt has engulfed me too. I am mad with myself as I think of that smile, his dry sense of humour. The way he looks at me deadpan serious when saying something silly. Oh, how I miss him already. Luca is so sweet, but he isn't Matt and that's the problem.

'Anyway, thank you for a lovely evening,' I say, after we have split the bill. 'It was so kind of you to bring me here.'

'*Arrivederci*,' says Luca.

I know, however, that we will never meet again. It was a bit of a disaster for both of us.

I head back to my hotel and sink into my pillow. Did flying turn me into someone who will never be satisfied? It has definitely changed me. I could never think of going back to a 9–5. A day's work might be long and often mean unexpected hours, but then you find yourself living in hotel rooms, eating and drinking amazing food. But there is also the downside. It can be lonely if you don't have a wonderful crew, which does happen from time to time. That is why Matt understands this life so well, and perhaps this is part of the attraction with him. Maybe this is why flight attendants often marry flight deck.

I am about to switch my phone off when it starts ringing. I can't imagine it is Luca; I think we both know how this evening went!

I sit up in my bed and see that it is Matt. I didn't expect to hear from him this evening.

'Hi,' I say.

'Hi. I can't sleep. I need to be open with you once and for all,' says Matt. How I have missed his voice. It's so nice to hear it on the other end of the phone. It feels like a comfort blanket.

'Go on.'

'I should have told you. The woman you saw me with is Francesca's sister. Lucille found it hard after she died and being around me seems to comfort her. I can assure you, it's all above board. I just wanted to protect her and not bring you into things.'

I haven't seen a photo of Francesca so have no idea if they look similar, or even if he is telling me the truth.

'Look, I didn't want Lucille knowing about us at this stage. I wasn't looking for a relationship, it just happened. I don't know how to handle any of this, quite honestly. It's been so unexpected. I hope you can understand that.'

'I think the feelings between us have come as a surprise for both of us. But that doesn't mean we can't be honest and you have to hide her from me, does it?' I say.

'Yup, I should have been honest with you. But I didn't want you being put off by the fact that Lucille and I are so close. It might seem a bit weird, perhaps. Sorry, I don't know what I am thinking right now.'

'Well, it has all been a bit of a rollercoaster, for sure,' I say.

'Penny, listen, I'd love a relationship with you. I really would. But if we are to have a proper relationship then perhaps you could meet Becky first and we can take it step by step. Could I arrange a dinner for us all and you could meet her?' he says.

I agree immediately, although part of me worries that he is too fragile for a relationship.

'I'd love to join you for dinner and to meet your daughter,' I say.

'That's brilliant. I'm so happy. But first, can I introduce you to my favourite Labrador?' asks Matt.

'Ha, yes, I'd very much like to meet lovely Lawrence,' I say.

My heart jumps for joy. The thought of meeting Matt's daughter and his favourite black lab makes me so incredibly happy, even if the thought of meeting Lawrence is far less intimidating than meeting Daddy's precious girl.

Chapter 27

Lawrence wags his tail and slobbers all over me when I meet him. He is such a friendly boy. I wonder why he is in the doggie refuge so I ask Matt what his story is. He tells me it is because his owner had a stroke and can no longer look after him.

'Poor Lawrence. I wish I could take you home,' I say.

'Me too. I'm hoping Becky might take him. She did say she wants to meet him,' says Matt.

'Oh, that would be amazing. I so hope she does. It's no place for an old boy like this to be in. How old is he? Twelve? Thirteen?'

You can see by his eyes that he is starting to look a little tired and sprouts of grey fur are starting to show through.

'Almost thirteen. His back legs are a bit sore. The vet thinks it's arthritis starting to set in. That's why he's been here for a few months. I think everyone who sees him is afraid of vet bills going forward.'

'Bless him. Such a sweetheart.'

We don't take Lawrence for a long walk. Instead, we take him for a drive and then stop at a park so that he can sit and watch the ducks. It is a lovely morning as Matt and I chat on a bench and Lawrence enjoys the view of the ducks. For anyone who didn't know us, they would think we were a happy family. But instead, I have to go home to Cardiff tonight and poor Lawrence has to return to his kennel. How I wish I could cuddle him in front of a roaring fire for the rest of his years. I wouldn't mind getting Matt in front of one too. Naked, of course! I laugh to myself.

'What's so funny?' asks Matt.

'Oh, nothing. I just thought of something silly,' I say.

'Go on, maybe I'll find it funny too,' he says.

'Um, no. You won't. Ooh, look, there's a swan,' I say.

Lawrence doesn't seem to like the look of the swan. As Matt is quite relaxed on the bench, Lawrence manages to pull the lead loose out of his hand. He rushes off towards the pond and chases the swan.

'Lawrence, come back!' we both shout.

It's no use, though. The next thing we know, Lawrence is in the water and the swan looks like he is about to attack him.

'Oh my gosh, do something, Matt,' I say.

I look in my handbag for the treats that I kept for Oreo and Willow. Luckily, I find some that have fallen out at the bottom of my bag.

Matt rolls up his trousers and gets in the pond to attempt to reach Lawrence. I then pass the treats over to Matt and Lawrence finally pays us some attention when he notices them. Good old chonky wonks; they never fail to make a dog do what you need them to.

'There's a good boy. Come on,' I say, as Matt leads Lawrence back to dry land.

The swan dawdles off and once they are both safely on the path, we see the funny side.

'We make a good team,' says Matt with his trousers rolled up.

All he needs is a handkerchief on his head and he would look like one of those characters on a British seaside postcard.

'There's a lovely country pub around the corner if you fancy lunch,' he says, rolling his trousers back down.

Lawrence wags his tail in agreement as if to say he would very much fancy lunch too.

'Sounds lovely,' I say.

When I see the food the waitress puts in front of us, I have to wonder if Matt has been to the pub before because he must know that the portion sizes are enormous. There will be plenty of scraps left for Lawrence.

I order bangers and mash, and there is enough for all three of us. I begin to regret not ordering a starter rather than a main course.

Matt tucks into his gammon and pineapple as I wrestle with three gigantic Cumberland sausages with heaps of mash and gravy. It is pure comfort food.

I am embarrassed that I can't manage to eat such a huge plate of food, so when Matt goes to the toilet, I sneakily give Lawrence a sausage. I don't have to worry about any evidence as he polishes it off in one mouthful.

'Shall I get another cider for you?' asks Matt when he gets back.

'Ooh, go on then. Just a half, though,' I say.

As he goes to the bar to get us more drinks, I see him take a call on his mobile. He looks quite serious as he speaks to whomever it is. I hope it isn't about the rumoured forced retirements. His face looks very concerned.

'Sorry, I'm going to have to leave. We're going to have to rush Lawrence back.' The thought of poor Lawrence having to go back to the dog shelter breaks my heart.

'What's happened? Everything okay?'

'Yes – well, no. It's Becky. She's in tears because the wedding dress shop has gone into liquidation. She is in a terrible state. I'm afraid that I have to get over to see her immediately.'

'Oh no, would you like me to come? I can talk woman to woman if that helps. I used to work in a store, perhaps I can talk to her about what happens to the stock in such a case?'

'That's very kind of you, but it's probably best you don't. I don't think she wants to see anyone right now. I've already paid the bill. You ready?'

Lawrence and I both look at each other, disappointed. We were having such a lovely day, but I suppose it is a real emergency for Becky given that her wedding day is fast approaching. That's the thing when you have to be both parents; even though Becky is not a child, Matt is still the one who has to do everything.

We head back to the dog pound and I promise Lawrence I will see him again soon.

'That's if nobody snaps you up before,' I tell him.

Lawrence leans into me as if he wants a hug. Oh bless. I think I might cry.

It seems I have won Lawrence's approval, but will I win Becky's?

Chapter 28

A couple of weeks later, Matt calls me to propose a date for dinner at his house, so that I can finally meet the famous Becky. Although I gladly agree, inside I am a walking wreck.

Since I don't have a daughter of my own and am unfamiliar with such relationships, I don't know how to approach her. I am assuming I will need to win her over, to get her approval before I can have a serious relationship with Matt. I suppose this is understandable; blood is thicker than water, after all. But it's not like she is a child and I can turn up with a big toy and she will instantly like me. What if she hates me? Matt assures me that she will adore me, just as much as he does, but what if she doesn't?

I decide to take her a bunch of lilies and a bottle of Welsh whisky for Matt. I have booked a motel near the village where Matt lives as it would be awkward to stay there with his daughter staying the night too. Fortunately, we get airline discounts at so many hotels.

As I walk from the hotel to Matt's house, I can see for myself the gorgeous chocolate-box village with quaint shops selling things like obscure cheeses and a local artist selling artwork of penguins – not that there are any around there. I am too late to catch the shops, but decide I will take a look around in the morning. I may even treat myself to a cute penguin painting for the living room to remind me of the first time I met Becky.

Matt has the most beautiful Georgian-style home with a mature garden, which has a wishing well and a pond with carp. No wonder he mentioned how everyone loves his garden. The fish look well fed too. I wonder who feeds them when he is flying.

I am not very good with the names of plants, but it doesn't take a gardener to work out that Matt spends a lot of time preening his bushes. I begin to think his property should be on the cover of a country lifestyle magazine. I must tell him he should do it if he hasn't already.

When I am closer to the front door, I spot Becky looking out the window and then disappear as we come eye to eye. Oh, bless her, she must have run straight to open the door. Hopefully she is excited about meeting me.

However, when I reach the door, it is still closed and I have to press the black old-fashioned doorbell which makes one of those classy, strong ding-dong sounds like you'd hear in a country manor. It makes me wonder if a butler is going to greet me instead of Becky. However, it is Matt who comes out. His hair is a little dishevelled and his cheeks are flushed. He still looks mightily cute, though. There is no sign of Becky, so I don't know what happened to her. I hope she didn't fall in her rush to open the door to me.

Matt doesn't kiss me as he usually does when he sees me, but I suspect that is because Becky is about, wherever she has disappeared to.

I hand him the whisky. He seems pleased with it. Phew, let's hope Becky likes the flowers as much.

'Becky, where are you? Penny's here,' shouts Matt.

I place my handbag down in the living room and take a seat while I wait.

'Glass of wine before dinner? I've prepared beef Wellington, it won't be long. It's Becky's favourite,' says Matt.

'Ooh, lovely,' I say, smiling. I can't help but think he could have asked me if I liked beef Wellington before I came for dinner. It's that niggling little doubt in my head again. Becky obviously comes before me, which is fair enough. But how far will he go to appease her over me? Is this something that could continue over our relationship if there was any future commitment? The dynamics of an adult stepchild is something I have never thought about before.

As soon as Becky meets me, I can clearly see in her face that she despises me. Despite the daggers she is giving me, I smile for Matt's sake and hand her the flowers.

'Here, I brought these for you,' I say. I thought the lilies would be a safe bet.

'I have hay fever,' she says. Then she dumps the flowers on a side table and walks out.

I am horrified. What if I have set her allergies off? I am sure it would be so much easier if she were a younger child. Surely a giant teddy would put any kid in a good mood?

'I can't apologise enough, I am so sorry,' I say to Matt.

I look out the living room window, annoyed with myself for choosing the wrong thing. But then I realise the garden is full of beautiful flowers so she must manage with those. I begin to wonder if whatever I would have brought wouldn't have been her thing. I had toyed with the idea of chocolates but thought as her wedding was coming up she may complain that she was on a diet. I really thought flowers would be a safe bet. Obviously not.

I take a big gulp of wine. I do hope Matt has a few bottles, if this is how the night is going to proceed.

I can hear Becky chatting to her dad in the kitchen. I try to listen to see if she is saying anything about me, but I can't quite make out their conversation as the house is so big.

Eventually, Matt calls me into the dining room. Like the rest of the house, it is just stunning. Hanging from the ceiling is a huge chandelier of candlesticks of different heights, all sat on a black iron ring. I suspect Francesca designed this room. The large oak dining table seats at least ten and is laid out with napkins, wine glasses and even water glasses. It makes me wonder if Matt and Francesca used to have swanky dinner parties with their pilot friends in here. If only these walls could talk.

I soon discover that Matt is a fantastic cook and everything is perfectly done. There is a huge platter of rainbow-coloured vegetables and some hasselback potatoes. He has carefully selected a vintage red wine for the beef and it is all very lovely. Becky, however, doesn't look impressed in the slightest. Every now and then she glances sneakily at me as if to size me up. The atmosphere is very tense, although Matt doesn't seem to notice.

'So, you're getting married, your dad tells me. That's exciting,' I say.

'Yeah,' answers Becky.

I try to think of something that will bring her out of her shell. Surely every woman is excited about their wedding dress.

'So, have you organised your wedding dress yet?' I ask.

As I say it, I realise what I have just done. Why did my brain not engage before saying anything? Of course she hasn't sorted her wedding dress out! It was one of those automatic stupid questions you ask a bride-to-be.

I want to retract the words, apologise for what I have just said. But I don't know how much knowledge I am supposed to have about the forthcoming nuptials. Matt looks at me, horrified.

'Don't talk to me about my wedding dress,' she says, enraged.

'Oh, sorry. I am so sorry if it's a sore subject.'

Oh no, someone please get me out of here.

'Umm, the venue? Do you have a nice venue lined up?'

'Yes, but sadly Mum wasn't here to help me choose it as I always thought she would be,' she says.

'Oh, I am sorry. My mum died too,' I say. Perhaps if she realises that I don't have a mum we might find some common ground.

'Yeah, well, you don't know what it feels like to be getting married without your mum and then your dad walks in with some flight-deck floozy he's picked up. I bet that never happened to you,' she says.

Flight-deck floozy! I am so shocked that I drop my fork on the floor. I watch as if in slow motion as it smashes down on the cream carpet and the red wine jus splashes off it.

'Mum chose that carpet,' snaps Becky.

'Oh, goodness, I am sorry. I'll clean it up.'

'Don't touch my mum's carpet!' screams Becky.

'Now, Becky. Come on, love, it was an accident,' says Matt.

I start to panic as Becky rushes out to the kitchen to get a cloth, leaving me unsure what I should do next.

'I'm so sorry. I am making a right mess of things, and not just your lovely carpet,' I say to Matt.

'It's okay. It's not your fault. Umm, look, I have some baklava I picked up in Istanbul if you'd like some. I'll just go and get it from the kitchen,' says Matt.

'Oh, no, I'm fine. Thank you, your beef Wellington was superb. I couldn't touch another thing,' I say.

I think we have bigger worries than having dessert right now.

Becky walks in with a damp cloth and makes a big deal of cleaning the carpet. She huffs and she puffs and then bursts into tears.

'Darling, Becks, what's wrong?' says Matt.

'It's just too much, Dad. I can't take seeing you with someone other than Mum. I'm sorry. It's just horrible.'

Matt gives Becky a hug and I make my way to the living room to get my handbag. It's clear to see that Becky isn't happy with me being here, so I attempt to sneak out without saying anything. Just as Matt did that morning in Paris. Now it's my turn to feel awkward and unsure what to say or do.

Matt catches up with me as I struggle with the heavy wooden front door.

'I'm sorry. To be honest, I was hoping you could be my plus one for the wedding. I thought if Becky met you now then it would break the ice. It's early days for her. I owe you an apology. She shouldn't have treated you like that. I can only thank you for being so graceful to her.'

'It's okay. I understand. I'm sure it isn't very nice for her to see you with someone else. Not to worry. I think it is probably best I go and we leave things where they are,' I say.

I walk down the garden path with tears in my eyes.

'There you go Becky, you had your way. Me and your dad are over,' I mutter to myself.

Getting back to the hotel, I order a drink at the bar. I need one. It is a relief to be a stranger in here. I feel like I need my anonymity after that; I am not in the mood for conversation with anyone. That was one of the most awkward experiences of my life, apart from that night I learned the truth about Geraint. Poor Becky. I do understand why it must have been horrible to see her dad with someone new, but I was innocent in the situation. It's not like I dragged her dad into the room and… Okay, well, maybe it's best she doesn't know the full story there.

Why are there always three people involved in my relationships though? I know it's very different, but first Alex got pregnant with my boyfriend's child and now Becky wants her dad to herself. Although I can understand that more than Geraint wanting a child with Alex.

I am in floods of tears when the waitress comes up to serve me.

'Did you want anything to eat? Oh, umm. Are you okay?' she asks when she sees the state I am in.

'It's just a man thing,' I say, snivelling.

'Oh, might have guessed. Don't talk to me about them. You need to look at the dessert menu. It's on the house,' she says with a wink.

I had noticed the dessert menu on the table and, as I skipped the baklava, I decide to opt for a massive chocolate sundae. It is one of those evenings when nothing else will do. Yet again, Penny Thomas is alone and eating way too much chocolate, although not frog shaped for once.

When I finish, I pay for the dessert and give the lady a nice tip. I promise her that I will leave a Facebook review.

It is not the hotel's fault that I have had a dreadful evening before coming here.

When I leave the hotel the next morning there is no sign of Matt. I secretly hoped that he might turn up to apologise, but nothing. I expect he had to stay with Becky and promise her that he will never date another 'flight-deck floozy'. I am disappointed that he didn't even text to say good night or good morning as he usually does.

I drive Dolly out of the village, sad that I may never see this pretty place again. As for the penguin paintings, I am so glad I never bought one. I don't think I would ever want a reminder of my disastrous meeting with Becky.

Chapter 29

My next flight is to Stockholm and I carefully look on the crew list to see who is flying the plane. It is a captain whose name I don't recognise. Matt didn't swap with another captain to surprise me, then. I shouldn't feel disappointed but it would be nice to have seen him and discussed what went on at his home, but I suppose that is it between us. Becky needs him more than I do, even if she is a grown woman.

The flight over to Stockholm is completely full. As I have the possibility to apply to work in business class shortly, my helpful supervisor, Anju, asks me if I want to help out in the business class cabin. Technically I probably shouldn't as I am not trained for it, but at least I can see how things work up there before I have to attend an interview for promotion, so this will give me a head start for any tricky questions. Also, as it is so different to economy, it makes me concentrate on something other than Matt. It is funny how quickly I have got used to my job.

I now know where everything is down the back of the aircraft, along with every noise and movement of the plane. Everything is different in the business class galley and the passengers seem quieter as they are busy on laptops. There is hardly enough room in economy to get a laptop out.

When I am handing out some cheesy snacks a Swedish man asks me for a glass of water.

'Thank you,' he says, as I rush back from the galley with his drink in a proper glass. Luckily Anju stopped me pouring it into a plastic glass as we do in the economy cabin.

'You're very welcome,' I say, smiling.

'Hey, what a nice accent you have. Where are you from?' he says.

'Wales,' I explain.

'Wales, a beautiful country. Like Sweden in some ways. I'm Johan, pleased to meet you.'

'Penny,' I say with a smile.

'Well, Penny, are you stopping over in Stockholm?'

'No, we go straight back,' I explain.

'Ah, that's a shame. I would have loved to have asked you to join me for a drink this evening,' says Johan.

'Oh, sorry, no can do. That's so nice of you to ask me though.' I smile. Even when I am not interested in going for a drink with someone, I still try to be polite. You never know, it might have taken all his courage so I don't really want to shout 'bugger off, you pervert!' in the middle of the aircraft.

'Well, here's my number. If you ever get a stopover, give me a shout,' says Johan.

'I will, thanks.' I stuff Johan's telephone number into my apron pocket and go back into the business class galley.

'Goodness, do men always give their phone numbers out in business class?' I ask Anju.

'No, not every flight,' she says, rolling her eyes.

The seat belt sign makes that double *bing* noise, meaning that we have to prepare the cabin for landing. I have to secure the economy cabin so I rush down the aisle to open the curtains between the cabins. It is then someone touches my arm. Oh goodness, what do they want now? It's too late to be asking for a rum and Coke or whatever it is they want at this time.

I turn to look at who it is and can hardly believe my eyes.

'Hello,' he says.

'What on earth are you doing on my flight?' I ask.

'Deadheading,' says Matt, smiling.

Deadheading is yet another of an airline's strange terminology, and it means that he is flying as a passenger and not that we are carrying a dead passenger's head.

'I'm picking up an aircraft in Stockholm to bring back to London,' says Matt.

'Oh, I can't get away from you then. Anyway, I have to secure the cabin, okay?' I say, and I rush back to my duties in economy.

I noticed some standby days on his roster; he must have been called out. Those naughty airline gods of love. My heart is thumping.

When we land in Stockholm, and all the passengers have departed, I spot Matt walking down the aisle.

'We need to talk. I'm sorry about Becky. She shouldn't have spoken to you like that, but I was stuck in the middle. Getting between two women has never been my thing. I didn't know what I should say. I'm really rubbish at this sort of stuff. I'm better with flight deck controls than females if I'm honest,' he says, smiling.

I can see he is stuck in the middle and, whilst I wish he had done something to help the evening go a little smoother, I understand he isn't the best at dealing with disputes between women. So I agree to giving him one final chance. We arrange to meet in London when we both get back as he has two tickets for an opera he has been dying to see. I don't admit that I prefer Def Leppard. Instead, I tell him that an opera sounds lovely.

I am on a high when I get back to base and even more delighted when I bump into Carys. After all this time, we are finally checking out of a flight beside each other.

She gives me a hug and kisses me on both cheeks. 'Great to see you. How's it going?' she asks.

'Oh, it's amazing. All settled in now and I even have a promotion coming up, fingers crossed,' I say.

'Oh, that's brilliant. You'd better get in quick though as there's a rumour they're putting promotions on hold for a while.'

'Oh no, I haven't heard that,' I say.

'Yup, lots of job insecurity at the mo. Hey, I'm off for a few days. Why don't we finally get a drink together and I can fill you in?' asks Carys.

'I'd really love that,' I say.

'Fab, I'll message you to arrange.'

It must be my lucky day. Drinks with Carys and a date with Matt. What could be better?

–

Matt looks dashing when I see him all dressed up for the opera in evening attire. I would even go so far as to say he looks like someone from a movie about some hot billionaire with the black dickie bow. I can just imagine me untying that and him standing there with it hanging down, as you see in these steamy movies. I curse my choice of a lemon strappy sundress. What was I thinking? I feel so underdressed. I really should have googled what people wear to the opera, but the last concert I went to was Bon Jovi when I wore jeans. At least I am wearing a dress.

Going to the opera is unlike anything I have ever done before. The opera house is so grown-up and opulent with its red swishy curtains and fancy balconies. I definitely don't feel as though I belong here. I order a gin and tonic, rather than a pint of cider, which I would secretly prefer. I don't think this is the type of place I would get away with dribbling half the pint down my dress. I am also secretly disappointed they don't have pork scratchings!

'I managed to get us wonderful seats,' says Matt.

'Oh great,' I say. I prefer standing usually at an event as you can dance away, but I guess this isn't that sort of place. Can you even bop away to opera music? I am about to find out!

An announcement tells us to take our seats and we follow the other crowds through an upper-level door. There are so many stairs that I am out of breath by the time we get there. I am glad to sit down at our exclusive seating and catch my breath.

'This is a beautiful place,' I tell Matt between deep breaths.

'It's one of my favourite places to come to,' says Matt.

I look around at the crowds of people. A lady sitting beside me wears a pale pink taffeta evening dress and she is holding some of those little binocular things on a stick. My goodness, I didn't see anyone with those at Bon Jovi.

Matt takes his phone out of his pocket to switch it off before the performance begins when it lights up in his hand.

'Oh, no, phone is ringing. I think it might be important,' he says.

Matt gets up to leave and take the call and I wait for him to come back. I look at the lady's gold binoculars. They look expensive. She is obviously an opera aficionado. I watch her to see how you are supposed to behave at such an event. I make a note that if I ever come again I will go clothes shopping, that's for certain.

The heavy velvet red curtains rise and the performance begins. Matt still hasn't returned.

Oh, my ears. This is so high-pitched. I am sure there is specific terminology for this sort of singing. Is the woman dressed in rags on stage some kind of soprano? I have seen the opera singers in Covent Garden and I prefer their voices. Perhaps that is because it is in the open air and I am normally eating pizza and slugging down wine or cider. This high-pitched squeak thing is bouncing off the walls and is already giving me a bit of a headache. Thank goodness I don't have the gin glass with me as it would probably shatter.

I can't understand any of this as it's in another language and I realise that opera is definitely not my thing, unfortunately. I am sure it is quite amazing if you are into it, but it's not for me.

The lady sat next to me is quite enraptured and she is in tears at one point. I don't understand how she can be in tears as I don't notice anything sad. I am obviously not following the story, although maybe that is because I am too concerned about where Matt is. There is no sign of him. He still hasn't returned. I desperately want to check my phone to see the time and see if there is any message from him.

However, the audience is so gripped that if I make a single noise, I fear I will get lynched. I do turn my head towards the entrance we came in though, just in case I see him creeping back in during the performance. But there is no sign of him. It makes me wonder if he is waiting for halftime so he doesn't disturb everyone. That must be what he is doing. I do hope operas *have* a halftime.

It feels as though it is five hours later when the curtain goes down and the lights slowly brighten. Phew, now I can find Matt.

I wonder if he's been waiting outside the door, desperate to come back in and find me, but there is no sign of him as I walk out. I consider that he might be nursing a drink in the bar as he waits for me. So I head there next. It is quite busy, but no matter how much I weave in between the crowds, I can't find him.

'Simplyyyy marvellous, what!' someone says in my ear.

I look to see who it is and notice it is the lady who was sitting beside me.

'Isn't it wonderfuuuul to come to an opera by oneself,' she says.

I want to tell her I shouldn't be by myself; I am with someone but he's disappeared. I can't be bothered though as I am more preoccupied with finding Matt.

'Oh, yes, it is. Wonderful show. It's almost as good as when I went to see *Rocky Horror Picture Show* years ago,' I say. I shouldn't have said this as then the 'Time Warp' song gets stuck in my head.

'Anyway, I am just dashing to the lavatory,' I say in my poshest voice.

As I head further away from the auditorium my phone picks up more bars from my network. I see a message from Matt. Hooray, he must be telling me where to meet him.

> I'm so sorry. Becky has an emergency and I've had to rush back home. Do enjoy the opera, won't you.

Matt has gone home and left me here alone! I can't believe it. I am fuming. It was him who wanted to come here. I would have been much more at home in my pyjamas watching chick flicks! Could he not have popped back in to tell me there had been an emergency instead of leaving me to waste two hours of my life that I can never get back? This is the last straw. Becky Garcia, you win. You can have your blooming dad!

Chapter 30

When I wake up and remember that I was left alone at the opera, it reminds me of the break-up with Geraint, waking up to the realisation that this relationship has run its course. Becky needs Matt right now, that much is clear. I feel flat as I make my coffee and get ready for the day ahead. I am so grateful that Carys and I decided to have drinks tonight. I can't wait to see her. But first I need to deal with Matt. Until Becky is married and happy there is no point continuing this and I need to make that clear. I have avoided his missed calls until I calmed down a bit, but now I need to speak to him.

'Penny, I'm so sorry about last night,' says Matt as soon as he answers.

'Look, it's not acceptable to leave someone in the opera alone and not even tell them you've left,' I say.

'I apologise, but I didn't want you to have to miss it because of me. I wanted you to enjoy your evening,' says Matt.

'Well, I didn't enjoy my evening. Not one bit,' I say.

'I'll make it up to you. I promise. My mate owns a barge on the Thames. How about we take it out? We could get lunch in a country pub and…'

Whilst it sounds perfect, I remember the last time we went to a nice pub for lunch and what happened then. It's no good. It's not going to work.

'You're just being optimistic. We both know this isn't going to work out. Becky needs you. She's getting married and needs you more than ever. There isn't room for both of us in your life right now.'

'Of course there is. It's just a bit difficult, that's all.'

'It's not going to work, Matt. Perhaps if we'd met later down the line, things would have been different. But I can't spend my life sitting at places alone because Becky needs you urgently.'

'But we're mole-mates,' says Matt, trying to make me laugh. It does make me smile as I think back to the first time we had sex together and Matt noticed that we had matching moles on our shoulder blades, but that doesn't help things right now.

'I know we are mole-mates, but I think you need to focus on Becky now. It's an important time in her life. There's nothing more to be said,' I say.

'I'm sorry to hear this. I really am,' says Matt.

'Me too, Matt. But I think it's for the best. I wish you well.' I put the phone down before I can change my mind.

We had our wonderful moments, but I cannot be strung along by someone again. It is all or nothing this time. I am too old to play games and be left alone in an opera, sitting there like a muppet, waiting for him to return.

When my phone rings again I worry it might be Matt begging me to change my mind, and I am not convinced I have the willpower to resist if he were to plead with me. I pray it isn't Carys cancelling the drinks we have planned for tonight either. I need a girl's night out more than anything.

But when I check my phone, it is the VW restorer that Matt had recommended to me a while back. It is the same company that did the work on his campervan so I trust that they will do an excellent job. The problem is that they are too good and didn't have any space for Dolly. I had put my name down on a waiting list as they told me that I would probably have to wait up to a year for them to be able to do the work.

I wonder why they are ringing me at eleven a.m. on a Friday morning.

'Hi, Ms Thomas?'

'Yes,' I say.

'We've had a cancellation. The next person on the waiting list has changed his mind as he can't afford the work. You know what it's like, just had a baby and all that.'

'Oh right, okay. I don't know what it's like to have a baby, not everyone does, but go on,' I say.

'Well, anyhow, it's just that one of my guys is dropping off a campervan in Cardiff right now so I thought I'd give you a ring. We can pick your Beetle up in about, say, thirty minutes, and bring her back with us.'

'Oh, wow. I wasn't expecting that. How long will you need her for?' I ask.

'Two, three weeks maximum. Once I've checked her over, I can give you more precise information.'

I will miss her but I can easily get a train up to the airport for work and I am relying on taxis tonight. So I agree and quickly run downstairs to empty out the glovebox of anything I will need.

'Oh Dolly, it's your big day,' I say.

I find packets of tissues and my airline uniform scarf in the glove compartment and remove them. Before I can check the boot at the front of the car, I see a tow truck driving slowly up the road. Then the driver spots the car. He arrived faster than I thought.

I stroke Dolly's steering wheel. I feel as though I am sending my dog to the vet for an operation. What if they find more rust than they thought and she doesn't make it through?

'Take care of her, won't you?' I say to the recovery truck driver.

'I will, love. You wait until you see her. She'll be tarted up as though she's brand spanking new.'

An image of one of the crew I flew with who had her lips done and those big funny eyebrow things girls seem to get tattooed on comes to mind. The ones that look like two slugs drawn on a face.

'I just want a little discreet touch-up, really,' I plead.

'Don't worry, love. You leave it to us.'

I watch as Dolly is strapped onto the tow truck and off she goes. I begin to wonder if I am doing the right thing even though I know the rust is making her weaker every day. I remind myself why she is going in. I don't really have a choice.

Later, when I get ready for drinks with Carys, I look at myself in the mirror. Should I get a little enhancement? I am starting to look tired after all those early morning flights. It is no secret that many of the crew get the best of the treatments and enhancements when they travel around the world. One of the crew mentioned that she flies to Casablanca for her Botox every few months as the only doctor she trusts is there. Apparently, he does a lot of Moroccan celebrities. Perhaps I will get my eyelashes tinted, to begin with. I suspect that will make me look a little bit more alive. That's enough for now though.

Carys suggested a trendy wine bar in the city for drinks. It is heaving and everyone seems so much younger than us. I don't know that I am so keen on these types of places any more. I prefer a country pub with a roaring fire and plenty of space to move. I tell myself that I must not think about country pubs. Everything is good. These are the places to be seen and be cool.

There is no space to sit down so Carys and I stand and try to chat in a small corner that we find. However, it is so loud that I can barely hear her.

'You want something to eat? Drinking on an empty stomach is never a good idea,' shouts Carys.

'Sounds like a plan,' I say.

'Fancy some tapas? I know a fab place,' she says.

'Great.'

We finish our drinks and head off to her favourite tapas place. As we get closer, I get a bad feeling we are heading to La Tapas. I haven't seen Miguel or the restaurant since that fateful night before my flying adventure began.

We turn the corner and there it is: La Tapas is right in front of us. Part of me thinks I should speak up and explain that I don't have good memories here. However, sometimes you have to face the past. This is my opportunity to lay it all to rest. Especially as Geraint is sitting right by the door with Alex!

Miguel sees me walk in and I am quite sure he is squirming in his latest trainers as he looks over towards Geraint and Alex.

'Hiya, Pen. You all right?' says Geraint when he sees me.

'Yeah, good. Thanks.'

'Cool. You remember my cycling buddy, Alex,' he says.

'Yes, of course I remember,' I say. I instinctively look at her flat stomach. I guess she went out cycling straight from giving birth.

'All right,' she says. At least she is looking uncomfortable. I wonder where the baby is.

'Out without the baby then?' I say.

'Yeah, Alex's mum's looking after her,' says Geraint.

'Oh right. It's a girl then,' I say.

Just like the one I always dreamed of having with him and taking shopping to Little Darlings.

'How old is she now? Must be about six months old?' I say.

'Almost a year,' says Geraint.

I look at him, shocked. She was much further along than he let on when he broke the news. No wonder he had to tell me quickly.

'Almost a year!' I say.

'Yeah, soz. I really should have told you before,' says Geraint. Alex looks away and fiddles with her phone.

'Yes, you should have. But I guess the timing worked out as then I wouldn't have got my new job,' I say.

'What you doing now then, babe?' says Geraint.

'Cabin crew.'

'Bloody hell. I should have dumped you earlier then. Alex always fancied that, didn't you?'

'Yeah, when I was a bit younger I did,' says Alex sheepishly.

'Anyway, look. Good to see you both looking so happy,' I say.

As I walk away from them, I make peace with it all. It might have hurt at the time, and it still hurts that I won't ever have the baby I longed for and they do. But I accept that for some reason, it wasn't what the universe wanted for me. I smile at Carys as we walk to our table. Exactly like her, I was meant to see the world and enjoy myself. It would be nicer if Matt was a part of my new life, but I have been alone before and I can be again.

I order a cocktail from Miguel which comes with the plastic flamingo stirrer. This time, instead of leaving it on the table, I put it in my bag and take it home. I'm going to keep it with all my other trinkets. The flamingo will always remind me of how my life took me on a completely different journey to the one I thought I was destined for. I just didn't realise it the last time I was here.

Chapter 31

Three weeks and a huge dent in my savings account later, Dolly is ready to be returned. It feels like Christmas as I wait on the doorstep for the tow truck to bring her home. I am so glad she is home safe. With everything that happened with Matt, it has been lonely and I have missed her. Dolly's return will cheer me up as much as possible under the circumstances.

I can see her sparkling from down the road.

The recovery truck driver hands me the keys and I walk around Dolly for a closer inspection.

'Oh, Dolly, you look amazing!' I say out loud.

The rust patches have been sanded down and you would never know she had been in such bad condition looking at her now. The interior has been patched up and where there were rips in the seats through wear and tear, these have been replaced with new covers that look as though they were always there in a shabby-chic kind of way.

I take some photos of her shiny body and immediately want to send them to Matt.

Of course I don't though, as we haven't been in touch. He will be busy with the wedding now I expect, since I am aware it is tomorrow. I don't know why I am thinking about Becky's wedding and what date it is, as it is nothing to do with me and certainly none of my business. I can't deny that I wish it *was* my business though, but as always, Penny Thomas has no choice but to plod on.

Although I now have a week's holiday time and could use my airline discount to jet off, I decided to stay home as I had been expecting Dolly back. I thought I could take her out on country rides on routes where there is no danger of coming across cows on the road. It will be just me and Dolly, like the old days.

However, our first stop as her new revitalised self is at the spa. Since Dolly is looking so well, I fancy a bit of pampering too. To lift my mood, I have made myself an appointment for a spa day which includes a new haircut, manicure, pedicure and, finally, some eyelash tinting.

The spa is at one of my favourite hotels. There is a pool, steam room and gym included in the spa day. I skip the gym and focus on the relaxation side of things. My tired feet, from practically walking all over Europe, are delighted with the pedicure. I never pamper myself, as I am always thinking of what I need to keep Dolly on the road, so this is a lovely treat. When my eyelashes are tinted I feel like a million dollars. Yay, I have eyes!

Now that Dolly is restored, I decide that this will become a regular investment since I spend so much money on the darkest of mascaras every time I walk through duty-free.

I lie by the poolside and scoff some lovely scones before I am called in for my hair makeover. I am so pleased I found this package on Groupon.

At the hair salon, the hairdresser shows me some hair photos that she thinks would suit me. I am surprised that they are quite a bit shorter than what I have always had, but I fancy a change. As I am off work, the hairdresser suggests we put in some funky colours that will wash out after a few washes. I have never had unicorn-coloured hair in my life but, for some reason, I am quite excited to try something so outlandishly different to the usual mousey blonde that I am.

One hour later I have a glossy bob with pinks, purples and blues running through it. Oh my goodness. Lucky I am not in work! The grooming department would never allow this with the uniform.

Not that I care, but I can't imagine Matt would appreciate it if I turned up at the opera looking like this. I feel as though I am rebelling against him. Not that it is any of his business what I do with my hair, not now, and not ever. It's a bit of fun for a few days though and I am thrilled with the result.

'What do you think?' says the stylist.

'I absolutely love it, thank you,' I say, smiling. I swing my bob about as I leave. Goodness, I feel almost as good as new; just like Dolly. Although it doesn't hide the fact that my heart is still broken, but at least I look okay. Thankfully, nobody can see what the inside of me feels like.

Thanks to the lavender mist I have been doused in at the spa, I sleep better than I have since I started flying. My sleep patterns are all over the place nowadays. I realise I am getting a little tired of not sleeping properly when I have to get up in the middle of the night to make my way to the airport. However, this morning, I look in the mirror and realise that, for the first time in months, I am not looking like exhausted me. I don't know if it is the eyelashes or the relaxation. Perhaps I needed this week off more than I realised.

I am considering how to spend my day off when I hear my phone ringing incessantly. I choose not to look at it as the operations department can sometimes ask if you want to come in on your week off if they are super short-staffed. What if everyone is sick and rostering are calling me to go in? I can say no, but I would worry it could affect my promotion if I am not cooperative. Crew members I have flown with have been talking about how it isn't looking likely any promotions will go through this year due to some airline restructuring. I don't think I will get the promotion this year, but I at least want to be seen as a team player in case anything changes.

I walk around the living room, unsure what to do. It is obviously something urgent as it keeps ringing and ringing.

I eventually look at the number and see Matt's name flash up. What on earth can he want? Why would he call me on his daughter's wedding day? Becky made it quite clear that I am very unwelcome anywhere near them; it is not as though they are going to send me a last-minute invite. We haven't even spoken for ages. I ignore the phone the first four times, but then I wonder what can be so urgent on such an important day. What if he is having a heart attack with all the excitement and wants to tell me how much he loved me from his hospital bed? This thought makes me finally pick up the phone.

'Hi,' I say.

'Hi, are you flying today?'

'No, I have a couple of days off. Why?'

'Oh, Penny. I am so sorry to do this to you. In fact, it is quite appalling of me, but I need to borrow you for an hour.'

'You need to borrow me?'

'Well, Dolly. I need to borrow Dolly… And you, if I may.'

'I don't get what you mean?'

'Becky's wedding car's broken down. A friend is driving the camper van for the bridesmaids, etc, but Becky should be arriving in a Beetle with me. The car's just broken down on the motorway. Would you by any teeny chance be able to come over and pick Becky up?'

'But you're two hours away. Won't I be too late?'

'No, the wedding isn't until one p.m. Luckily, the car broke down on the way back from another run it was doing so we have a bit of notice. I don't know who else to ask. You don't deserve this, I know.'

I look at my Snoopy pyjamas. I was planning on a chill-out morning before doing something later. After the way Becky spoke to me and the trouble she has caused, I really don't know that she deserves a helping hand. But no matter how mean she was, this is a bride's big day. What choice do I have?

'Okay, I'll get to yours as soon as I can,' I say.

I hurry about the house getting ready. What on earth can I wear to be a chauffeur? Well, madam Becky, I don't have a flat cap, so a pair of trousers and a blouse will have to do. I am not going that far for her.

I quickly head off on the motorway. I can't say I am not nervous about going to that house again. Will Becky even be nice to me? And how is Matt going to react? I have no idea what to expect from any of this.

Dolly does me proud and I manage to arrive at Matt's ten minutes before we have to leave for the church. I don't see Becky as she is upstairs getting ready, but Matt is beaming like a proud dad when he opens the door to me. He looks so dashing in his morning suit and my heart absolutely leaps when I see him. I didn't think he could look any more handsome than when he is in his uniform or dressed for the opera, but by gosh, he is one stunning man. I try not to think about it. I am here purely as a chauffeur.

'Oh, Penny. Thank you so much for doing this,' says Matt.

'It's okay,' I say, smiling.

'No, it's not okay. I owe you so much. You are truly fantastic, you know that?'

I can feel my face heating up and I try to avoid eye contact.

Then I spot Lawrence bounding out of the door to greet me. He is looking very handsome also. He has a bow tie around his collar and sits up straight while I pat his head.

'Lawrence, what are you doing here?' I say.

'By the look on your face, you're more pleased to see Lawrence than me,' says Matt.

'Well, I didn't know he would be here. What a fabulous surprise,' I say.

'Becky decided to take him. But he stays with me sometimes as he loves sniffing around the garden.'

I am so thrilled he got his happy ever after. What a shame we didn't.

'Can I just tell you again that you are the most amazing person? You could have easily told us to shove off after what's happened,' says Matt.

'It's her special day, I couldn't do that,' I say.

Matt hugs me and I feel that tingle once again. Why, oh why, does this man affect me in ways nobody has ever done before? Something in my brain tells me that it is because he is not only a mole-mate but also my soulmate. Even if the timing is all wrong and we never get our fairy-tale ending, I know in my heart that we belong together.

That is what all the sparkly beams of electric between us is all about.

'You did something to your hair, it looks different,' says Matt.

Does it take having four different bright colours for a man to notice a change in hairstyle?

'Dad, Dad, is she here yet?' I hear Becky's voice shout from upstairs.

'Yes, she's here. I told you she wouldn't let you down,' he says.

'Thank you, Penny. You are an angel!' I hear Becky shout.

Ha, she didn't call me that last time she was near me. I was more flight-deck floozy than angel then!

Whilst Becky finishes off getting ready, we pop outside to quickly transform Dolly into a wedding car.

'Wow! You had the restoration done,' says Matt.

'Yup, I used your guys. I wanted to send you photos, but…'

I look away and take the big white bow that Matt has managed to remove from Nigella so that we can put it on the front of Dolly. She looks so beautiful when we finish with her, just as Becky does when she comes down the stairs finally.

'Mum would be so proud,' says Matt to Becky.

I can't help but feel awkward as I stand around as they both have a few tears over Francesca. It is incredibly sad that her mum isn't here to see her on her wedding day. I totally understand why meeting me must have been so awful for her and why she seemed to want to sabotage everything.

Becky looks at me and I can see the tears still shimmering in her eyes.

'Thank you,' she says, her voice low. 'Thank you so much for doing this for me.' I can feel her sincerity and I see a glimpse of the Becky she is with everyone who isn't trying to get with her dad. I actually see her as a human, emotional, the Becky who has tragically lost her mum.

'Oh, I couldn't let you down,' I say.

'Are we ready then?' says Matt.

'We are, Dad,' says Becky, smiling.

I run ahead and open the car doors for them both and once Becky's dress is safely inside, I close the door gently.

Then I help the VIP guest, Lawrence, jump into the front seat and pop his doggie seat belt on. Lawrence just about fits inside Dolly and scrapes his head on the top of the car as he looks out the window.

Praying I don't stall in front of all the neighbours, who have come out to watch, I drive off carefully. In the mirror, I can see Matt's campervan chugging away behind me with a friend of his driving and the bridesmaids safely on-board. I have awful visions of it slamming into the back of us if I have to brake too hard, so I take it slowly all the way to the church. Matt gives me the directions, which is probably a good thing as I would hate to end up on the wrong roads like the last time I used my satnav. Luckily, it doesn't take long to reach the church and we all get there in one piece. What a responsibility! I don't know how limo drivers keep their nerves on such a special day.

I open the doors for Becky, Matt and Lawrence, and wish them the best of luck. I turn to leave, but Matt calls me back.

'This is very embarrassing, but Becky and Rufus will need a lift to the hotel, where we're holding the reception. Would you be able to hang around a bit and take them there? I'm so sorry. I promise to make it up to you,' says Matt.

Looking at Matt with Lawrence beside him, I agree. I can't really let the blushing bride walk to the hotel.

'Sure,' I say.

'You're a lifesaver, really,' says Matt. He reaches over and kisses me on the forehead. That same zap of electricity rushes through me.

'Enjoy your special day. I'll wait out here,' I say.

Becky walks in with her dad, and one of the ushers comes out to take Lawrence inside. It looks like a beautiful wedding. Nothing but the best for Becky and Rufus, I expect.

I can hear the organ music from outside and the invited guests singing hymns as I walk around the church grounds looking at the graves. I have always found headstones interesting to read and I look at the names and the ages that are inscribed. It is so sad when you see some of the young ages and I like to pay my respects. Some of the graves here date back to the 1800s. The average age was around forty. Thank goodness life expectancies have increased.

I read one of the headstones that belongs to a baby from the 1800s. Just three months old. How incredibly sad.

As there is a small shop selling bits and pieces opposite the church, I run over and ask if they have any little teddies. The shopkeeper shows me some small toys and I find just what I am looking for.

As I am placing the little brown teddy on the baby's grave, I hear the church doors open. Confetti flies everywhere and Becky and Rufus are married. Although I try to stay out of the way, a few bits of confetti fly onto my hair thanks to the breeze that is starting to whip up.

When the happy couple have finished talking to guests, they are ready to leave. Once again, I make sure Becky's dress is in the car safely and drive them to their destination. Fortunately, I looked up where the hotel was whilst they were in the church as I didn't want to quiz Becky too much. I decide to let her speak to me if she wants and not to speak unless I am spoken to. I am merely her chauffeur, after all.

Becky and Rufus have a bit of a smooch in the back of the car and then she finally turns to me.

'Thank you again for saving the day.'

'That's okay. No problem,' I say, keeping my eyes on the road ahead of me.

'I love your hair,' she says.

'Oh, thank you.'

I can feel she is really trying to make an effort with me but I don't quite know how I should speak to her. I am still terrified of saying the wrong thing. Imagine if I made her burst into tears on her wedding day!

'Look, umm, I know you're not dressed for it. But you can come to the party this evening if you'd like. You'd be very welcome,' says Becky.

'Thanks, that's very kind of you, but I need to head back,' I say.

'Dad would love it if you did stay,' she says.

I almost stall at some traffic lights at this news.

'Ha, I am not so sure,' I say.

'Of course he would. He really adores you. It was the first time I had seen him smile since Mum's, you know, accident,' she says.

'Thanks,' I say quietly.

'Look, I need to apologise to you. I can see you're not a flight-deck floozy. And I know that Dad was so excited about going to the opera with you and then I purposely made up a drama so he would come home. I thought it was what Mum would have wanted. I was trying to protect Dad from hurtling into some relationship with the first person that came along. I also knew it would break my aunty Lucille's heart to see him with someone other than Mum. I thought I was protecting them both and all I did was hurt Dad. He was genuinely happy with you and now he's just a miserable old git.'

Rufus laughs at this last bit.

'He has been like a bear with a sore head, hasn't he, Becks?' says Rufus.

'Yeah, in fact, he's been getting on my nerves a bit. It would be nice if you two could finally make things work. I know I'm to blame for all of this,' says Becky.

'That's nice of you to say, thanks Becky. I appreciate the apology,' I say.

As Dolly's new tyres scrunch up the gravel driveway of the fancy hotel, Matt is waiting with Lawrence on the front steps for Becky and Rufus, along with the brides-maids. Becky and Rufus head off inside.

'Thanks again. Becky's wedding would have been a complete disaster without you,' says Matt.

'It was nothing, don't worry.'

'Please say you'll come in and have a drink with us, at least.'

'In fairness, Becky already invited me. I need to head back, though. I have plans tonight,' I say.

'Oh, of course. A Saturday night. Why would I not think you're going on a hot date, or whatever it is,' says Matt.

The truth is that all I will do tonight is sit at home eating a takeaway in my pyjamas. I might even push the boat out and pop my Snoopy ones in the wash. I don't want Matt to know any of this, though.

'Well, I wouldn't say that,' I reply.

Matt is about to speak when a harassed-looking wedding planner rushes up to him.

'Have you seen Becky? I need to run something past her,' she says.

'Listen. I can see you're busy. I'd better shoot off,' I say.

'Thanks again, Penny. And a huge thank you to Dolly for saving the wedding of the year,' says Matt.

'It was nothing; sometimes an older model is all that is needed,' I say, smiling.

'Isn't that the truth,' he replies, laughing.

As Matt turns to go inside with the wedding planner, I bid him farewell and begin my drive home. I leave the family to enjoy their celebrations. I felt like an outsider, despite their invitation to join them.

Dolly and I dawdle all the way back in the slow lane of the motorway. After all, we have nothing to rush home for.

Chapter 32

I don't expect any messages or calls from Matt this evening. He already said his thank you to me. I assume he will be catching up with long-lost cousins and Francesca's family, who were no doubt invited to the wedding. I am glad I didn't bump into Lucille; I think that might have been a bit too much for everyone on such an emotional day.

So it is a surprise to be interrupted by Matt sending me messages when I am in the middle of catching up on Saturday night telly.

> I wish you could have stayed

> Never mind. It was more of a family affair. I'd have felt awkward.

> Can I be forward and ask you if you've met someone else? Am I interrupting you?

If he could see me now with my bed socks on nice and cosy, he would know that I am definitely not seeing anyone in this state.

No, I'm not with anyone else.

I'm so relieved. Can I meet you tomorrow?
Could I drive down to Cardiff and spend
the day with you?

That would be nice, but doesn't Becky
need you just after the wedding?

I don't want to go back to having to play second fiddle
again. There is no way I am going to go to the trouble of
hoovering the house and ironing the tea towels and then
he doesn't even turn up because of a Becky emergency!
Although, I don't normally iron my tea towels; that's only
for very special visitors. Visitors I want to impress, like
Matt. Whether we are able to rekindle things or not, I
don't know, but at least I have ironed tea towels.

Rufus can deal with any of her dramas. It's
my turn to enjoy my life and that, if I may
say, is to try and work things out with you.
Even Becky agrees with that.

Well, if I may say, that sounds positively
splendid. I'd like that very much.

Great. Well, we check out of here around eleven a.m. tomorrow, so I can be with you just after lunch. By the time I bid everyone goodbye and make my way down, it might be more like two p.m. if that's okay.

That's perfect.

I look around the house at the mess I am going to have to tidy. I need all the time I can get.

Oh, just one thing though

Here we go.

Do you mind if Lawrence comes along for the drive? I'm dog-sitting while Becky and Rufus head off to Tobago on honeymoon.

The thought of Lawrence visiting makes me so happy. I wonder if he wants to stay over with me for my holiday. I could almost run out now and get him a basket in case. How lovely it would be to have a doggy sleepover. A Matt one would be nice too. I message Matt back trying to drop a hint.

It's a bit of a drive with Lawrence, so if you want to bring some things you're welcome to stay over

It would be so nice to wake up to Matt and Lawrence here. It would be like being part of a proper family unit. Would he rush off though, as he usually does? I can't quite trust him yet, no matter what he says at this stage. He needs to demonstrate he means it this time. There are no more chances.

> Sounds like a plan. Will bring Lawrence's favourite toy and some dog food with me

> Great.

> Yikes, the buffet's ready and Lawrence is already eyeing it up. I'd better go before he pulls the whole thing down off the tablecloth. See you tomorrow, my lovely Penny. Thanks again for being such a kind and wonderful woman.

I sit back, happy that once again Matt is in my life, and pray we can make it work once and for all. This time there would be a bonus with Lawrence tagging along too.

–

When I wake up, I wonder if I had dreamed the whole thing. But as I see the *Good morning gorgeous* message on my phone, I realise that the day did happen as I thought yesterday. Matt confirms his estimated time of arrival (always the pilot), so I have a quick coffee and, unlike my usual lazy mornings when not at work, I rush around the house tidying everything up, hiding away my corn plasters and bed socks.

I just about manage to get everything done and am plumping up the cushions when the doorbell rings.

Matt stands at the door with a bouquet of white long-stemmed roses.

'Oh, my absolute favourite. Thank you.'

'They're from Lawrence,' says Matt coyly.

'Well, that's very thoughtful of you,' I say to Lawrence. He seems desperate to get in and investigate where he is.

I put the kettle on whilst Lawrence wanders around from room to room doing his bit of exploring. I only hope he doesn't walk out of the bathroom with a pair of knickers I have forgotten to put away, but I think I have covered all the bases. Lawrence doesn't seem the type of dog to knock the washing basket over. At least I hope not. Still, I remain on edge until he comes into sight again, since this is the first time Matt is staying at mine.

I give Matt his coffee and Lawrence a new toy carrot I have managed to pick up. Hopefully, that will make sure he stays away from my pants.

We chat politely about the wedding, how it was such a beautiful day and how everything went smoothly after the car fiasco. Things are still a little strained between us after all our ups and downs, and we were more relaxed on the phone than we are face to face. Then we head to Cardiff Castle with Lawrence and any awkwardness between us resolves. I try calling Little Darlings before we go into the castle to see if I can catch Jane. Again though, I am disappointed that she is not in the shop. I would have liked to have introduced Matt to her. I leave her another message and hope that we can catch up before too long.

Lawrence isn't allowed in all the parts of the castle. So, as I want Matt to see it in all its glory, I sit outside with Lawrence for a while as Matt explores it further. I had hoped that Jane may call whilst we wait, but there is nothing. I expect she is busy. When Matt returns, I take them both to the Victorian market where we walk together underneath the overhead lanterns.

Matt loves food from different places so I am excited to take him into the central market and get some laverbread and cockles.

'Oh, these are good,' says Matt as he devours a cockle covered in vinegar on a cocktail stick.

'They're one of my favourites,' I say.

There is so much good food in the market. We even manage to pick up a doggie Welsh cake in the shape of a bone for Lawrence. He is, of course, thrilled to bits and eats it in two bites.

We sit down for a while to give Lawrence a rest and then eventually think about heading home. I would have liked to have introduced Matt to one of the fabulous snazzy restaurants that Cardiff has to offer, but I don't like the thought of Lawrence having to be left alone at mine for too long in case he gets nervous. So, despite eating for most of the day, we pick up a curry when we are eventually on the way home.

'This dish reminds me of a wonderful restaurant in Delhi. They did the best Malabar fish curry. It was cooked in coconut and curry leaves, and it was divine,' says Matt, as we tuck into the takeaway.

'I'd love to fly long-haul, but I think I'll probably be stuck on the European routes now. Especially with the promotion on hold. What is Delhi like?'

'It's fantastic. All the sights and sounds, the vibrant colours in the markets. There were snake charmers and fortune tellers on the street. I found it quite a mystical place, I suppose.'

'You're so interesting. You know about everything. This is why I love you so much,' I say. 'I mean, I love talking to you so much,' I quickly add.

'Ha. Well, if it's any consolation, I love you to bits,' says Matt.

'Really?' I ask.

'Of course I do. Why do you think I was so miserable without you? I know Becky told you I wasn't the best of company when we fell out.'

'She told you about the chat we had in the car then,' I say.

'Yes, she said you didn't say much in response, though. She wasn't really sure how you felt about me.'

'Okay, well maybe I should tell you then.'

I pause for a moment and then say it as it is.

'I love you. I really do.'

'Then come here, because I have bloody missed you,' says Matt.

'Let's never fall out again, okay?' I say.

'I absolutely promise,' says Matt.

I stand up from the kitchen chair and Matt pulls me into his arms.

'Shall we leave this for later?' he says, looking at our takeaway feast.

'That might be an idea,' I say grinning. 'Oh! What about Lawrence?' I ask, as we head to the bedroom.

'He'll be okay. Look at him,' says Matt.

Lawrence has fallen asleep with his head on his carrot and is using it as a pillow. He looks so adorable.

I shut the bedroom door and, for a moment, I stop worrying about Lawrence.

Chapter 33

I only have cornflakes to offer Matt in the morning, and, even then, they are all the crumbly bits at the bottom of the packet. I was so busy getting the house cleaned and getting Lawrence a present that I forgot to get some things in for breakfast. I would have loved to have bought croissants and fancy cheeses just as we eat in Paris, but I suppose now we are officially together he will have to find out my true unorganised colours at some point.

As we finish up the measly breakfast I split between us, Matt's phone rings. He looks at it and rushes out. My first thought is that Becky is up to her old tricks again. What if there is a drama on her honeymoon and Matt has to fly out to Tobago!

I get a knot in my stomach. Lawrence is happily chomping away on a bone, oblivious to my imagination that is telling me that something is going to go wrong now that I am back with Matt.

When he walks back into the room, Matt's face looks white as a sheet. His usual tanned face is drained.

'Everything okay?' I ask.

'Yes, all fine,' he says.

'Was it Becky? Everything all right on honeymoon?'

'No, not Becky. Long story.'

The hairs stand up on the back of my neck when he says this. I am always cautious of Matt's long stories.

'We have plenty of time. I'll make us more coffee and you can tell me,' I say.

'No, it's nothing. Just something I have to think about, I suppose. There's nothing to say at this point.'

I wonder what it could be.

I want to ask if it was something to do with work. What if there has been an incident I am not aware of? I try to push it further but Matt doesn't seem to want to open up. I don't want an argument now that we have just got back together, so I figure if he wants to tell me, then he will.

'I was thinking… I know I'm supposed to head back home today with Lawrence, but how do you fancy popping down to St David's for the night? You've never stayed in Nigella yet, have you?'

Matt seems to cheer up at the thought of a night in Nigella.

'Well, that sounds gorgeous. How exciting. I love doing things spur of the moment,' I say.

We pack up Lawrence's toys and I get a few bits and pieces together before we head on our campervan adventure. I am so excited at the thought of staying in a campervan for the first time. We stop in a supermarket on the way down, but Matt won't let me see what he picks up. He says he is arranging dinner tonight and has managed to pre-book a campsite that has space for us. Apparently, they have shepherd's huts there too. I suppose that's handy to know if the campervan gets too cold at night.

The scenery on the way down to the campsite is just stunning. How beautiful it is down in rural west Wales. I watch from the passenger seat as we drive alongside the sea as it crashes on rocks and dogs run carefree around the beach.

'I could retire here,' says Matt.

'I can't imagine you retiring,' I say, laughing.

'One day, when I stop flying, I'll have a dog running alongside me on the beach, like those people out there. Then a beautiful woman to share my retirement with. I think I'd adjust pretty well. Wouldn't you like that too?' says Matt.

'Well, that does sound lovely. Shame you have to give Lawrence back to Becky,' I say.

I don't say anything about the beautiful woman. I think he is talking about me, but you can never assume anything in this life.

'Yes, it's sad, but Lawrence has settled really well over there. Rufus adores him and they can give him more time than I can. It's only fair to Lawrence, really.'

'Yes, I suppose at least I can jump on a flight if I want to see you. Poor Lawrence can't.'

'Oh, that reminds me,' says Matt. 'I have to use up some staff travel tickets. How do you fancy coming to Paris with me for a night or two? I could get us two first class tickets and I know this great hotel in Paris. You may know it,' says Matt, laughing.

'You're full of surprises today, Captain Garcia!'

'You haven't seen the last of them, either,' he says.

'Oh, now you have me really intrigued.'

Surely there are no other surprises.

'This evening. You'll have to wait a bit longer,' he says. 'Though I don't know how you're going to take it.'

'Oh no, don't frighten me.'

Lawrence starts barking at some dogs in a car that is next to us at the traffic lights and it becomes impossible to find out more.

'Let's discuss it later,' says Matt.

At the campsite, Lawrence has a good old stretch as we sort out the booking with the farm owner. The campsite is on the edge of a cliff and the sea extends out in front of the huge drop below. It is breathtaking. I only hope the handbrake on Nigella doesn't give out.

'Why don't you go and explore whilst I get dinner ready?' says Matt.

'Oh, is that fair?' I ask.

'Of course it is. Relax, let me spoil you for the evening. But I will warn you, it won't be cordon bleu cookery. Unfortunately, this Nigella isn't quite as well equipped as her namesake.'

I come back from the walk to the smell of burgers and sausages on the BBQ and find Nigella has been transformed into a magical cavern. There are twinkling fairy lights hanging over the seating area and the seats are covered in cosy fluffy blankets. A bottle of champagne in an ice chiller is laid out on Nigella's pull-down table.

'Oh, Matt. This is just gorgeous – and you even have an ice bucket!'

I throw my arms around him.

'Thank you. What more could I ask for?' I say.

I notice the smell of burning while I am kissing him.

'Do you smell that?'

'My sausages are on fire!' exclaims Matt.

He rushes to the BBQ and sorts out the fire by removing a fire extinguisher from Nigella. That's the good thing with a pilot: always calm in the face of adversity and very often found with a fire extinguisher somewhere handy.

'Good job I haven't put the burgers on yet. At least we can salvage something. We still have champagne and crisps too. Lawrence will be disappointed about the sausages though,' says Matt.

He pours us some champagne while the burgers cook and I thank my lucky stars for how perfect everything is in my life.

We are about to finish our bottle of champagne when Matt takes my hand in his.

'So, you know I wanted to tell you something?' he says.

'Oh, yes, what was your surprise?'

'Well, it's not really a surprise, more of a confession.'

My stomach lurches and I start to worry.

'What? Oh no, just tell me.'

'That was an airline in the Middle East on the phone this morning,' says Matt.

'Oh, okay. Why would they be calling you from the Middle East?'

'You know I have this fear that one day Calm Air are going to retire me. I can't help it. It's just this hunch as I get older. I worry about keeping my job. So, something happened whilst we were apart.'

'Oh. Like what?'

'Well, Becky was getting married and I could see that she had her own life now. Even Lucille is becoming stronger and not so reliant on me. I only have a few years of flying left. I have to make the most of these few years before I won't be allowed to fly any longer.'

'And what has this to do with the airline in the Middle East? Please tell me it isn't what I think you're going to say.'

'I've been offered a fantastic opportunity. It's too good to turn down.'

'Well, that's great news that it's a good offer, but I mean surely you can't move to the other side of the world!'

'Well, that's the thing. I have to move to Dubai. It's a position as a captain on a private jet. It's something I've always wanted. When we were apart, I thought I would apply. Do you know Tom? He was a first officer with Calm Air, he's with them already.'

I remember Tom from my first flight. He was obsessed with flying privately.

My head starts to spin.

'I know it probably comes as a bit of a shock. I had a shock myself this morning when they told me the job was mine. I'd really love to accept the position but I also don't want to leave you. This is a lot to ask of you, but I wondered…Would you think of coming with me?'

Oh, aeroplane gods of love, what are you trying to do to us?

Chapter 34

Once Becky returns from her honeymoon, and Lawrence goes back home, Matt begins the plans for our Paris trip. I am aware that when we return, he will be starting to pack up and get ready for his relocation to Dubai. How fast things can change. He has already stopped flying for Calm Air so I am grateful we have the flight tickets so that at least we can do one last trip together.

Matt desperately wants me to go to Dubai with him, but it would mean giving up the job I love, putting Dolly into storage and giving up my place. There is so much to think about. He has enquired about a job for me, and apparently they are currently looking for cabin crew as well as flight deck positions, so this could be my chance of working on private jets for the rest of my flying days too. It is like a huge promotion, something that I am not going to get where I am for a long time. Matt reassures me that the job is as good as mine as he is friendly with Annika, the head of cabin services, who used to fly with Calm Air a few years ago.

I think back to those glamourous women who sat in the hotel in Geneva. They had Hermes bags and designer clothes. I have never been one for designer stuff and I worry that I may not fit in. However, Matt reassures me that, within a few days, I would know everyone and that Annika isn't materialistic. Apparently, she is very down to earth. She is there for the perpetual sunshine and tax-free salary. Matt says that if we do this for a few years we can easily retire to our dream home overlooking the sea near St David's. I have told him I will make my decision on the trip. It is a lot to think about in such a short space of time.

It seems odd checking in at the airport as a passenger. There is no crew passport and security control to skip the large queues and we stand patiently as we wait to go through. I was told to dress smartly as we still represent the airline with our free tickets. So, I wear an elegant navy trouser suit that makes me look like a businesswoman who would be used to sitting in business class.

Still, I am slightly embarrassed when I sit down with the full-fare-paying passengers in business class, having not paid a penny for the flight. Matt tells me not to be though; it is simply a perk of the job and that we work hard for this.

It is certainly not hard work now as I sit back and one of the crew, Annamarie, serves me champagne. We flew together to Italy once and visited the Leaning Tower of Pisa. She was great fun to fly with.

'Didn't know you two were an item,' she says.

'Yes, very much so,' says Matt, taking my hand.

I am so pleased he feels we can be open about our relationship finally.

'Aw, well, you look fab together. Well suited. Now drink up. Got to fill your boots on a free ticket,' she teases.

As I am about to switch my phone off for take-off, I see a message from Jane.

'Sorry I keep missing you. I didn't want to tell you over text, but I can't wait any longer. We put an offer in for a house in the Cayman Islands and it's been accepted. I'm selling up, Pen!'

Attached is a photo of the most beautiful villa with its own private swimming pool. Oh my!

I take my glass of champagne and toast her good fortune. What a way to retire. I am delighted for her and so glad I didn't stay in the shop. Had I stayed I would now be unemployed.

–

Even though it is such a short flight, after take-off Annamarie ensures Matt and I aren't short on drinks. I seem to be drinking far too much champagne at the moment. However, when it is being handed to you for free, it would be a shame to say no.

'So, have you decided if you are coming to Dubai with me? Can I persuade you to fly on private jets with a handful of passengers? Imagine, you would no longer have to serve hundreds of demanding people. Just three or four very demanding ones,' he says, laughing.

It certainly seems like the offer of a lifetime. I have never been on a private jet. Imagine having that on your CV! But I love the different passengers we have at Calm Air. All the people I work with. Also, I remember Gavin on my first flight saying how the family you fly for call all the shots. It is up to them how long you stay away. You can't tell them that it is time to head back to base when you have had enough. Despite this though, a life in the sun flying on private jets does sound appealing. I am still only flying short haul, which means many of my flights are turnarounds with occasional night stops and I would like to see a bit more of the world. The only thing putting me off is fear of the unknown.

'I just can't decide,' I say to Matt.

I look around at the familiar Calm Air colours on the plane. What a different experience the Dubai opportunity would be for me. Then I think of Jane and that swimming pool. She is much older than me and has taken a huge leap into the unknown.

'I want to be with you and we're so happy. But what if I don't like it? I could lose my job and not be able to go back home again.'

'How about if you take unpaid leave for a bit? They've been asking the crew to do that as the slower months are coming up. That way you could try it and if you don't like it and you're not happy, you can come back? What do you think? I'm pretty sure you'd be able to do that. Then you have nothing to lose.'

'That does sound like a good way to try it,' I say.

Maybe the bubbles and the oxygen levels at 33,000 feet mess with my rational thinking, but I make my decision. If I hadn't taken any chances then I would never have gone to Calm Air in the first place. I can't begin to imagine how much I would have missed out in life had I stayed. So I make a brave decision and hope it is the right one.

'I'll come to Dubai with you. Ask Annika about the position. Flying on a private jet does sound quite amazing,' I say.

'I promise you won't regret this. We already have the best job in the world, this will just take us to the next step,' says Matt.

Any apprehension I have is replaced with excitement as Matt talks about the airline. It is going to be a wonderful experience for sure. I bet my mum and dad never imagined their daughter flying on a private jet. I wonder what they would have thought. Sadly, they never had the chance to see the world and that's why I believe in some ways I am having these chances. To live the life they should have had. I wish I could tell the flickering chandelier. I am pretty sure it would have flashed on and off in approval of this news.

Matt continues to tell me that, with a private airline, we could fly anywhere in the world. One of the flight deck he knows flies for royalty and stays in guest palaces sometimes. Anything can happen. I must confess, the more he talks about it, the more I can't wait to get out there. We are so lucky that, unlike many of the private jet recruiters, this family prefer slightly older crew, rather than glamourous young ladies as the prerequisite. This is a once in a lifetime opportunity.

By the time we reach the hotel, the effects of the champagne have worked off a little. I should have taken it a little easier. It was all Annamarie's fault, although granted, I didn't have to guzzle it down.

We are staying at the crew hotel in Paris that the airline normally uses as we managed to get a great airline discount on the room and they have even upgraded us.

We throw our bags down in the room and decide to have a snooze before hitting Paris for sunset. The champagne in the business class lounge and the plane has made us both a little woozy.

As we snuggle in together and I lie in Matt's arms in the queen-size bed, I think about how I could never let him go. I know that I have made the right decision about going to Dubai and I look forward to our new adventure together.

When we wake up from our blissful nap, Matt suggests we go for a walk before dinner. I agree as we do seem to be eating and drinking a lot at the moment. Where better to work off all our overindulging than around the beguiling streets of Paris?

We start our walk along the Seine. The Eiffel Tower overlooks us ahead.

We walk past little food stalls and souvenir shops. I am so tempted by the smells of the street food, but we have a reservation at the restaurant we went to last time on the Champs Elysees. I know how good the food is there, so I want to leave room for it all.

When we pass a souvenir shop selling touristy stuff, Matt stops. I didn't think it would be his kind of place, but he tells me that he wants to get a little something for Becky. I hate to tell him that she probably won't be happy with anything he finds in there, but he goes in with a big grin on his face.

He soon comes out stuffing something into his pocket.

'Can't be that big, whatever you got her,' I say.

'Easy to take home. Always pack smart,' he says.

Matt is always the height of practicality. I should have known.

He takes my hand and we walk further along until we reach the bottom of the Eiffel Tower, just as the sun starts going down.

'Want to go up?' says Matt.

'Not really. You know I'm not the best with heights,' I say.

I look up at the Eiffel Tower. My goodness, it is high. No, I definitely don't want to go up there.

When I finish gazing up, I see Matt going down on one knee and landing in a puddle.

'Oh my gosh, are you okay? Did your knee go?'

I suppose anything can happen now he's heading towards sixty.

'What's wrong?' I say.

'Can you be quiet for a moment? I am trying to propose,' says Matt, laughing.

'What about Becky? What would she say?'

'She knows. I told her. She already asked if she could help plan your hen night if you say yes.'

I have a flashback to that night in La Tapas. I never thought my name and 'hen night' would ever be said in the same sentence.

'Oh, that's very kind of her.'

'Look, never mind Becky, or my knees, for a moment. I'd like to ask you, Penny Thomas, will you marry me?'

Matt puts his hand in his pocket and pulls something out.

'Sorry, I didn't know what type of ring you'd like so I thought this could do for now. Plus, I couldn't assume you'd say yes and that would be an awful waste of money if you said no. I mean, I am looking ahead at retirement,' teases Matt.

I can't stop laughing as Matt hands me a tiny model of the Eiffel Tower.

'I know it's not a ring, but I thought it looked like it was made of gold, or something. Sorry, it's not very romantic, is it? I picked it up in that shop back there. A bit last minute. If you say yes, then obviously we can go ring shopping together right away.'

Matt seems to be babbling now. For a man who is always so calm, he seems incredibly nervous.

'It's so cute. I'll keep it forever. I'll put it next to the model of Dolly beside the bed.'

'But are you sure about this? Are you ready to marry again?' I say.

I need to be sure before we reach this final commitment.

'Of course I am. Come on, I mean we love adventure, dogs, old Volkswagens, planes and we even have the same taste in operas. We're soulmates and mole-mates. A match made in heaven,' says Matt.

'Yeah, about the opera…' I say.

'Shh, it's okay. Just teasing you. I know it's not your thing,' says Matt.

He knew! Perhaps it is the collection of heavy metal music I have on my phone that was a giveaway.

'Well, in that case, Captain Matteo Garcia, I would love to marry you.'

He takes me by the waist and kisses me.

'You have made me a very happy man, Penny,' says Matt.

As Matt holds me tight in his arms, we look just as in love as the other couples as we embrace in front of the Eiffel Tower at sunset.

Only we are two soulmates who are a little bit older than the others around us, and are about to begin the next chapter of our lives on the other side of the world.

A letter from Helga

Thank you so much for picking up *Fly Me to Paris*. As always, when I write a book, I hope the reader will enjoy the story and join me on an adventure to escape the real world and have fun for a while.

This story is very special to me as I was fortunate to be cabin crew when I was 21 and flew for the most fantastic airline called Gulf Air. It was a changing point in my life when I met friends for life and found myself. I truly belonged there, as many of us who flew for Gulf Air have realised over the years. The crew I flew with were amazing and we all made the best team. Some of the flight deck were rather nice too, thus I simply had to write a rom-com with a hunky captain involved! In addition, my lovely publisher wanted me to write something about flying, so how could I resist?

Being long-haul cabin crew was undoubtedly a dream come true. We flew to the most wonderful destinations such as Zanzibar, Delhi, Singapore, Melbourne and many European destinations including Paris. During my flights, I met the most intriguing passengers with so many stories. I believe that every passenger has a story – you just never know whom you are sitting next to on a flight. (I have been reminded by my good flying friend that not all passengers on flights want to talk though!)

At the time of writing this book, there are British airlines hiring slightly older cabin crew, so if you are over forty and reading this, you could follow in Penny's footsteps. After all, as I try to portray in all my books, it is never too late to fulfil your dreams.

I do hope you will enjoy meeting Penny and her friends. As always, the biggest thank you for picking up one of my books. I truly hope you enjoy *Fly Me to Paris*.

If you enjoy the story, do feel free to contact me on social media, where I am usually found at all hours of the day!

You can contact me via:

www.twitter.com/HelgaJensenF
www.facebook.com/helgajensenfordeauthor
www.instagram.com/helgajensenauthor

Acknowledgements

I must start by saying the hugest of thank you's to Keshini Naidoo at Hera Books for believing in my stories. I am so lucky to have renewed my contract with Hera/Canelo to allow me to write another two books so that *Fly Me to Paris* could come to life.

Also, a big thank you to the most incredible editor, Jennie Ayres, for all her editorial help and for whipping everything into shape. Books would be so different without the support of wonderful editors like Keshini and Jennie. Thank you also to Jennifer Davies for a sparkling line edit and all the staff at Hera/Canelo for being so amazing.

Of course, a book wouldn't be a book without a gorgeous cover and so my enormous gratitude to Diane of D Meacham Design for another stunning cover. Diane always gets the essence of my books and the covers always come out exactly how I would have envisioned.

To my fantastic writing friend Jenny, I don't know what I would do without you. Thank you for listening to me bash out ideas and work out plot holes. Every writer needs a Jenny in their lives!

Thank you to JK who has kept me fed and has progressed from fish fingers in the study whilst I work, to ginormous Sunday lunches with lots of roast potatoes and no veggies spared. If anyone knows someone at Cirque

De Soleil, please put a good word in for him as he is also a talented performer when not feeding me!

Thank you to Mr B for increasing my Instagram followers, we all know it's the labradoodle photos everyone follows me for.

Huge thank you, as ever, to all my amazing friends for their support. To my Gulf Air girls and everyone else that I love dearly. To my Twitter and RNA friends too. The writing community on Twitter is just incredible.

Last, but definitely not least, thank you to the wonderful readers who pick up my books. Without the reader authors would cease to exist, so my heartfelt thank you to every single one of you who has bought a copy of my books.

Happy reading

xxxxx